# GRACE & GRAVITY

# GRACE & GRAVITY

A NOVEL BASED ON THE MOVIE

S.E. CLANCY

This is a work of fiction. All characters and events portrayed in this novel are either fictitious or used fictitiously.

GRACE AND GRAVITY



Based on the film *Grace & Gravity*



WhiteFire Publishing

13607 Bedford Rd NE

Cumberland, MD 21502

ISBN: 978-1-941720-58-5 (print)

978-1-941720-59-2 (digital)

Yes, Jesus loves me.
Yes, Jesus loves me.
Yes, Jesus loves me…the Bible tells me so.
It's time.

# CHAPTER 1

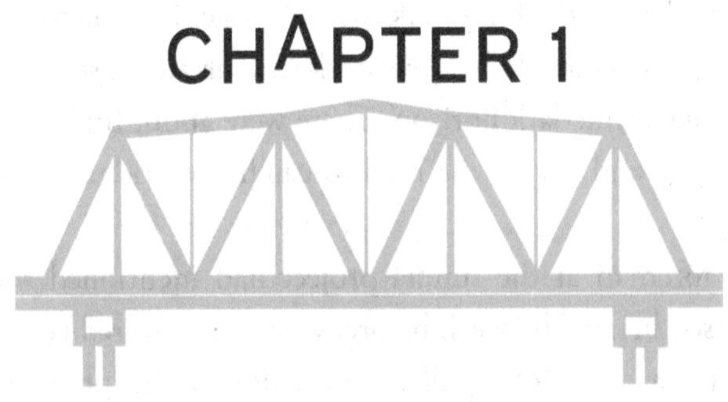

## FIRST LIGHT

*John*

**THE BEEPING ALARM ROUSED JOHN PALMER FROM HIS** medicated sleep. He rolled over and swiped his phone with a groan. Through the sheer curtain of his rented walk-up flat, the sky was dark.

"Perfect," he whispered, voice still hoarse. After a silent countdown, John rocked up and swung his legs over the edge of the bed. His toes touched the laminate and curled, the chilly flooring waking him as he scrubbed his face with both hands. He needed to shave.

Another groan pushed through his lips when he shoved up from the mattress. Mrs. Pottifer promised to have the heat fixed no later than the previous day. The fourth morning of an icy apartment made John grateful that his meds allowed a deep slumber through the night, even if his back ached by morning. Maybe he'd add in a couple of ibuprofen with his daily vitamins.

In the bathroom, John checked his upside-down boots on the electric dryer he'd had sent to him from the States. At least his feet would be dry for the long walk to the bridge. Electric toothbrush vibrating in his mouth, he drew back the curtain. A sliver of color snaked across the dark horizon. There were about fifteen minutes to finish up and get on the road to catch the bridge at the ideal lighting.

His foreman at the tunnel project had mentioned the timber trussed bridge the week before, when they toured two nearby highway crossings. John pulled up the note on his phone to look over the directions again. There was no way he was going to miss capturing one of the oldest remaining British wooden bridges before he went back to California after this project wrapped in a few weeks.

After dressing and shoving a granola bar into his camera bag, John heard his cell phone ring from the nightstand. It vibrated across the glass top. Both features were turned on so that he didn't miss a call from home.

John grabbed the phone and stared. The cracked screen displayed his wife's photo from last year's Christmas party. He plopped onto the mattress watching her picture as it buzzed in his hands. Two cleansing breaths later, he swiped open her video chat.

Joy smiled into the camera. "Hi, sweetie. What's up?" The speaker distorted her voice. No amount of covering the phone in rice could fix the damage of an English spring deluge. Or three.

He leaned closer, as if to smell the same perfume she'd always worn for twenty-six years. "What time is it there?" he asked. She hadn't changed much—her blond hair still hung to her shoulders, and the cracks in the screen hid any of the lines she complained about.

"Ten at night."

John glanced to the window. The horizon blossomed. "The

sun is barely rising here." He had to get a move on to catch the dawn rays.

Her eyebrows dipped together. "And you're up already?"

"Yeah. I want to catch that first light."

"Huh, that's a surprise." She turned her head sideways. Static squelched through the speaker and John nearly didn't hear her next words. "Since when do you ever get out of bed this early for anything?"

He switched the call to audio and cradled the phone to his ear. "Joy? Honey? Can you hear me?"

"Hello? What's going on?"

The new telephoto lens sat in its bag near the lamp. John removed it with care. "I'm rushing to catch that light." It weighed less than he thought it would. But then again, who really looked at the weight when ordering online? "There's this amazing old bridge nearby, but I have to hurry." He placed it on the bedspread, turning it over to look at the features.

"You have to hurry?" She used that tone of voice when their daughter Jenny was leaving without eating breakfast. Or when he had to work out of town for a few weeks.

Dawn woke outside, spilling onto the hills. "Joy, you know I love that stuff."

They'd met at an art exhibition in college. He'd shirked around the corners, trying not to bump into anyone he knew from the engineering department. She'd found him at a collection of black and white prints of brick buildings, near her own watercolor lilies.

"Yeah, I know you love that stuff." The edge still hung on her tone, even through the static, all the way from the other side of the globe.

"It's my only day off. Aren't I entitled to a little bit of fun?" Between weather delays and the company being slapped with fines after an inspection, it most definitely had *not* been a good week at work.

Joy sighed into the phone. He'd heard that sigh so many times in the last few months. Resignation. Defeat. Acceptance.

"So, you've got your coat?"

John stood and rounded the bed, depositing the new lens into his black camera bag. "Of course, I have a jacket."

"All right," she said.

"This is England, for crying out loud." He continued into the bathroom, his voice bouncing off of the tiny tiled walls.

She sighed again. The static rattled his eardrums. "I wish I was there."

John reached down to pick up a tissue that had missed the trash can. "Yeah, I wish you were here, too."

"I love you."

He threw the tissue into the toilet and closed the lid.

"John? What? You won't say that you love me, too?"

"No. Of course, I can say it." He flushed the toilet on his way out of the bathroom. "I love you, too." It was too fast, too clipped. And she knew it as well as he did.

"Are you there?" Joy sounded like she was speaking through a kazoo. "Don't forget Jenny's gonna call."

Next to the bed, his Bible lay on a wooden tray that doubled as his dining table when he ate in. If he took time to read the devotion for the day, he'd miss the shots altogether. He grabbed the worn Bible tract that sat haphazardly on top of his Bible. John always kept it in his shirt pocket, just in case he needed to remind himself about forgiveness. He slid it into the pocket of his plaid flannel under his jacket. Layers were the key to staying warm and mostly dry. Maybe he'd have time to read it again after he took his pictures of the bridge. He really needed to work on memorizing the verses inside the tract he'd picked up before his trip.

"What time will she call?"

Joy hummed, and it tickled John's ear. "I don't know. Maybe around one o'clock, when she gets back?"

"One a.m.!" John sat on the edge of the bed again. "What's she doing until one a.m.?"

Joy scoffed. "It's her birthday, John—" The phone slid from John's ear to the floor and bounced on the carpet. He grabbed the phone and Joy was still talking. "She's going out to a show and then going to a club—" Whatever she said after that was swallowed by static.

"Joy?" He moved to the end of the bed. Sometimes that helped with reception.

"Did you even remember Jenny's birthday?"

John's muscles went rigid. She just had to dredge it up. Again. "No, I'm a terrible father." He distracted himself by grabbing something, anything from the camera bag. An extra useless strap. "Of course I remembered." He shoved the strap into the other pocket of his flannel and stood.

"Just don't let her down. You promised, okay?"

"Yes, I'm very aware that I forgot her birthday last year." Cell service was spotty in that part of Montana, and it didn't help that he'd been called to bail out two of his employees from jail. Add in the time it took to recover the truck from the towing company… and yeah, he forgot. "Thank you for always bringing that up." John shrugged on his jacket. Same conversation, different day. At least the bridge wouldn't rehash his mistake. As if he needed help with that every single time he saw Joy calling.

"You're blowing it out of proportion, John. She was hurt. She waited for that call."

John snorted in disbelief. "Forgive me for being so busy trying to be a godly provider."

"Please don't do this, John. I'm sorry I brought it up." She sniffed into the phone.

Great, he'd made her cry. He closed his eyes, trying to focus. Could he ever get things right between them again?

"Joy," he said tenderly. "Joy…Joy."

"I just wish that you two would talk like you used to. Or go to the movies." He wasn't sure if she was crying or if it was static.

For years, every Friday or Saturday, they had a daddy-daughter date. Waffles at Kate's Diner, then a movie. Sometimes she'd drag him to see the latest Star Wars movie six weeks in a row.

He squashed the phone to his ear. "I can't help it. I tried." It took Jenny days to return his apology text because she wouldn't answer his calls. And when the Montana job ended, she always had something else to do rather than catch a movie. "She's the one who wouldn't talk to me after that."

"It was just a phase." Right. A phase that lasted for months and months. It was a wonder Jenny would call today at all.

"Yeah. I know she blames me for everything, and you just allow it," he said. Joy would never stick up for him. It would mean that she'd have to tell Jenny—

"Did you tell her?" Joy's distorted voice sounded even smaller, more hesitant.

He paced to the end of the bed, rubbing his forehead with his free hand. "I told you I would never tell her anything about that." They'd sworn to secrecy, to keep Jenny in the dark. It was…less messy that way. "Look, I really have to go." The sun peeked over the horizon now.

"All right," Joy said. "Well…"

"Okay." The line went dead. He held the phone out and glanced at the black screen. "Bye," he said to the empty room.

Gathering the camera bags and tripod, John headed down the three flights of stairs. His rental was parked a block away, wedged between a delivery truck and another tiny car. John dropped his equipment into the passenger seat and started the engine. "Drive on the wrong side," he whispered, maneuvering the two-door sedan to the roadway.

He glanced through the windshield as the trees blurred by and the sun rose higher. He still had sixteen minutes to go, according to the lady robot voice on his phone's map. It wouldn't be the light he'd wanted to capture, but it'd still be close enough to play with the aperture and depth of field. If there was a breeze, he could even get a few long exposures to catch the movement around the trestle.

The map directed John to a small dirt turnout, where a gate barred the way on a tumbled gravel road into the woods. "Okay," he said, cutting the engine. "I'm up for a hike."

Throwing a camera bag on each shoulder, John slipped his phone into his pocket before grabbing the tripod and locking the car. The tall grass and sparse trees soon blended into a carpet of ferns and mossy tree trunks. John sped his steps, trying to get to the bridge before his shots were blown by locals or tourists.

A random apple tree draped over the narrowing path. The bottom branches were stripped bare, probably by people on their way to the creek. But nestled behind a thick set of leaves, a red-tinged green apple weighed down its branch, just aching to be plucked. John obliged after a quick glance around to make sure no one would see. He polished it against his jacket. Launching into the crisp skin, he immediately spit the sour bite out, regretting his thievery, and tossed the apple into the tall ferns. Then he heard the creek far away.

The tree line broke, and John found himself on a typical English hillside, overlooking the dark timber trussed bridge. Tall grasses and ferns filled the field, the trail disappearing over the edge. John descended the hill, and the creek grew louder.

Large cobblestones and white birches lined the creek bed. Because the bridge sat in a valley, the brightest light hadn't bathed the area. John hurried to set up the tripod. He still had time to catch the light he wanted.

After switching to his trusty wide-angle lens, John crouched to check the tripod's height adjustment. An upward angle would work perfectly.

Rays of sunlight spilled through the trees to the east, streaking across the bridge. John leaned into the viewfinder to line everything up, when from the corner of the frame, a man in a white suit walked into the shot.

John dropped his head and rubbed his forehead. When he looked back up, the man kept walking toward the center of the bridge. "Come on, buddy," John whispered.

Since the intruder didn't seem to be interested in leaving, John took the time to fasten his camera bag closed. He didn't want his new lens to fall out and break.

The man finally stopped, dead center on the bridge. Of course. John bent forward as the guy did something with his shoes. Was he taking them off?

John grabbed his camera and zoomed in as much as the wide angle would go. His stomach dropped as the man in white climbed onto the railing and held onto the sides, pausing to look up into the sky.

He was going to jump.

# CHAPTER 2

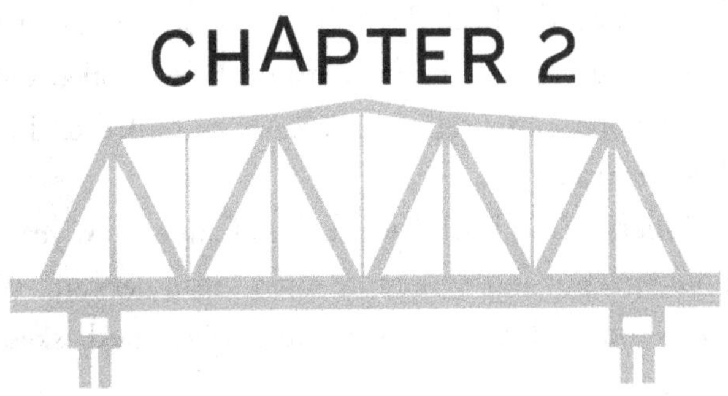

## SLIP-ONS

*Chris*

**CHRIS STEPPED BACK AND LOOKED AT THE ENVELOPE** propped on the spotless kitchen counter. Yes, that'd work. Chloe would see it when she came round. All the directions she would need. She would see it when she came by eventually. If nothing else, he'd taught her to be observant. All of those times they'd trudged through the park looking at flowers or identifying insects. She could spot a honeybee across the church yard.

And the envelope was blue—sky blue, her favorite color. Hopefully it'd help her when she read the note inside. Even just a little. She could forgive him.

With a quick nod to the envelope, Chris backtracked through the flat to his bedroom. The narrow bed took up most of the space. His pressed linen suit was laid across the bed, like he'd crawled out of the clothes and left them behind. Chris considered and reconsidered his shoes. Not that it mattered. The hands on his wristwatch tracked time exactly, and it was essential.

Through the thin walls, Chris heard the tune announcing the

morning news on the Beeb. Probably more of the same rubbish, despair, recycled stories. The same reason he'd stopped watching it months before. Chris rolled his eyes as he pulled on his black shirt, then his trousers.

The trainers were a birthday gift from Chloe a few years back. "You should get out and walk more often," read her card. Well, he would walk today, along the quiet bridge where he'd asked Carol to marry him.

Chris tugged on the first shoe with ease. The second one was a bit snug. When he yanked on the shoestrings, one side snapped.

"Great," he muttered at the useless material. Glancing at his bedside clock, he kicked both shoes off and stuffed them under the bed.

In the wardrobe, his slip-ons were jammed into a corner. He hadn't worn them in ages. The last time he saw his wife Carol, in fact. The soles were worn bare of tread and the white leather scuffed, but they would work. Chris slid them on, flexing his toes. Still fit after all this time.

He rang a taxi company, but no one picked up. Of course. Could anything actually go according to plan? With a huff, Chris yanked open his laptop and waited for it to load. And waited and waited because the thing was nearly ten years old and barely connected to the internet. After much searching, he found a local taxi company that didn't require a smart phone. Those things confused him and needed updates. He booked a ride to the bridge and then the website required his credit card to prepay.

"Are you kidding me?" he ranted to the empty flat, stomping into the kitchen to retrieve his wallet.

When the transaction was paid for, Chris closed his internet and tried to turn off the laptop. It instructed him not to turn it off while updating. "What now?" He left the screen open and placed it near the pillow. Blasted thing.

Slipping into the jacket that matched the trousers, Chris double-checked the envelope and made sure the flat keys were hanging on their hook. He wouldn't need them today. According to the time, the driver would only be a few minutes away, so Chris turned off the lights and grabbed the front door handle.

It jammed.

Chris pulled, twisted, leaned. He spat out words he'd never use in front of Carol or Chloe. He kicked the door. And it was the moment that he growled and turned the handle with all of his might, that it opened without any resistance.

"You stupid piece of wood!" he seethed, yanking it closed. He couldn't care less if the lock worked.

Carol would have laughed at his temper tantrum.

She always seemed to have a knack at rounding out his bluntness. After all, she'd been the one to drag him to church for their second date. It changed his life. He hadn't even known that he'd grabbed her hand during the sermon until after they were the only ones left in the pews.

"Are you all right?" she whispered, the stone walls snatching away any echoes.

"I don't know." Had the minister known about his home life? The way Chris gulped alcohol to dull the pain? Or the way he cringed when he saw other people's joy? "I don't rightly know."

"Would you like to talk to the pastor?"

Chris swiveled his head to face Carol. "Who?"

She giggled. "The man who preached today."

"No." He definitely did *not* want to talk about the way the fellow seemed to peer into his soul. If they talked then he might not know how to steer the conversation. Chris stood. "Fancy some lunch?" He looked at their joined hands and squeezed. Better to fake that he knew what he was doing. Right. He tacked on a big smile.

It was mirrored when Carol rose from the wooden bench. "Would love some, but it's Sunday and the shops are closed." She brushed a stray hair from her cheek.

"I suppose we could pop across town to the new Chinese restaurant."

"I'm fairly certain my father would not allow me to 'pop across town' with an airman he hasn't met yet."

"Point taken." They meandered toward the church door, fingers intertwined. "I didn't plan this out very well, did I?" Chris reached up with his free hand and scratched his fresh haircut.

"That really takes the biscuit." Carol moved alongside him. "I pegged you for a man who plotted it all out."

Outside of the church, Chris ducked past the pastor who was talking to another couple. He nearly pulled Carol down in his hurry to avoid the man. And his sermon. And the way it stuck to his brain like old porridge. *Finding joy when everything seems wrong.*

He straightened his tie and slowed his steps to match her shorter strides. He drew in a deep breath to ask her out to dinner next Saturday when she spoke.

"Dad and I are supposed to have supper later—shepherd's pie. I can fix you up a plate and you can meet my father." Her eyes dropped. His gaze followed and stayed on the cracked pavement.

Chris sniffed now and moved his slip-on to cover the cracked concrete at the flat's stoop. Carol. Love of his life. She left him, and nothing he said or promised stopped her. Not even the church that took up so many years of their lives helped him in the end.

The taxi pulled up to the curb. The driver rolled down the window, the interior light shining off his bearded face. "Chris?"

"Yup." He pulled on the car door handle, and it was locked. Figured. He tried a second time and it still held fast. "The doors?" he said, incessantly tugging on the handle like a child.

"Sorry about that." The locks popped up, and Chris slid onto the cracked vinyl back seat.

"Good day for a walk in the countryside." The young man adjusted his mirror and checked over his shoulder before merging into the sparse traffic before sunrise on a Saturday. "Have you been before?"

Chris turned toward the window. He didn't need chit chat. The sliver of dawn through the dark clouds and blurred buildings matched his mood. The driver caught on and turned up the radio a tad. Some old jazz station. Reminded him of Carol's dad and the music he kept on while he washed the dishes by hand every night. Right up until the day his heart stopped.

Seemed like everything was determined to throw Carol back into his thoughts. The universe wanted to crush Chris under its heel. Again.

The city thinned out as the car tires hummed along the new tarmac. Construction on the new bridge slowed them, but only for ten or so minutes. The driver stayed silent. That suited Chris just fine.

The car pulled into the gravel turnout and parked at the beginning of the trail to the bridge. Since Chris had prepaid the driver, he exited the car without a word. "Thank you—" he heard as he slammed the car door closed. In the burgeoning dawn, Chris could barely make out the path to the bridge. But he knew the way.

The "No Trespassing" sign had fallen over a decade before and lay in the tall grass. His slip-ons weren't ideal, and Chris could feel every rock underfoot. Once he reached the trees, he stopped for breath. The smell of moss and the damp ground under the ferns weighed each lungful of air. He should have used the trainers and walked more often. But Chloe wouldn't care now. She hadn't spoken to him in weeks. No, months. According to her, his only child and the light of his world, everything wrong in her life was because of him.

Chris pushed on after that thought, turning their arguments over in his mind. The last time he'd reached out to her, Chloe had quelled all hope. "Never call me again."

It wasn't until a low-hanging apple thudded into his forehead that he stopped thinking about Chloe. "Ouch," he said, rubbing the sore spot and swatting at the fruit. It was too early in the season for it to be ripe. But overhead, he could faintly smell the ripe apples. Of course he could. It was the only smell in the world that reminded him of his wife.

Those years in the Royal Air Force before meeting Carol, Chris breathed and slept precision. From the tucked bed corners to the uniform inspections, there was something comforting, even now, about having a routine.

She blew into his life like an apple-perfumed tornado, reckless of schedules and ironed clothes. As much as he tried to ignore her across the lawn at a backyard party at another airman's home, along with her tittering laugh that seemed to start up as soon as it ended, Chris ended up catching her glance more than a handful of times. When Carol marched up to him, eyes locked like a homing beacon, Chris steeled himself.

"I'm Carol Graham," she said, thrusting her hand out.

She smelled like an entire flower shop. Her dark eyes were

nearly black under sassy brown bobbed hair. And her smile lifted his own mood.

"Chris Arnold." He was surprised that she shook his hand firmly. Most girls were limp-handed and clammy.

"I haven't seen you at any of James's picnics before. First time?"

Naturally, Chris looked around for James or any of the guys from the base. Women were not his forte. The all-boys boarding school had hammered out any social elegance other than polite answers.

Chris went with his gut. "Yes, madam."

Carol snorted before her laughter climbed again. "Let me guess. Boarding school. Holidays at the school. Straight to the RAF." Her pink polished nails tapped her bicep when she crossed her arms.

He cleared his throat. "Yes…exactly." Clasping his hands behind his back was an easy way to keep from fidgeting.

His father was a busy barrister. Mother relentlessly made it clear that she had not chosen to have a child. It was his father's choice, and she'd given up a year of her life in the fashion industry to accommodate him. Summers home were for working and staying out of the way.

"You need some fun." Carol latched onto Chris's hand and dragged him toward the dance area. By some miracle, James found the pair, and Chris didn't have to admit that he didn't know how to dance.

A nearby bird launched into song, pulling Chris from the long-ago party where he met his wife and best friend. His feet plodded along the memorized path. He never tempered her laughter but helped her learn scheduling. In turn, she gave him a reason to find joy and perhaps the best gift of all—their daughter Chloe. But no matter how Carol tried to swerve Chris from his accuracy in most areas, he remained dedicated to the lifelong art of thoroughness.

And so, it was with that planned out meticulousness that Chris climbed the path to the bridge. He slipped off his shoes and lined them up at the edge of the bridge, toes pointed out over the stream bed. Unfastening his watch, he noted the time, before laying it into the right shoe. Fishing into the inner pocket of his jacket, Chris grabbed the folded note for the authorities and placed it into the opposite shoe. He shrugged off the jacket. A sigh escaped through his lips. Chris cleared his throat and pushed on, folding his jacket into particular corners before depositing it to cover the slip-ons. Neat and tidy.

Across the small hill, above the stream bed. Chris heard something tromping through the field. Possibly a deer. He shook away the thought. The rough wooden braces of the bridge fit perfectly into each hand. Chris grunted as he placed his left foot up and then hauled his body up onto the railing.

The sunrise was light enough to show the rocks in the stream far below. Water gurgled between the cobblestones on the edges, and it was certainly deeper in the middle. This would be the easiest way, he reasoned with himself, swaying back and forth from one foot to the other to test his balance. Without Carol and Chloe, there was no purpose in the universe.

He glanced up to the clouds.

The universe would be fine without him.

# CHAPTER 3

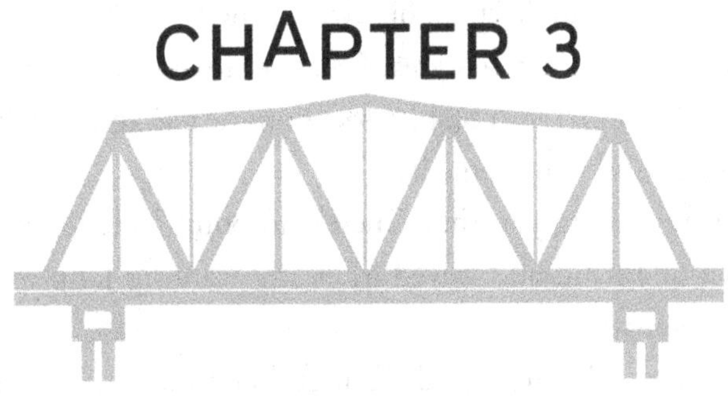

## THE AMERICAN

*John*

**"HEY!" JOHN STOOD AND YELLED, BOTH HANDS CUPPED** around his mouth.

High above and out of hearing range, the man widened his grip on the railing, the suit in stark contrast to the dark timbers. He kept his gaze on the creek bed.

John bolted forward, his left arm knocking the camera and tripod to the ground. "Hey!"

The jumper hesitated as John stumbled down the steep banks, still shouting. "Hang on, just don't let go, please!" John raised his hands, as if it would convince the man that he'd catch him. And so, John kept his arms up while he tripped over tree roots and rocks, until he stood under the trestle. What should he say? He needed to make a decision, quick. Basic. Keep it simple.

"My name's John—John Palmer—and I'm an American! And you are?"

"Not interested." Definitely British. No one else would be caught dead in that combo of a nearly white suit and black shirt.

"Oh," John said, keeping his eyes on the man, "the British humor thing! I like it…that's great!" Stay positive and upbeat even if it sounded dumb. Don't let him focus on the bad things, whatever they were. "And your name is?"

"I'm not telling you that. There's no point." He let go of the rail with one hand and waved it, clearly wanting John to move, to clear the path.

But John was determined. "But I'd like to know. I'm interested." Interested in saving this guy's life, or at least not having to call for an ambulance. John couldn't think about that part.

"Okay. I'll tell you my name if you promise to leave me alone."

"Fine," John said, a flat out lie. Jesus would totally forgive this one. He had no intention of going anywhere. No one was dying today. Not on his watch.

"Right. I'm Chris, now go."

"Chris." John smiled up to him. "That wasn't so hard! We're off to a great start." He took a step back, dropping his nearly numb arms but keeping his eyes up on the bridge span. "So why don't you just come down and we can talk?" That didn't come out how he wanted it to.

Chris shook his head back and forth, his dark hair alternately covering and revealing his face. "No, no, no." He sounded exhausted. John remembered the feeling after he and Joy…

Time to change tactics, just like he'd learned from the counselor back home. "I'll come up." There was a muddy track to the left, threading through the ferns and trees up the hill. Seemed to be in the right direction to reach Chris on the bridge.

"You come up, I'll jump." He held out his hand in a warning.

"No! I don't want to see that!" John looked around. There was no way to climb up from the aged trestle. Besides, he didn't want to climb up the supports and be known as "The American who collapsed the oldest wooden bridge in England."

Overhead, Chris groaned. He scrubbed his face with his free hand, then shifted his attention to the creek. "I want this."

John took a step toward the path, trying to figure out the quickest way to Chris. If he could only stall him. "I…I know you may think that you want this, but—"

"You don't know what I think!" Chris's yell echoed down the small valley. Birds flitted from their hiding spaces. "You've no idea. You haven't a clue."

John could almost feel Chris's desperation. His chest tightened. He'd tasted that wine from the bottom of the barrel. "Then tell me." Another step up the embankment.

"There's no point."

"I'm listening, I won't say anything."

"Doubtful. You've done nothing but talk since you arrived."

John nodded. "Fair point. Just five minutes. I want to listen."

Chris sighed loud enough for John to hear it over the creek. "There's nothing to say."

"I'll come up." And before Chris could protest again, John scrambled up the path. He ignored the ringing phone in his pocket. Crawling on both hands when he slipped, John shoved through the greenery and brambles to emerge on a gravel path at the edge of the bridge.

Chris leaned against the inside of the rails now, fastening a watch onto his wrist. He made no move other than to tuck a folded piece of paper into the inside pocket of his jacket as John brushed off his jeans and yelped.

"Just wait," John said, approaching with both hands out. They stung from the thorns he'd unwittingly grabbed during his ascent.

And the bridge was a lot longer than it looked from down at the creek. As long as he stayed in the middle, it'd be okay.

Chris slid his black sock clad feet into the shoes he'd removed earlier.

"Help me, Lord," John muttered, shaking his hands to lessen the pain. He marched up to Chris, who waited in the center of the bridge. "I need your help, please." Nothing extinguished the fire in his palms.

Shaking his head, Chris plucked the most obvious thorns from John's right hand. "Great," he muttered. His plain gold wedding band looked nearly identical to John's.

John's lungs burned. He needed to exercise more often. "I almost didn't make it up."

Chris dropped John's hand. "I'll leave you to it then." He strolled in the direction he'd come from before, jamming his hands into the pockets of his trousers.

"Hey, wait, Chris." John loped behind the stranger, picking out thorns. "Chris, wait, just five minutes." When Chris failed to stop, John's desperation made his mouth blurt questions. "What about friends? What about your family? There has to be someone."

That did it. Chris paused, head hung low. "There was someone," he muttered.

The air in John's lungs didn't squeeze from the climb now. Chris used past tense for that someone.

The ringing and buzzing started from John's breast pocket once more. Chris turned around, glaring as John removed it to look at the screen.

"I'm sorry, it's my wife. You know how wives can be."

Chris closed his eyes and tilted his chin to the sky. A heavy sigh pressed through his nose. John silenced the phone and shoved it back into his pocket, unseen thorns snagging on his shirt. Joy would have to wait. Again. Hopefully, she'd understand this time. And not conjure up some crazy imagined story.

The phone scratched up against something in his pocket. The tract. John slipped it out and held it in front of him. The orange sunshine on the front stood out against the gray English morning. Maybe this would work, and Jesus would be able to help Chris, like he'd helped John.

"You know, I believe there's a purpose to living." The more he spoke, the greater John's confidence grew. Jesus definitely could save Chris from his misery. "Can I share something with you?"

Chris rolled his head on his shoulders before looking at the flimsy tract. He squeezed his eyes and grunted. "Is that what I think it is?" His accent made the question sound even more belittling to John.

"You see, I'm a Christian—"

"Oh great."

John shook his head a little. "What?"

Chris scoffed. "You're joking, aren't you?"

"No." John's hope for Chris faltered.

"Of all the bridges I choose… Just what I need."

"Come on," John said, waving the tract like a flag of truce and opening the flaps. "Let me share this with you."

Chris squared his shoulders and jutted his bottom jaw to the side. "You're really gonna do this, aren't you?" He took two steps toward the rails. Man, he had long legs.

"Yeah, just listen." If John could get through it, he was sure that Jesus would do the rest. But something was off. "It's in Spanish." He flipped the tract. "Oh, here we go. They write these things in two languages, and I had the Spanish side out." His words ran together the more nervous he became.

John dragged his finger down the first column, not finding what he needed at the top. "Here we go." He held the tract out for Chris to read while he pointed, extending his arm and trying not to move forward toward the edge of the bridge. "It says here that there is a creator of the world, John chapter one verse one. In the beginning was the Word—"

"And the Word was with God and the Word was God."

Well hallelujah, Chris was already halfway there! John slapped Chris's shoulder. "Amen, bro."

Chris wagged his head, scowling. "I am *not* your bro." The wind swirled debris at their ankles, but he focused his stare on John. "You really don't have a clue, do you?"

"You know about Jesus?" John asked. This would be much easier if Chris did, since John was new to this evangelism stuff. It was simpler to stay quiet. But Chris needed to hear a reminder. "Well, good! That's good. Maybe if you listen, then you'll understand that there's hope."

Chris closed his eyes again. His chin dropped, and he took a deep breath before letting it go. "Don't." He took the last step and grabbed the railing.

"I…I have to." Jesus could do it with the Pharisees, and this guy had the attitude of an entire bunch of them. "You have to understand that He can save you." John took the terrifying paces to Chris's side, keeping his eyes level.

The muscles in Chris's face relaxed when he opened his eyes again. "I don't have to understand *anything*."

"But," John started, then stopped. It shouldn't be this hard. This was almost worse than fighting with Joy or Jenny. But this was Chris's soul. "If you just listen, I mean, what have you got to lose?"

"Okay." Chris shoved back from the railing, walking backward toward the middle of the bridge. "Okay 'buddy bro.' Give me your best shot." He nodded, his tone dripping in sarcasm. "Give me the gospel. Tell me your good news so I can be another jewel in your crown, another feather in your witnessing cap." Chris turned on his heel and continued to the opposite railing. He scoffed at nothing but the air. He faced John once more and pointed his thin finger.

"Then you can go back to your megachurch in Middle America with its Starbucks in the lobby. And you can tell everybody about the poor mixed up Brit who you led to Jesus with your tiny little scrap of paper that you'd forgotten was written in Spanish." Chris crossed his arms. "Yeah, go for it, *bro*."

John shifted from one foot to the other. Well, that was unexpected.

Chris had no idea what John had been through. How dare he mock him? As if his accent made him superior or something.

John could play that game, too. "Okay, sure, whatever you say." He kept his tone as cynical as Chris's.

Crossing the bridge to face his adversary, John cleared his throat and held the tract in front of him, hoping that Chris couldn't tell he was shaking. If this man wanted to be treated like one of the workers who needed it straight from the book, John would read it that way. No misunderstandings or misconstrued words.

Except that it didn't feel right. This guy wasn't a worker, he was a guy who'd just thought of ending his own life. John knew what that felt like. Chris needed hope. John tucked the tract next to his phone. The sound of the creek below made his heart race. He placed a hand on the railing, ignoring the stinging pain, and prayed this would work.

"Well, in the Bible it says that God made the world perfect. And He made man, and they had a perfect loving relationship together." John wove his own fingers to make a point. "That's how it was meant to be. But then we sinned. Man did wrong things that broke that perfect relationship." He pulled his hands apart. They prickled from the bits of thorn dug in deep.

"But God had a plan. He sent Jesus, His one and only begotten Son, to live as a man here on this earth. And He suffered."

Chris stared at John, blinking and passive. He probably hadn't shaved in a day or two and probably didn't care. John took a breath and plowed on.

"Jesus died on the cross. He rose again and ascended into heaven." John pointed up to the gray clouds. Chris looked away. "Now, His death on the cross paid the penalty for sin."

John smiled. He loved this part. "If you trust on the Lord Jesus and ask Him to forgive you, you will have a brand-new relationship with God. And everlasting life." He paused long enough for Chris to look back and make eye contact. "And a friend who will never fail you."

It was enough to shrug about. John lifted a shoulder. "So, what do you think? It's pretty cool, isn't it?"

He'd done it! He'd gotten through the entire presentation without mistakes. Now Chris could cling to the same hope John grasped with every fiber of his being.

When Chris's sad eyes bored into his, something deep inside of John wished he could help. Chris raised both hands and clapped slowly with disdain. But he remained silent.

John felt his smile melt. Chris placed both of his hands on the railing and peered down to the creek. John used the chance to sneak a glance at the tract again. He really didn't mess it up *that* bad. It went back into his pocket.

"I didn't mean to offend you," John sighed. "I just...I can see you're in need." He stood next to the railing beside Chris.

"Not of religion," Chris snapped. His jaw worked, but he didn't say anything more.

"Christianity isn't religion, it's true faith. It offers real hope."

Chris pushed back with one hand, angling his body toward John. "And you think I'm in need of real hope?"

John jerked his hand back. Was this guy for real? "You're the one who's about to jump off of a bridge, Chris."

# CHAPTER 4

## A PROPER WRECK

*Chris*

HE SHOULD'VE KNOWN IT WOULD BE MUCKED UP. AND by an American no less. One who would not stop talking from the moment he yelled across the gorge. Chris couldn't even get this done right. Everything he did failed.

Now the guy, John, was reading a tract word for word, babbling on about Jesus. What did Jesus ever do for Chris other than take his life away piece by piece?

John blathered on, and Chris held his tongue. This guy was unreal. That or he really, truly believed this nonsense. A book that was supposedly written by a bunch of men inspired by God thousands of years ago.

Carol believed it. With every part of her being. No, her soul. Even more than this pathetic man who couldn't take a hint. His speech about a brand-new relationship with God and everlasting life could convince a passel of nuns to convert.

"So, what do you think? It's pretty cool, isn't it?" John smiled one shoulder hiked high.

Chris stared at John, unblinking. With measured slowness, he raised his hands and clapped at the ridiculous presentation. As if Jesus actually loved him after all he'd done. Chris applauded with every ounce of scorn that had been stored for years. Hopefully John would shut up.

When the man's grin drooped, pulling his eyes down, Chris turned and held onto the railing. The stream below lured his gaze. He couldn't count the times he'd stacked those rocks, making a castle for Chloe or digging deep in the sand to search for the gold Carol was certain they'd find. Those were the simple times. Picnics, bring and shares, and tea parties.

"I didn't mean to offend you," John said behind him. He sighed and moved to Chris's side. "I just…I can see you're in need."

"Not of religion!" The last shred of patience snapped inside of Chris. This stranger hadn't a clue. And this was not some kind of spill-your-guts moment for Chris. As if this "bro" could feel the way Chris hoarded the last pieces of his broken heart like an orphan with his tattered favorite toy.

John shifted his stance. "Christianity isn't religion, it's true faith. It offers real hope." Every word dripped desperation.

This needed to end. Chris wanted to finish what he'd started this morning. The plan needed follow through and a conclusion. John could go back to his family and go on about his life. He'd forget all about this day.

Chris twisted his body to halfway face his rather homely opponent. Time to make this man saunter off and repeat his tract to someone who cared.

"And you think I'm in need of real hope?"

John flinched as if he'd been struck. He stared and blinked like sand was in his eyes. "You're the one who's about to jump off a bridge, Chris."

Chris held his breath, resting both forearms of the cool wood rail. An arm's length away, John's fingers drummed against his thighs. Carol took up crocheting when she started that habit. His favorite cardigan she'd made, with a tan body and black sleeves, was back in his wardrobe. Perhaps Chloe would keep it. Maybe she'd even remember the story her mum would repeat about running out of the beige wool. "A proper wreck," was the official name of the jumper. Fitting, right down to the crooked buttons.

And what he wouldn't give to have the cardigan instead of this bloke interrupting destiny. John's eyebrows were arched high. He had one foot poised in front of the other, as if to hurry and block Chris should he bolt forward.

"Yes," Chris huffed, "and the only good reason I haven't is because you won't leave me alone."

Alone.

The mantra of his life for the last couple of years. Well-meaning people who pushed him to get out and live a little. He was quite content to allow the emptiness to swallow him whole. Silent flat, quiet phone, and an uninterrupted plan. Until now.

John shuffled closer and smiled. "Well, that's good, isn't it?" He smiled a lot. It thoroughly annoyed Chris's countenance.

"No. No. It's not good." Chris squinted at the American. "It's not good at all." He nodded to the valley floor. "Anyone would jump off this bridge rather than stand here listening to you!"

Yes, Chris preferred the mute rocks below. They would be less irritating than this incessant drivel.

Out of the corner of his eye, Chris saw John put up both hands. "Okay, I get it. Excuse me." He pulled the syllables long to mock Chris before he took a step backwards.

The nerve. He had no right to be here, to interject his beliefs and ruin the moment. Utterly exhausting.

"Why?" Chris pushed his body from the rail. "Why do you Americans always do this? You go in when you're not invited, and you cause more harm than good."

Americans. Always thinking their country was the best. Trigger warnings on everything. Asking how you're doing when they don't know you. Even their pessimism was cheery. The inherent need to feel bigger and better than everyone else.

Chris shook his head. "If I wanted to hear about your faith, I'd ask you." He spoke in the general direction of the stream. Maybe the rocks would listen. All he wanted was to complete what he'd set out to do this morning.

John coughed behind him. "Well, I can't not speak about my faith because it's true." John grabbed the railing next to Chris. "There is a God, and He will judge you."

Chris glanced up. John's face was pinched in earnest concern.

"I have to warn you," John said, "I'm compelled by Christ who lives within me to offer you hope." He swung one fist forward in tempo with his words, as if to hammer them home.

Would he never stop?

Standing tall, Chris towered over the man in his shriveled jacket. "Oh, he lives within you, does he?" There was not enough contempt in the world to make John get the point. "You really believe in a divine creator of the universe?" He dropped the bait, knowing it would be swallowed whole.

John nodded, his face brightening. "Yeah!"

"And whose decision to cure evil was to come down and visit our tiny insignificant speck of a world." Chris paused and pinched his fingers together. "And have himself killed."

John opened his mouth and Chris launched into the second punch.

"Then to cap it all and come and live with you." He threw both hands into the air. "It's insulting to the universe and small-minded." Chris turned away from his counterpart. "Not to mention preposterous."

Behind him, the gravel crunched as John shifted. "Hey. Now you're getting personal."

"Well, what do you expect?"

If it took getting personal with John's version of God to make him leave, that was exactly what Chris would do. He was good at making people leave, making them feel unloved and bitter. Even the landlady preferred his payments to be dropped into the slot, rather than being cornered with the litany of problems he found in the flat.

Down in the valley, he imagined Carol lying on a blanket, another covering her legs because she was perpetually cold. She read one of her books from the public library, the one next to the tattoo parlor, where they knew her by name. They finally stopped ringing the house asking when she'd be around for her books on hold when Chris tossed her card onto their countertop.

Getting personal? That he could do.

John sighed. "Look. I know you're in despair, and there's real hope."

Chris shook his head back and forth, chin dropping toward his chest. "You haven't a clue."

"The Bible says, in the book of Isaiah, 'For I know the plans I have for you, plans for a future and a hope.'"

"That's funny. What a lot of tosh." Chris chuckled and faced John again, a grin teasing the corners of his mouth. Americans. So confident. So wrong.

"What?" John's eyebrows drooped and he glanced to the sky. "No. I—I said it right."

Chris hesitated before answering, giving John time. When a puzzled look remained, Chris crossed his arms. "Jeremiah."

"Huh?"

"It's in Jeremiah."

John's confusion grew, etched into the lines of his face. "Well, I, um…"

After a long draw of air, Chris settled. "Written in the sixth century B.C. as a message to the people of Judah in exile at Babylon." Chew on that, mister know-it-all. There was no part of this era of history that Chris did not know by rote.

"Wow! Impressive!" John smiled, yet again, and nearly punched Chris's arm before drawing up short. "The man knows his Bible." His face turned serious again, intense and focused. "But what it says is true. God brings hope."

Stuff and nonsense. Chris closed his eyes. Perhaps John would disappear. And for a glorious moment, he didn't speak at all. The babbling stream sounded below. Birds darted about.

Chris returned to leaning on the railing. "Why am I getting drawn into all of this?" he mumbled.

When John left, which was certainly soon, Chris would be alone again and on the path to release. Nothing John had to say could stop him. There was nothing new under the sun to learn from a man who had to speak from a tract and quoted the wrong scripture.

"Because you care," John answered in nearly a whisper.

Chris did *not* care. And he would prove it.

"It also says in Jeremiah, 'The Lord has not sent you. You persuaded people to trust in lies.'"

John looked like a child whose favorite toy had been snatched away. His mouth was slack before he found his bumbled words. "It's not lies. You have to believe on the Lord Jesus."

Chris adjusted back to standing. Crossing his arms once more, he sniffed, settling on crushing his opponent with equal text.

"Phillip says in Acts chapter eight, 'If you believe with all your heart, you can be baptized." He waited for John's mind to catch up. "And the Ethiopian he is with replies, 'I believe that Jesus is the Son of God.'"

Really. This was too easy to do. Chris watched John's confusion bloom into excitement. It would be satisfying to cut his proverbial legs out from under him.

"That's my point exactly!"

"But 'believe that Jesus is the Son of God' is cut out of most translations."

John drew back. "Well…well there are different translations, and I know that all of them—"

"Do you believe in the Trinity?" Chris knew this minefield. Had it memorized. John, obviously, would trip his way through it and end up destroyed.

"Amen, I do!" There was that blasted grin.

"The Trinity is only mentioned once." Chris held up his index finger, nearly nicking the tip of John's nose. "Once. And that's in the first Epistle of John."

Immediate confusion clouded John's face, his crossed eyes trained on Chris's finger. He hummed ambivalently.

"'For 'there are three that bear record in heaven. These three are one.'"

Chris could still hear Carol's minister reciting the passage, holding an egg of all things. He used the egg to illustrate the three parts of the Trinity, yet they all composed the same egg. All Chris could imagine was dropping the egg. Would the Trinity become edible? And as if the man in the pulpit could read his thoughts, he answered. "Even if the parts were mixed, scrambled if you will, they are still parts of a whole."

"This part," Chris continued, "is cut out of most manuscripts as well, which is proof that the Trinity doesn't exist." In the end, it was all a breakfast analogy, and a poor one at that.

It was John's turn to cross his arms. "No." He shook his head hard enough that his chin alternately touched each side of his jacket collar. "Nope. I refuse to believe that."

"But you don't know what you believe, do you?" Here is where John's religion went to join Abraham's bosom, or so they said. "So, you can quote the Bible. A bit." Chris held up his fingers barely spaced apart. Then he shrugged. "Who cares? So can I."

Memorizing things had never been a struggle for Chris. His cursed visual recall slipped each day. Even he was surprised the passages sprang forward in his mind. Why could he spout Bible verses and not remember Carol's favorite song? Her Boxing Day birthday never slipped. But the day she told him she was pregnant or the exact words she said when she left? Lost forever.

"Besides," Chris said, "it's just an old story book." His heart pulled down, weighted with his heavy words. Better to cut off the load and be free. "You know, we've moved on and so have human rights. I mean, how can you believe in a god that condones slavery and stoning to death?"

Deep inside John's pocket, a phone vibrated in tune with a ringtone. John fished it out, eyes instantly on the screen. He blew out his breath through pursed lips. The moment he was interrupted, John lost interest.

Chris snorted. "Well, that's convenient." He nodded toward the phone.

John looked up, his fingers were poised, ready to swipe. A small protesting sound came from the back of his throat. "It's my wife, for crying out loud." For a measure of privacy, John turned his back and walked toward the middle of the bridge.

Just like that, Chris looked at the stranger's back. Like anyone else who had any interest in Chris's pathetic life. "You're no different than the others," he muttered.

A crisp breeze tossed some leaves across the bridge and over the edge. Chris watched them float down, dancing in their descent. This was the opportunity he needed. Success would come, no matter the cost. And if John remembered this as the most horrible day in his dismal life, so be it.

The wooden crossbeams were still cooled from the night and fit neatly across both palms. It was this one time, worth the end result no matter how hard his heart rioted inside of his chest. He took a deep breath and heaved a leg onto the railing to follow his fate.

# CHAPTER 5

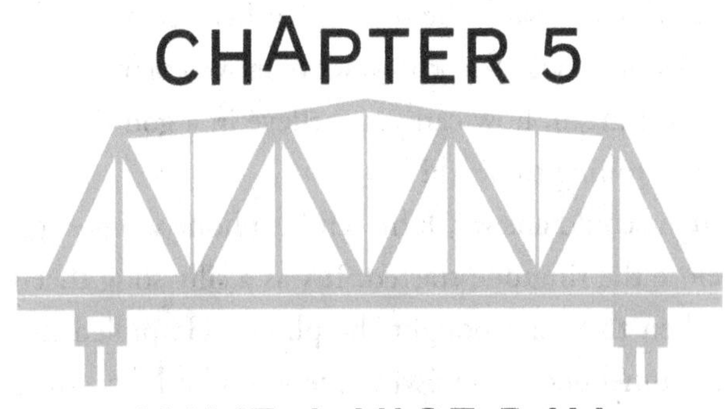

## HAVE A NICE DAY

*John*

**A BIRD WARBLED ITS CHIPPER SONG, OBLIVIOUS TO THE** men facing each other on the bridge. Chris's folded arms rubbed together, the material on his sleeves sounding like a miniature motorcycle in the distance.

"But you don't know what you believe, do you?" he languished, all nasal and snobbish. "So you can quote the Bible. A bit." He indicated the tiny bit with two fingers and shrugged. "Who cares? So can I."

John faltered. Sure, he could recite John 3:16 and some verses from Romans. Those were the ones he learned in Sunday School as a kid. But Chris was right. John didn't know much. He'd only started really trying to memorize verses a few months ago. And it certainly wasn't in case he found someone ready to jump from a bridge.

His mouth was suddenly dry, and he struggled for something to say. Anything at this point. Maybe he could compliment Chris's outfit.

"Besides," Chris said, the muscles in his face going slack, "it's just an old story book. You know, we've moved on and so have human rights. I mean, how can you believe in a god that condones slavery and stoning to death?"

Before he could answer, John felt his phone vibrate against his chest before the ringtone started. It was a silly song that Joy had picked when they first bought the phone. He pulled the phone from his flannel pocket, knowing the scorn he'd face for ignoring her earlier call.

"Well, that's convenient." Chris stared down John's phone like a hawk ready to strike.

John didn't answer right away but kept his finger above the screen. This guy had a superiority complex bigger than the size of the United Kingdom. No, bigger than Texas.

"It's my wife, for crying out loud," John said, turning away from the colossal judgement radiating across the small bridge.

Before he could slide the bar to answer, the ringing stopped. Great. John let his head fall back. She'd start imagining things again. He needed to call her and explain. Sending a text about finding a guy on a bridge would just make her suspicious or she'd reply a bazillion times asking for details.

Chris didn't need questioning. Exhaustion and weariness dulled his eyes. His unshaven face hung in bitterness above the surprisingly pressed suit. No, the guy didn't need a judge and jury, he needed a friend even though he was looking for a fight.

John slid the phone back into his pocket. He'd call Joy later. He didn't care if she believed him or not. This was the moment he needed to be in.

A noise behind him made John look over his shoulder. Chris hoisted a leg onto the railing, hands grabbing the bridge supports on either side. A grunt escaped the British man as he lifted the other foot from the deck.

John scrambled across the gravel and latched both arms around Chris's middle. He didn't expect so much fight. Either Chris had been a wrestler or he was just squirmy. He fought like a rabid badger. The two men twisted, one desperate to leap and the other just as determined to pull him back.

John's head ended up in Chris's armpit, the latter slapping even after John had pulled him back to the gravel. John held fast, despite the fact that one hand ended up near Chris's ear. When the other man stilled, John looked up and then followed his gaze.

Far below, a plump hiker with a crooked stick who looked like a hipster version of a wizard stared at the pair. The man adjusted his glasses and offered a hesitant half-wave.

"Morning!" Chris yelled. He elbowed John in the ear. "This is like a bad joke," he said in a low voice. "Say nothing."

Chris cleared his throat and waved with a free hand. "He's American. I'm showing him the sights."

Looking down at the hiker made John's breathing speed up and red spots pricked his vision. If he could just wedge one foot to keep from toppling over. He shifted his weight back and Chris resisted. Maybe he could switch Chris's attention to move them back to safer ground. He took a deep breath to chase back his nerves.

"Hey!" John shouted, trying to catch his breath and sound chipper. He awkwardly waved his free fingers near Chris's cheek to help sell the ruse. "I'm taking pictures. The view is spectacular." He tried in vain to wave his pinned hand.

The hiker remained rooted to his spot.

"Yankee doodle dandy!" John ripped one arm free and waved.

"Have a nice day!" British people always were uncomfortable when he said that.

It proved true for Hipster Gandalf, who presented a half-salute to the men with his staff and continued on his trek.

John tugged his head free at the same time Chris pushed him away.

"Have a nice day?" Chris said, raking his fingers through his hair. "Have a nice day? Really?"

The Brit staggered two steps backwards, toward the middle of the bridge. There was no way he'd make it through John, who dropped his shoulders and held both arms wide. The worst game of Red Rover ever.

Chris scoffed and looked over his shoulder. He snapped his jacket straight with both hands. "You do know there are two sides to every bridge?"

John felt his stance deflate. He heaved a frustrated sigh. Two sides to everything. Even with his marriage. The hidden parts that weren't shown at the church picnics or family get-togethers. Secrets that Joy held onto with both hands at times to protect their daughter.

Across the bridge deck, John's phone buzzed and bounced across the gravel. He patted his shirt pocket. He'd never even felt it fall out. Stretching his neck, he could see Jenny's face across the screen. That picture was from years ago at the ice-skating rink. They'd gone to the diner afterwards for stacks of pancakes and hot chocolate. Jenny slipped her hand into his on the drive home and fell asleep with her head against the window. He drove for over an hour so that she could sleep. She loved to sleep.

Which is why he couldn't believe she was still awake at one in the morning. John reached his hand toward the skittering phone—

"Don't." Chris held up one finger, like a parent chastising a child.

"I have to!" John inched closer to the phone.

Chris still held out his warning. "You answer it, I jump."

John's heart rammed into hyper speed. Jenny would hate him if he didn't answer. She'd never talk to him again!

"It's my daughter, and it's her birthday!"

"So?" Chris shrugged, nonplussed and annoyed by the way his voice pitched up. "Call her back."

The phone rattled again. "It's…it's late over there." Surely, he had to understand. "She's already going to sleep."

"It's a phone call!" Chris raised his voice and hands, shaking his head side to side in indifference.

Suddenly, the phone stilled. The screen blipped to black, like part of John's heart. No. Oh, no. Maybe she would be so tired that she'd forget he didn't answer. But then again, Jenny didn't forget much. Like Joy, the pair loved to relive the *other* forgotten birthday phone call as often as possible. No, Jenny wouldn't forget this one either.

That's what he got for trying to help. John covered his face with both hands. It didn't help.

"Great," he mumbled through his fingers before dropping them to his sides. "Thank you very much." Every muscle ached when John retrieved his silent phone. "Wonderful. You've just wrecked my family." Every part that he'd tried so hard to repair now ripped back open. The counseling and agreements. He'd be the villain again.

"I promised her, man," John said, voice cracking. He stared at the dark screen, wishing—no praying, that Jenny would call again. *Just one more try, honey. Daddy will answer this time.* He could patch up the rough spots and promise to go on that road trip to Zion National Park, like she'd wanted to as a kid. Or maybe Joy would join them and go to the coast. Although Joy didn't like sleeping in tents. If only Jenny would call again.

Gravel churned behind him. "What is it with you and that stupid phone? If your family can't leave you alone for one minute, let alone a few hours or days, you've got a real problem."

John turned to see Chris walk away, on a diagonal course for the opposite rail. This guy was really going to jump if Chris didn't stop him.

"You're right!" John said. "You're right. I'll put the phone away." He paused, waiting for Chris to turn. Once John had his attention, Chris followed his path a few steps. "Let's just talk a little more. This can wait." He held up his phone, torn between the jumper and his daughter.

This was a man's life. She would understand.

"I'm putting it away now." John extended the phone out so Chris could watch his exaggerated motions. He kept his eyes on Chris in case he bolted. It was harder to find the pocket on the flannel without looking.

The phone dinged twice. Chris's face twisted into sour disgust. "It's just a voicemail," John said. "I'll check it later. Putting the phone away now."

Before John could slide the phone back into his pocket, it chimed again. His eyes strayed to the screen. Joy. Ten texts. Two voicemails. And probably climbing the walls in anxiety, wondering who John was spending time with.

John glanced up to Chris. "It's my wife. Can I at least answer her?" Talk her off the ledge. Just like the man in front of him.

Chris held out his empty palm, face slack. "Give me the phone." He motioned with his fingers for John to obey.

John collected the phone close to his chest. This lifeline helped rebuild his trust with Joy. It helped him keep his promises…up till now.

"Give me the phone, or I jump."

Chris took two steps toward the railing. He was within jumping distance. John bolted forward, phone stretched out. It vibrated and Joy's picture lit up the screen. She'd understand once he told her the entire story. She'd have to because he couldn't just watch a man kill himself.

"Give me the phone!" Chris yelled.

John jerked his hand. He stared at Joy until Chris's hand wrapped around the screen. Chris scanned the phone before he swiped Joy's smile into oblivion. With a smug frown, he deposited the phone into the inner pocket of that stupid linen suit.

And like a boulder heaved from the bridge, John's chance of reconciling with his family plummeted into despair. It took *months* for Joy to look him in the eye during a conversation. Those text messages he made sure to send her every time he was out of town? Didn't matter anymore.

Jenny might not know the details, but she could sense something was off between her parents. Always a smart cookie, she could usually size up a situation and person before John had the chance to say "hello." But missing her birthday calls two years in a row would probably sever the last thread between him and his most cherished person. No flowers or number of apologies would fix this, even though it was a man's desperate existence.

John stared at Chris's suit, right where his phone rested. "Wonderful," he muttered, throwing his hands up, letting them fall like a dead weight against his thighs. Tears pricked the corners of his eyes. Jenny was twenty-one now. She didn't need him much anymore. "You've just ruined my life."

For the first time in his life, John didn't mind the walk to the edge of the bridge. His mantra felt as useless as the harnesses he required for job sites. No, his ironic basophobia, fear of falling from heights, lay as flat as his hopes for Joy and Jenny understanding why he chose a stranger's life over their phone calls.

John grabbed the railing and peered over and recited the words in his mind.

*Prepare yourself.*

*Take it slow.*

*Visualize success.*

*Breathe.*

*Take it easy on yourself.*

The mantra he'd developed over the years seemed rather pathetic now.

"I may as well jump, too."

John wondered where the hiker disappeared to as he looked down. Not sure anyone in their right mind would hike alongside a running creek lined with slick river rocks and bordered by vicious thorny bushes. But the British, as he learned, were a different breed than his family and friends.

"Right," Chris said to John's right side. "Now it's my turn."

John's chin dropped to his chest before he scrubbed his face with both hands. One leftover thorn burned in his palm. He pushed off the railing and crossed his arms, facing the one who probably forever ruined his well-fought-for happily ever after.

"What's that supposed to mean?" John asked. This guy had already extracted every ounce of patience, cost him his camera, and now his family.

Chris mirrored John's stance. "Well so far, it's all been about you." He had a way of squinting his eyes just a tad that made John feel even more criticized.

"Oh, right."

This ought to be good.

"Now it's my turn to speak," Chris started, dropping his hands to his pockets and his tone to something almost friendly. "And all you have to do is listen."

He was worse than Jenny when she was seventeen and knew it all!

"Whatever you say, I got all the time in the world now, buddy." John mentally kicked himself for not calling Chris *bro* again. He looked at the sky, thinking of everything he'd just undone by ignoring those calls. "My wife is probably throwing my stuff out the front door as we speak."

Although he got the words out, he nearly cracked on the last part. "For better or for worse," they'd promised and been reminded by the counselor. And he blew it.

The breath he inhaled made his chest hurt. Or was that his heart?

Either way, his British counterpart waited until John looked at him again. Probably to turn another cruel trick.

Chris gave a quick nod. "I used to be a pastor."

# CHAPTER 6

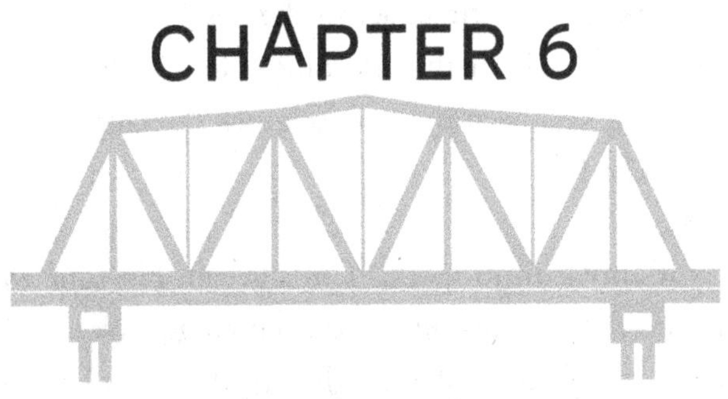

## OLD TREE ROOTS

*Chris*

**NOW THAT JOHN'S EVER-RINGING PHONE WAS OUT OF** the way, Chris wouldn't be interrupted. They might have a proper conversation. Mobiles were an obsession for Americans. Noses always stuck to the screen instead of being with the people around them. Even worse was an entire group plastered to their addictions.

"Wonderful," John said, moping like a half-deflated balloon. "You've just ruined my life."

Chris squeezed his eyes together and shook his head. How utterly pathetic. When he looked back up at John, the man grabbed the railing of the bridge, head hung low. He surveyed the drop below. "I may as well jump, too."

And he was dramatic also. Well, Chris could play that tune. After all, he was born and bred in the land of Shakespeare, Byron, and Wordsworth.

Chris squared his shoulders. "Oh, right."

John raised his eyes, and it nearly knocked Chris over. He'd seen that look so many times across the desk. Desperation. Loss. The same thing he'd felt this morning. He felt almost perfectly awful knowing he'd been the one to knock the chipperness right out from under John.

Almost.

"Now it's my turn to speak," Chris began. His tone was even and even a bit cheery, just like he'd been taught. Not too cheery, but enough to try and make it right. "And all you have to do is listen."

John scoffed. "Whatever you say." A fake smile snaked across his face, and he tossed his hands wide. "I got all the time in the world now, buddy. My wife is probably throwing my stuff out the front door as we speak." He glanced to the sky, as if lightning would strike him dead at the admission.

Poor bloke. Probably had one too many nights away from home. Jobs that took him overseas and left her alone, wondering where he was—who he was with. Ah, and that's why she called him over and over. What a pitiful position to be in all the way across the globe.

Nothing like what he and Carol had. There wasn't a day he concerned himself over her whereabouts, nor she doubting who he was with. Every night they'd sit at the kitchen table with tea and talk about their day, before rinsing their cups and sleeping side by side. Only three times in twenty-eight years had they been apart, and that was while she was in hospital with Chloe and twice for retreats. The longest nights of his life.

Chris glanced over to John's sad puppy dog face. Perhaps now that John's wife and daughter were silenced, he would never leave Chris alone. Unlikely. The two of them were so different, but Chris remembered that feeling of enthusiasm. The initial push of adrenaline to help someone in need. To be the one who could solve their problems.

It'd all been so long ago. And he could almost feel Carol at his elbow, pressing herself against him as a nudge to move forward. When John lowered his gaze from the overhead clouds, the tears in his eyes prodded Chris. He needed to set the facts straight.

It was the simple truth, he reminded himself while he cleared his throat. The reality that would resolve this mess and allow John to walk away into his own proverbial or literal sunset.

So why was it so hard to admit? Chris kicked a piece of gravel with his toe and watched it bounce across the bridge.

"I used to be a pastor."

There. The truth. He hadn't told a soul for years!

John's chuckle ended in a snort. "And I used to be Santa Claus." He held up a hand and used air quotes. "Or is it Father Christmas?"

For a moment, Chris remembered Chloe sitting on the lap of Father Christmas when she was five. She squinted at his beard before casting a glance to Chris. He'd shaken his head, silently praying she wouldn't yank the horrible fake thing from his face. She nodded once and returned her attention to the man, diligently repeating her list: a pony, art supplies, a bow and arrows, and a new *Peter Pan* book since the pages in her old one were falling out.

"Oh, ho, ho!" Father Christmas said, throwing his head back. "Did you drop your book in a puddle?"

Chloe's eyebrows dropped and her pert nose wrinkled. "No. It was my father's, and we read it every night." She slid from his lap. "I think I'll ask Dad to fix it instead."

Chris sighed. "I used to believe in all the things you talked about." He shrugged when John looked up. "But then I came to my senses."

"Yeah, well maybe you didn't really believe in the first place," John shot back, venom tainting each word.

"Oh, I believed." Counseling. Seminary. Theology classes online. "I believed all right."

Then came the sleepless nights when church members needed him. Or when their confessions shook every cognitive thought. The volunteer serving in the church who lived a second life, while professing righteousness.

Chris straightened, and a couple of cracks and pops came from his back. "Then I realized that Christianity is a bigoted and misinformed religion."

John held up one hand and pretended to have a puppet. "Blah, blah, blah."

What happened to the man who'd run through brambles to help? He was just as shallow as the rest of the people who'd filled the pews.

"Yes, and your genuine lack of care, Jim—"

"It's John."

"Is living proof of Christianity's hypocrisy." That got his attention. John swiveled his entire body toward Chris as he continued. "You tried to give me hope with some happy clappy clichés that you learned at some evangelical seminar."

John took a breath but didn't respond. He knew he'd been caught.

Chris continued. "But right here, right now, a suicidal man just wants someone to listen and the best you can come up with is 'blah, blah, blah.'"

The groan that came from John's throat caught Chris off guard. John covered his face with both hands and shook his head. And as if to reset himself, he dropped his arms, stood tall, and gave his entire body a wiggle.

"All right. I'm listening." John cleared his throat. "Were you really a pastor?" He squinted at Chris the same way Chloe inspected Father Christmas.

"For ten years." Hard to believe such a huge chunk of his life was thrown away to that congregation.

"Wow." John's face lifted, as if he'd expected far less.

"It was an old evangelical church in Liverpool." He paused. The man was a visitor and American and probably needed help on location. "You know, the Liver birds, football, the Beatles—"

"I got that one."

"It was only a small church, forty members, a joke by your American standards. And they were all misfits."

Mrs. Black who played the slightly off-key piano each week as if she were a concert pianist. Hamish McDermott, the plumber who moved from Glasgow after finding a job that ended up with him mostly discounting his services to the elderly. The Bennett family, with their two special needs children whom everyone loved enough to ignore their behavior during service. Dylan Prewett, keeper of the grounds, keys, and history of the small church.

Chris could see them all in his mind. He shook himself from the memories, back to the bridge. "But somehow, I believed it all." The thought of Carol's smile warmed him. "I was drawn in."

That first thought of leading worship, of shepherding souls, came well after their wedding. Chloe was a toddler. Carol left her position at the telephone company and Chris crunched numbers as an accountant. It was a steady life with his girls. Though he couldn't remember the day, Chris could recall with distinct clarity when he floated the question of seminary to Carol.

"I've been praying for you," she said, nabbing a toy from the carpet. "You have a knack, my love. I believe you'll make a fine pastor."

"What about you?" he asked, looking at their daughter babbling to her dolly.

"Me?" Carol wrapped her arms around his waist and kissed him. "I'll make a fine pastor's wife."

It surprised Chris how the past crept in all around him on this bridge.

"I think I was too frightened to question it all." Yes, the way he accepted it all the second time he went to church with Carol. Bible studies that filled his mind with suggestions. And above it all, Carol's unwavering support and attempts to get him involved.

John shifted from one foot to the other. "What…what made you change your mind?"

"My wife died."

"You know," John started, "sometimes grief can hurt a guy so deeply that he blames it all on God."

"Don't." Chris clamped his teeth down. How dare he? "You have no idea."

The gaping spot in his middle. The gnawing guilt. The way he tried everything else to fill it.

"So tell me." John nodded, as if to encourage Chris. He smiled ever so condescendingly, like Chris was a child on a bicycle.

The silence between the men was only interrupted by the sound of the breeze and the birds. The sun that had broken through the clouds for a moment, dropped behind the veil of gray. Chris remained mute.

"That's okay, ignore it," John said, shrugging, palms up.

"I was free," Chris nearly whispered.

"Well, that's…that's tragic."

"I hated them all, and I walked away." Molten anger that had lain dormant for months bubbled up within Chris. "The lady who only came to church when her daughter was in town telling me that my wife would be sorely missed. Everyone saying that we could rejoice that she was with the Lord in heaven." An angry tear slipped out, and he swiped it away with the back of his hand.

"And then how they all avoided me. Went on with life. 'Here's a work order, Pastor. It's for the repairs. You'll need to sign here.'" Chris flourished a signature in the air. "Asking me how I was holding up, like I was a rafter and not a man without his wife."

John stayed silent. He shuffled forward a half step. "Then what?"

"Then I walked away. I finally stopped feeling guilty and realized that God doesn't exist." He opened his arms wide. "For the first time in my life I felt truly free. Left the manse, the ever-ringing mobile, and the choking expectations to move on."

"What happened to your church?"

Chris shrugged. "Gone." He sniffed, indignant. He didn't care, he reminded himself with a quick tug of his jacket. "Closed a couple of years later. It's been converted into flats now."

He'd driven by several times after leaving, tamping down the twinge in his heart when the door handles were secured with a chain and lock. It didn't take long for the new owner to remove the stained-glass window above the front doors. If fact, he didn't even know what it had been transformed into until an advert caught his eye a year later: new flats in a converted historical church.

Part of him was sad. Chloe had been baptized there. Ten years of Christmas plays and spring bring and shares. Pews with bronze dedication placards screwed to the back. The pulpit that had been transported all the way from Israel by the founding pastor. Too bad the new owner would have to put up with the old tree roots in the sewage system.

Those reflections plunged Chris's heart down, so much that he leaned forward onto the railing with both elbows.

"That's sad." John took a deep breath and slowly let it out before mimicking Chris's position on the railing. The coloring in his face took on an ashen hue, and he kept his gaze anywhere but the stream below.

"Sad." Chris pulled his lips into a tight smirk. "Sad is losing the love of my life. Sad is having her ripped from her daughter. Sad is thinking there is some god that would allow that, to give such meaning to a person and then yank it away like a petulant child."

The silence between the men stretched taut.

"Well," John started, his voice low and unsteady, "I know in my heart that God does exist." The more words he spoke, the stronger the conviction in his tone. He folded his hands together and nodded.

"So did I." Chris let his chin fall to his chest. All of the sermons. The baptisms. Weddings. Funerals. "So did I."

A white, round piece of gravel caught Chris's eye. It was so out of place among the gray jagged rocks. As a girl, Chloe would've scooped up the treasure and pocketed it, and it would've ended up in the wash, knocking around the washing machine. But she wasn't here, and this day was for an entirely different ending.

Using his slip-on, Chris nudged the pale stone until it tumbled from the platform. He watched until it splashed into the water below. Peaceful finality for that bit, resting at the bottom of the water, undisturbed.

John cleared his throat. He stared down where the rock had disappeared. "Not the way I'd like to go."

He held onto the rail and pushed back some, then looked at the stream again. He gripped the rail and looked both ways on the sides of the shoreline, as if he was looking for clearance or a particular spot. Was he actually thinking of jumping?

"Are you sure this is high enough to do the job?"

# CHAPTER 7

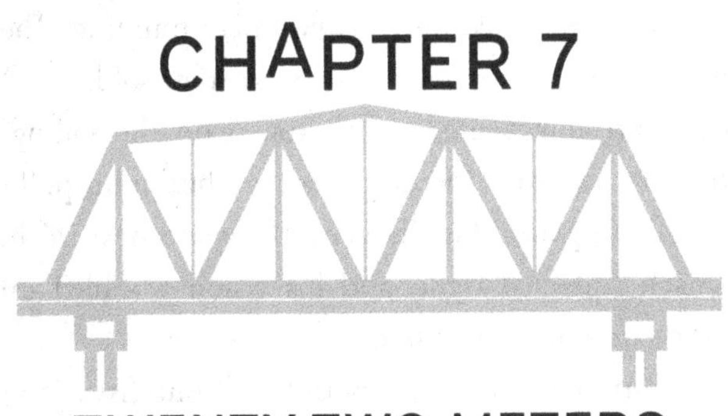

## TWENTY-TWO METERS

*John*

"THEN I WALKED AWAY. I FINALLY STOPPED FEELING guilty and realized that God doesn't exist." Chris opened his arms wide, like he was going to start singing about climbing every mountain. "For the first time in my life I felt truly free. Left the manse, the ever-ringing mobile, and the choking expectations to move on." Though he really laid on the conviction thick, his face wrinkled in worry.

"What happened to your church?" John asked, half not wanting to know the answer. There were some crazy confessions going on.

"Gone." Chris lifted his chin and brows—the perfect picture of snobbery. "Closed a couple of years later. It's been converted into flats now."

Converted into flats? People lived in a church? Or maybe they somehow transformed the space. Either way, tragic for the people who used to attend there. John could only imagine seeing a beloved church transformed into an apartment building. The sanctuary divided into bedrooms. Pews discarded or sold.

"Sad," John commented. Chris rested on the railing, head hung low. He needed a friend, not a preacher. John pulled in a deep breath and placed his elbow on the wood next to the Brit. His stomach squeezed tight, and his vision wobbled until he looked at the top of the tree line.

Next to him, Chris bunched both hands into fists. "Sad." His words were nasal and condescending. "Sad is losing the love of my life. Sad is having her ripped from her daughter. Sad is thinking there is some god that would allow that, to give such meaning to a person and then yank it away like a petulant child."

It knocked the fight right out of John. This man had already lost so much. It was the bottom of his barrel. But John had been there too. The bottom meant that the only way was up. And as cliché as it sounded, it'd worked for him. Maybe God made John reach the bottom so he could help Chris from his. It was worth a shot, would make having missed the phone calls from Joy and Jenny mean something.

"Well," John started. No. He'd have to be more confident for Chris. "I know in my heart that God does exist."

A soft grunt came from Chris before his head lowered once more. "So did I. So did I."

Chris moved around gravel with his loafer. Now that John got a look at them, they seemed rather expensive. Scuffed and well-worn, but still nice. Nothing that he'd ever even try on. He'd rather be caught in the unused cowboy boots Joy bought him years ago to wear to the local rodeo.

John watched Chris single out a round white rock with his toe and push it off the bridge. Though his unreasonable fear of falling clawed at his throat, John couldn't help but watch the stone plummet.

It plopped into the creek far below.

Still, the birds carried on and the wind blew. So much to live for.

"Not the way I'd want to go," he said, eyebrows arched high. He'd seen so many accidents throughout the years. Definitely not the way to maim yourself.

John stood back and examined the railing and then the drop again. Eh. This wasn't right. There were too many variables. "Are you sure this is high enough to do the job?"

The angles were off. Not to mention the possibility of slipping on the railing. He'd certainly feel better if there were a harness. Or at least a rope.

Chris made an incredulous sound. "Anything over twenty-two meters is high enough."

Stomach churning in hunger and dread, John motioned to the expanse below them. "What if you hit the water?"

"I'll aim for the ground." Chris angled both of his hands toward the bank.

"Oh," John said, cringing. "That's tough. You really have to swing wide." Maybe he could talk Chris out of this preposterous idea using facts. Anything to save his life.

"I'll manage."

John hummed a nonchalant sound. Time to reel this fish into shore. Maybe there'd still be time to call Jenny and wish her a happy birthday.

For a moment, he remembered her birthday party with a farm theme. Hay bales and everything. He'd hung a rope swing from a branch of the big oak tree. Sometimes, years later, he'd find her there swaying back and forth in the backyard, eyes closed and far away. He missed that and needed to get back to her.

"Honestly, I'm not convinced this is high enough to do the job."

"I checked on the internet." Chris straightened and crossed his arms. "It says anything over twenty-two meters is fatal."

"Twenty-two meters, huh? That's about seventy-five feet." John stood up tall, a bit irritated that he wasn't taller at that very moment. "Wow. That's over two seconds before you hit the ground."

Chris squinted and glared. "What?"

"You'll be falling for more than two seconds." John lifted his chin toward the railing. It'd make him look smarter if he couldn't be taller. "The acceleration in gravity is equal to thirty-two feet per second squared."

"Right!" Chris nodded once before his face morphed into confusion. "Wait. Did you say thirty-two feet per second squared? Isn't that thirty-two times thirty-two?" The more he talked, the deeper the creases between his eyes.

"Sort of. You'd fall about sixteen feet in that first second because you're accelerating from zero to thirty-two feet per second in that first second. You'd accelerate to sixty-four feet per second in the *second* second. And for a short time, your distance would match your velocity at sixty-four feet."

In John's mind, a mutiny of thunderous applause sounded. His college professors all gave him thumbs up. It paid off to be smart. And it paid well. Take that, Mr. Snobbery.

Chris resembled a fish, mouth working open and closed. "How…how do you know that?" His tone practically accused John of witchcraft.

John shrugged his shoulders and smirked. "Surprise, surprise, I'm an engineer. I've taken my fair share of physics." He'd paid off the student loans to prove that degree. It allowed him to travel and see not only the wild and wondrous United States landscape, but other countries as well. Places he promised to bring his girls on vacation to see. It just hadn't worked out that way yet.

"Well...well what if I went headfirst?" Chris was worse than a five-year old school yard bully, trying to one-up another kid.

"Well, you'd definitely hurt yourself. But what if you flipped and landed feet first?"

Chris sniffed and looked up to the clouds. "I think it's going to rain."

"This is England. It always rains."

John had been so underprepared for the copious rainfall amounts in England. His normal work boots that had travelled from Washington state to Canada and down to Mexico were a feeble attempt to keep his feet dry. Everything felt damp. Even sunny days were muggy. Thank the Lord he'd thought to order an electric boot dryer—they should sell them by the boatload here, much as they needed them—though he would leave it behind. No need for it in California.

A scoff escaped Chris. "It was sunny this morning." He searched the sky for the hidden glowing orb.

"You guys are always talking about the weather." John rested his hands on his hips.

Chris levelled his eyes to John. "Are you stereotyping?"

John wedged his lips sideways to keep from laughing at Chris's stereotypical sneer. "No, I just noticed it."

"It's *called* polite conversation."

"I believe it might rain, old boy." John wagged his head side to side while donning a faux British accent. "I could murder a cup of tea. Ta, ta!"

"Well," Chris exploded, "at least we're not rude!"

Oh, here we go. A fire kindled down in John's belly. He'd been anything but rude! He was trying to save this guy's life, for heaven's sake.

"And all Americans are rude?"

Chris jerked his head forward, his shaggy hair falling into his eyes until he raked it back. "Well, loud and brash. In your face and, yeah, rude." He swept his arms out. "Then of course there's the whole eating in your car phenomenon. Burgers, hot dogs, donuts," he ticked off each item with a long bony finger, "all washed down with a drive-thru mega bucket. What a *fantastic* contribution to world cuisine that is."

Before John had the chance to launch back his reply, a quiet stillness settled in his mind. Perhaps Chris's desperation made him so bitter. He was lost and hurting. John didn't have to lash out. He drew in a long breath through his nostrils. The air smelled sweet and damp. It was all he needed to resettle his course of action. Maybe humour would help.

"Speaking of which, because of you, I missed my breakfast this morning." Would've been the granola bar in his camera bag across the field. Or a cinnamon roll from the bakery down the block if he didn't have to walk in the rain.

Chris's eyebrows stretched upward. "Don't let me keep you." He motioned for John to leave the bridge.

John couldn't leave. He couldn't abandon hope. Not after all he'd been through with Joy. His bottom of the barrel hadn't been so long ago.

"You know, when you die, it's not the end." John immediately thought of Mrs. Lacy's flannel board in Sunday School where he helped out when he was home. The old-fashioned cut-outs of angels with harps over blurry gold bricks. It was going to be better than the flannel board, that was for sure.

"You believe in hell." Chris pulled his head back a bit.

"Yes. But you don't?"

"Oh, I do." Both corners of Chris's lips turned down. "I do, believe me." He pointed to the trees before spreading both arms out wide, like he was presenting a prize—of himself. "This. This is hell right here, right now. It doesn't get any worse than this."

Chris sauntered to the railing and leaned onto both elbows. "And when I die, it ends. The pain, the suffering, the heartache. Snuffed out in a single moment. Hmm, glorious. Now you see, if there really was a god, that would be the one thing he got right. That really is the peace that surpasses all understanding. Peace, lasting peace."

Deep within Chris's jacket pocket, John recognized Joy's ringtone. Chris removed the phone and swiped it to silent without even looking at the screen. John's heart notched down a couple of steps. She would be so worried. Chris replaced the phone back where it came from.

Chris continued. "Live life and be happy. And if you can't, die quickly and be done."

His admission sucked the air out of John's lungs. Surely, he couldn't believe that. He was a pastor. He knew the Bible and about God's peace. It was like Chris was taking God's words and twisting them to fit his mood.

Even at his lowest, John never thought this way. He couldn't do that to Jenny. The thought of leaving her with that legacy kiboshed any thoughts of ending his own life. A kid without a dad. No. He'd seen what that had done to his cousin, Wayne. It became Wayne's excuse to fail at life: no college because his dad didn't leave an inheritance, job hopping because he drank to chase away his dad's ghost, or whatever the excuse happened to be that week.

Not to mention, John recalled his own mom's reaction to her brother's suicide. With her constant alternating between despondency and rage, John became adept at gauging which questions to ask his mom and when to simply remain quiet.

A vacuum filled John's life for a time after his uncle died. It took time for normal things to come back. But it'd left a mark on everyone in the family. And his mom didn't even drag God into it.

John stuffed his chilled hands into his pockets. "That is so empty, man."

Chris turned to look at John. "Of course it's empty. But then you've never had to face the fear of an empty existence." He looked John up and down. "You've always run away from it."

The fire that had died earlier flared up inside John. Who did this guy think he was? He had no idea how many times he'd faced fear. Sure, maybe not an empty existence, but fear nonetheless. The difference between him and Chris was that he chose to keep going, even after wallowing in the lowest part of his life. John scraped and scratched his way up. He slid back and had to start over. But run away?

Again, that surreal peace blanketed John's mind—a reminder. Yes, he'd made it this far. With help. Time and time again, he'd called out for help and moved beyond the fear of the moment.

John fought to control his voice, swallowing past the lump in his throat. No one knew what he'd been through except God. A small, fiery push of bravery made him speak.

"My God delivers me from my fears."

Chris glared, nonplussed. "Oh, does he?"

"He gives me true peace. Not the stuff people talk about at Christmas or when there's a news story. It's a true, lasting peace." John wouldn't let Chris warp this into something else.

"So," Chris said, "let's find out how he works for you, shall we?" There was something menacing in his tone. He turned to rest his rear on the rail. Pulling his jacket straight, he tilted his head to the side. "Tell me about your relationship with your family."

In an instant, John's mind tumbled down, down, down and splashed into the creek bed about twenty-two meters below. Of all of the things he could've said, Chris pulled that one out of the thin grey air. God's peace felt like a joke at the moment as John's mind ping-ponged for an answer to the smug Brit who recrossed his arms, like he'd won the victory.

Well, not today. Or ever. John silently threw up a quick prayer for peace and anything else God could spare. Wisdom would be good, too.

"Well," John started, pulling his hands out and wringing them together, "it was great until this morning. Right up until the time you took my phone. Joy is a good wife. I love my daughter, too." A nod helped him believe it.

"Oh, come on. You sound like one of the people from my old church."

Chris snorted. John's heart stuttered. He'd walked right into whatever trap Chris set.

"At least be honest, John."

# CHAPTER 8

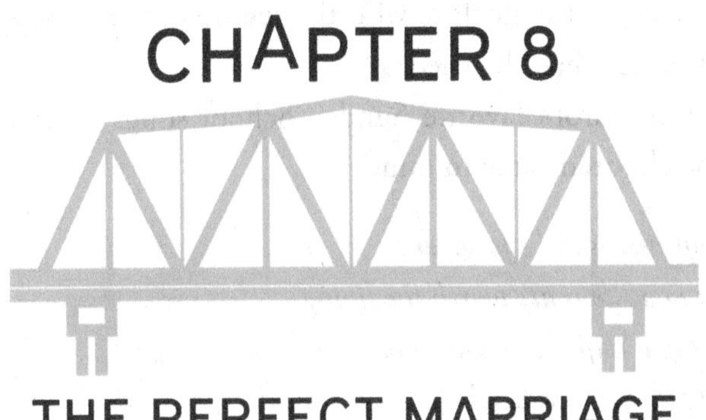

## THE PERFECT MARRIAGE

*Chris*

"YOU KNOW WHEN YOU DIE, IT'S NOT THE END." THE CONviction in the American's voice was downright daft. He simply repeated the rhetoric he'd heard in whatever mega church he attended back home. Or maybe he'd read about it on those daily reminders that'd pop through on his mobile. A verse a day keeps Satan away kind of thing.

Chris grew bored of John's interference. "You believe in hell." Not a question, but a statement. He'd lead John to the same conclusions, even if he had to drag him there by the proverbial verses.

"But you don't?" John's question half stuttered out in confusion.

"Oh, I do."

During the past years, Chris figured out more about hell than he ever had in any seminary class or book. The world was an awful place. Happiness was a mist that pleasantly settled over a person and would eventually blow away. Poof into oblivion. He'd been left more alone than before with the tendrils of joy disappearing no matter how hard he tried.

One of Carol's favorite Sunday School songs that she sang with the children came to mind:

*Happiness is to be forgiven,*
*Living a life that's worth the living*
*Taking a trip that leads to heaven*
*Happiness is the Lord.*

Rubbish. His happiness was beneath a granite headstone in West Derby Cemetery, near the sea that she loved to visit as often as they could. Watching Carol struggle for every breath at the end, begging him to sing "Jesus Loves Me" one more time until she left him alone. More alone than he'd ever been.

"I do, believe me," Chris said, opening his arms to the pitiful scene around them. "This. This is hell right here, right now. It doesn't get any worse than this."

Chris walked over to the railing and leaned down onto his elbows. A perfect drop. He'd aim for the bank and make sure to go headfirst. It'd be successful, no matter what Mr. Engineer had to say about it.

"And when I die," Chris continued, looking to the spot where he'd land, "it ends. The pain, the suffering, the heartache. Snuffed out in a single moment. Hmm, glorious. Now you see, if there really was a god, that would be the one thing he got right. That really is the peace that surpasses all understanding. Peace, lasting peace."

There'd be a blip and then nothing. That's what Chris believed. No matter how hard he had to talk himself into that belief time and time again. Didn't matter that it could be blackness or a floating sense of nothingness. All of the searches online turned up thousands of options. Even reincarnation. Any one of those random answers seemed far greater than a god who allowed cancer. This all-knowing god, whom he'd dedicated years of his life to, even allowed his own creation to have free will, to *not* choose a life dedicated to him. How ludicrous was that type of god?

Everyone who'd clapped his shoulder and said Carol "was in a better place" drove a wedge between Chris and Jesus Christ. Sympathy cards rang as hollow as the dip in her pillow where her head last rested. There was no peace or love when she died. Not even when the children's choir sent him hand-drawn pictures of her in heaven. He felt like a man on a dinghy, floating farther and farther from shore. Jesus didn't reach out for Chris then. And by the time he remotely cared enough to try and paddle back, he realized Jesus didn't care a whit.

Against his chest, vibrations started just before a silly tune sounded. The stupid mobile that John would barely give up. Just how many times did they have to call one another? Must be in a tight spot, having to make hourly check-ins. Chris pulled the mobile from his pocket and swiped the screen to make it stop repeating the annoying ringtone. John looked like a man who'd been sentenced to prison as he watched Chris slide the phone back into his jacket.

"Live life and be happy," Chris said once the phone fell into place. Back to the task at hand. "And if you can't, die quickly and be done." It sounded like a bumper sticker campaign gone wrong. Carol would turn over in her grave to hear those words from his lips. She'd done her best to help him understand that God's plan was perfect, that cancer was His will. Obviously, she believed the gold streets of heaven were real. Chris didn't believe that anymore. It was pointless.

Carol deserved her streets of gold. Chris, on the other hand, did not. He didn't even want to see them. It was far easier to forget about everything he'd learned and taught from the Bible, no matter how often he was reminded of God. Everything became "coincidence" and "lucky." And not reading the Bible every day was beyond easy. Once Chris stopped reading and began figuring things out for himself, it was simpler to sink into the grayness of life. Busy nothingness. Each day of hell on earth without his wife pushed him to this place, to the bridge.

"That is so empty, man." John shoved his hands into his pockets. He looked at Chris like a poor, broken thing—an abandoned kitten in the gutter.

"Of course it's empty." Chris felt another vibration against his chest. No doubt a voicemail. "But then you've never had to face the fear of an empty existence. You've always run away from it."

Chris watched John's face morph into horror. Oh, he'd guessed right! Trouble in paradise. Must be the reason for the incessant phone calls. It'd been such a long time since he'd been chuffed to bits that Chris felt a tad embarrassed by his deduction. Sherlock Holmes would've been proud.

John's entire body gave a quick shake, almost as if to reset himself. He cleared his throat. "My God delivers me from my fears."

"Oh, does he?"

John nodded like one of those bobble head toys. "He gives me true peace. Not the stuff people talk about at Christmas or when there's a news story. It's a true, lasting peace." His smile grew the more he talked. It felt like a pebble in Chris's shoe, how easily John could find something to smile about.

There should be no smiling on a bridge where a man would soon take his own life. With that in mind, Chris prepared to knock this ignorant man back to where he came from so that he could get on with it.

"So, let's find out how he works for you, shall we?" Chris pulled his lapels straight, feeling the mobile bounce against his chest. This would definitely hurt John more than it would hurt him. Delightful. "Tell me about your relationship with your family."

It was almost tragic to see John's face muscles relax before pulling together in sorrow. No, he couldn't run away from this existence.

"Well," John said, twisting his hands together, "it was great until this morning." He looked at Chris's jacket. "Right up until the time you took my phone."

Classic defensive response. Chris had heard it countless times during counseling sessions or from Chloe when she'd been caught in a lie. It was all about the tone and posture, the manner in which John nearly snapped his words like a cornered dog.

It was all too preposterous and made Chris huff.

John straightened a tad, as if mustering his confidence. "Joy is a good wife. I love my daughter, too." He added a convincing nod.

Right. The age old "saying it out loud makes it true" approach. Time to face this head on.

"Oh, come on. You sound like one of the people from my old church." Those men and women who prattled on about how Jesus would see them through and held his hand after Carol died, as if it was comforting. In fact, it was all a big lie. "At least be honest, John."

The American lifted his chin a tick. "Every family has its problems."

Oh-ho! The chink in the armor.

"Well of course," Chris said, narrowing his eyes. "But what difference does your faith in God make?" He paused for simple dramatic effect. Call it leftover pastoral prerogative. "None."

"Faith isn't a free pass from pain and problems." Anger tainted John's tone. His jaw muscle bulged. "Sometimes my faith is the only reason I carry on." Pink spilled into John's cheeks, and Chris knew the fireworks were coming. Not many men could keep their anger at bay once it was allowed into the arena.

"Well don't tell me you've considered suicide." Chris didn't want a sidekick in this venture.

"No!" John waved both hands flat in front of him. "Never," he added, bringing his shaking voice back into check. He rolled his fingers into fists and lowered them to his sides. "I mean, I carry on with my work, my church, my family—"

"Your family," Chris interrupted. Time to send this chap along to deal with his own problems and leave him here to finish. "I told you the perfect Christian family was too good to be true."

"I never used the word perfect." John kicked a pebble across the bridge deck.

Ah, he hadn't said perfect. Chris was remembering all of the times congregation members and friends called *his* marriage perfect. He never disagreed. The vows they took as a young man and woman fashioned their lives. He absolutely loved Carol with every fiber of his body. Even when she folded his socks the wrong way. She was something out of a fairytale book: cooking, cleaning, raising their daughter, and growing a garden. Carol worked with the poor, prayed with the women in their church, and smiled with ease. Yes, "perfect" was a word that many people associated with their marriage.

A horrid realization hit Chris, one he never had to fathom in all of his marriage with Carol. They'd lived side by side, working and playing together throughout their lives, rarely away from one another because they loved being together. Truly. If she wanted to paint the living room and he had to study for a sermon, he'd move his books to the couch. Most sermons were clobbered together on the kitchen table while Carol baked or cooked for their family or others in the church. She was the first one to hear passages, to give feedback, or ask for clarification. Give correction, if needed. Carol was the air in Chris's lungs. He'd been dying one day at a time without her.

John, on the other hand …

The phone calls. Working across the globe. The defensive state.

"Your wife doesn't trust you."

For an instant, silence blanketed the bridge. There were no birds, no breeze to ruffle the leaves. Time stopped with Chris's dreadful revelation until John gritted his teeth, tipped his head back, and tossed forced laughter into the void.

"That's a laugh, man." John slapped his denim jeans with one open palm.

Yet, it was an itch Chris wouldn't let go. He'd get to the bottom of this. Show this tract-toting, brash American what a flat-out joke his god and his life was. Some kind of warped civic duty to reveal the stripped-down truth of it all before he jumped with the hope that it would be a blip and not the fire and brimstone he used to preach.

"She phones you every five minutes."

John looked straight forward. "So?"

"So, all of those trips away have taken their toll, John. She doesn't trust you."

Twice in their marriage, Carol had stayed at home while Chris traveled. One time, she was over eight months pregnant with Chloe and he had a presentation at a pastor's convention in Peterborough. True, he had the radio dial all to himself, but the stations seemed boring without someone to banter with. When he arrived and parked the car, Chris hated the feeling of going into the hotel alone. Party of one, single bed. The tiny room seemed empty. And though they couldn't afford it, he made one phone call just to hear Carol's voice and tell her that he'd made it safely.

"I already miss you," he confessed, hand gripping his suitcase in case she needed him back.

"Christopher Arnold." She laughed into the receiver. "You need to unpack and get to it. I'll see you in a few days." Those days marched on in tediousness until he was speeding home again.

The other time he left on a solo trip, Chloe was recovering from pneumonia. They were the longest two weeks of his life. Though he roomed with another pastor friend, it wasn't the same. He decided to write Carol love letters every day he was away and send them by mail. She giggled when he hauled her in for a passionate kiss upon his return. "I should send you away by yourself more often," she teased.

Carol trusted him implicitly. And he trusted her more.

Chloe would find those letters soon and see that he wasn't such a twit. He simply had lost his way without her mother. Plain and simple.

John shifted from one foot to the other. He cleared his throat. "It's personal."

"Well, cheating often is."

# CHAPTER 9

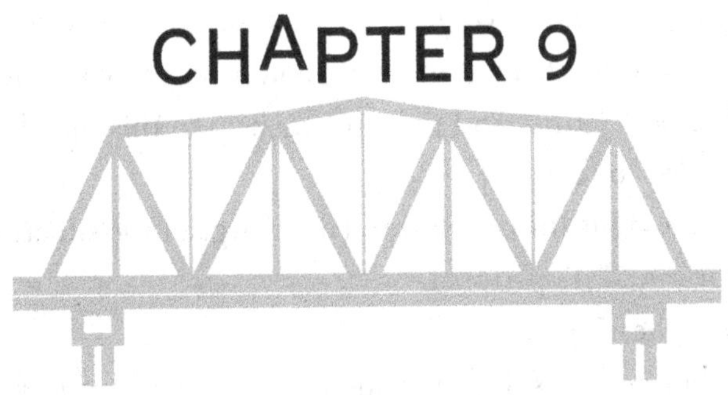

## PROMISE KEPT

*John*

"YOUR WIFE DOESN'T TRUST YOU."

"She phones you every five minutes."

"All of those trips have taken their toll, John. She doesn't trust you."

*"She doesn't trust you,"* echoed in John's head, causing him to nearly stagger. He'd fought too hard to let some stranger tear down all of the progress he and Joy had made.

Inside, he fought for control. No need for anyone else to know what happened. That was long ago. Months. Practically ages ago. Since then, John had moved inches forward, never dwelling in the pain that blanketed their marriage.

*Tell me something I don't know!* John screamed in his mind. Instead, he glanced down the bridge. He should've let this guy jump. His camera was going to be ruined if it started raining. It would be easier to leave now.

So why did his feet stay planted in the gravel? God certainly didn't mean for John to learn something from this deranged, bitter ex-pastor who derived great joy from bringing pain to others. There was a lesson here, John knew, and he knew that to learn it, he had to help Chris. And to be of any help to this suicidal man, John needed to focus.

He cleared his throat. Now to take charge of the situation and move forward. "It's personal."

"Well, cheating often is."

Red hot anger exploded inside of John. "You are *way* out of line, my friend." He ground his words through gritted teeth, heart smashing against his rib cage in rage. He'd never punched a man, but this was drifting closer and closer to the limits that he could handle. No one had any idea of what he'd been through.

"Well, that's not very Christian, is it?" Chris hummed and crossed his arms. John wanted to knock that smirk right off his smug face.

Hovering just below his anger, John's anxiety poked its straying fingers into his train of thought. If those two feelings bumped elbows and were set loose, John would lose control, like he had before.

Chris cocked his head forward, as if trying to gaze into John's tormented soul. "You cheated on your wife, didn't you, John?"

A whooshing sound muffled everything. John's fingertips grew cold, and he knew that if he didn't react, he'd end up unconscious. His basophobia had taught him the warning signs. But never had any person caused it. John breathed in through his nose and out through his mouth, flexing both hands open and closed, until the sound faded and birdsong returned.

Little gray birds flitted from branch to branch. It'd be nice to be so carefree, like the bird in the field from the book of Matthew, without any worries. No overlording, presumptive man butting in on life, trying to stir up things from the past.

John remembered the verse he needed from counseling. The words that quieted the doubts. *Trust in the Lord with all of your heart and lean not on your own understanding. Acknowledge the Lord in all of your ways and He will make your paths straight.*

The peace that surpasses all understanding that Chris had just mocked didn't wallop John or wrap its warm embrace around him either. It didn't even wash away John's fears. But he knew it was there. And that was enough for right now.

"I've never cheated on my wife."

"Oh, come on!" Chris snapped, flinging a hand out. "You wouldn't be the first guy in the world."

As if she'd sensed their conversation, Joy's ringtone sounded again from deep in Chris's pocket. Both men stared at each other, gridlocked in their opinions. John glanced toward the sound. Chris reached in ever so slowly and stopped just shy of removing the phone.

"Let me take that," John begged. Joy was probably climbing the walls by now. It'd be a miracle if she hadn't called his supervisor or the police. It was crazy how quickly she assumed the worst now.

"No." Chris remained frozen, hand suspended over his pocket, shaking his head side to side.

"I promise—"

"No. No."

Desperation clawed John's throat. "I won't tell her a thing about you." Joy didn't need to be burdened with this crazy guy's opinions and outlook on life. He just needed to tell her that he was okay and not avoiding her.

Chris's lips turned down. "No." He inched out the phone and held it just out of reach.

"I, I…I promise on everything I believe in!" Even God would

understand this promise. It wasn't swearing on His name, but it was close.

The phone balanced on Chris's hand.

"Just, please." John outstretched his palm. Maybe, just maybe, Chris would have a heart. Cut a guy some slack.

A miracle happened when Chris offered the phone to John.

"Thank you," John said. He'd make it right with Joy and calm her down.

He held up the phone. She was trying to video chat. The cracks across the screen distorted her photo.

It was another miracle the phone screen hadn't fallen off altogether and that the phone actually still worked. The rage he kept a tight lid on had caused that calamity, among others. Not even the cheap case saved the screen from John's wrath when he chucked it at the refrigerator. He should replace it when he got home.

John swiped the video call open. Joy's pixelated face cleared up. "Oh, there you are," she said, voice scrambled. One step to the middle of the bridge and John had three bars of coverage. "Thank the Lord." He took one more step away from Chris for privacy before swiping the screen.

"Hi, Joy."

"Hi." Her face was divided by cracks. "How come you didn't pick up earlier?"

There was his wife in a question. In attack position instead of even asking if he was all right. She'd lost the softness in her voice whenever they'd talk. It was business. Everything by rote. There had to be a way out of this rut.

"I'm sorry, honey. I just wasn't able to." It wasn't a lie. He'd promised never to lie to her. It was more like editing.

Joy craned her neck toward the screen, as if she could see past his camera view. “So, what are you up to?” Her voice screeched with distortion on speakerphone.

“I—” John looked up and around. “I’m…I’m on that bridge I told you about.” He angled his phone so that she could see the wooden guardrail. Hopefully that’d be clear enough on the other end of the call.

“It’s late here. Jenny said that she tried calling and you didn’t pick up.” The pitch of distortion grated his hearing, but he didn’t miss her accusatory tone. Even the Atlantic Ocean couldn’t hide it.

“I know, I know,” he said, his free hand making motions for her to calm down. “I promise as soon as we hang up, I’ll call her.”

Jenny wouldn’t answer. He knew she wouldn’t. She’d hang onto the fact that he hadn’t answered and hang it over his head like a noose. If she only knew how hard he was fighting to keep his family together, maybe she’d forgive him.

“Is there someone there with you?”

Joy’s accusation bolted through him. He glanced up to Chris, who stared back like a hawk ready to strike.

“I…I told you I’m on that bridge.” He held his phone camera over his shoulder to show her the opposite side from where Chris stood. Promise kept.

When John brought the phone screen back into view, Joy’s video skipped and pasted her face like a Picasso painting before setting it all together again.

She sighed and it sounded like a kazoo. “You know, there’s something going on here. There’s something between us.” Joy moved her hand back and forth between herself and the camera before moving closer to her phone. “Do you love me?”

Always the same question. Every time. She knew how to cut the legs out from under him. And when John looked up from the phone, remembering Chris was there, he found himself being examined.

John walked a couple of steps farther. "Look, Joy," he said, voice hushed, "this isn't the right time."

There'd been plenty of times he'd been a spectacle when she'd clamp onto his arm at a work function or become emotional at a family dinner. It wouldn't be in front of this bitter Brit, though. Not if he could help it.

Joy said something but it came out garbled. "Why do you love me?" she asked, all pitched and distorted.

"I…" John scrambled for an answer. There were several to choose from. Counseling had filled his toolbox, so to say.

"Hello?" Joy snapped her question faster than an alligator. Or was it a crocodile? "Can you answer me?" Though her features scrambled together, John could imagine the way her eyebrows furrowed together. She always did that when her frustration reached a certain level.

He remembered sitting side by side at Pastor Ryan's office with Joy, miles apart. He initially regretted going, feeling the guilt heaped on his shoulders. It wasn't until Pastor Ryan gave him time to speak without being interrupted that John felt the layers peel away. He could go back to loving his wife. "Fall in love with her again," Pastor Ryan encouraged. John reached over and grabbed her hand. She squeezed his, and they both had tears in their eyes.

John looked at his wife on the phone screen. "Because I choose to." Today, that was the best he could do.

"You choose to?"

"We're married, Joy. I'm committed to you."

John knew this conversation was quickly turning into a dumpster fire. He'd carry the blame. Again.. Joy would be like the Titanic full-steam, knowing there was an iceberg dead ahead and refusing to change course until the last possible moment.

"I..." John began, pulling the phone closer. "I love you. I truly do."

Joy's response was lost to squelch. The phone only had one bar of coverage now.

"Now will you please—"

She interrupted him again, but he couldn't understand and shook his head. If only she'd realize how much going backwards hurt. She could trust him entirely.

"I think I really need to call Jenny." Changing the topic to their daughter usually helped reel her anxiety back in.

"Yeah, make sure you do." The defeat in her voice weighed on John. "You know, we're losing her."

Joy would never stop. Not until he groveled and begged for forgiveness. Everything circled back around to John's fault. His decisions had led them to this path. John had already argued with the suicidal man behind him on the bridge. What was one more useless argument?

"Eh, and when did that begin?" he seethed. His squeezed the phone too tightly and lost the picture around the edges.

"You blame me for this, don't you?"

"No, I'm just saying the way it is."

"What? You're going to blame me for it now? I mean...long distance?" Her face split into colored blocks across the screen and the rest of her words jumbled into chopped up sounds. Of course, the phone would lose coverage right then. Exactly when he needed to respond.

"Joy."

"Are you there?" Her forehead appeared, then her chin, before they both scrambled again.

One tiny bar held the futile conversation together.

"We're breaking up," John said.

"You blame me for this, don't you?"

"Can you hear me, Joy?"

"Quit being so mean," she cried. "You said you cared."

Pops of anger burst in John's mind. "Hey, I'm not the bad guy here. Since when am *I* the bad guy?" His hand shook and he felt the fury breaking past every careful excuse and apology. "I do care. I care about you and I care about Jenny. I care about every single thing."

"I care about you," Joy whined back. He knew that it was out of habit.

And it broke his heart.

"The truth is," John said, voice shaking, "if not for you, everything would be fine and happy!"

"You know what?" Joy's tone was saturated in sass. "Don't be so cruel."

"I'm cruel?" John exploded. "I'm the guy who's trying to fix everything! I'm sorry and I've said I'm sorry. It's too late to be sorry."

Blind anger loosened his tongue and John raged on. "You cheated on me and every time you look at me, like everything's supposed to be normal, I gotta deal with that."

Not even Pastor Ryan heard this pent-up frustration. And here he was, yelling it for the entire English countryside and Mr. Tell-Me-About-Your-Family.

So, let him hear.

"Every time I look across the church, and there he is all 'Hallelujah,' I gotta deal with that. Every time you go, 'Oh honey, I'm cold. Put your arm around me,' I gotta think about his arms around you."

His heart was beating so hard against his chest that it ached.

Even the birds were silent after his outburst. But there it was. Finally. No more hiding or pretending that he was over it. Endless apologies for endless accusations. Yes, if you squinted, he played a part. And he owned it. But this having to live under the weight of suspicion needed to end. Right now.

The phone tweedled and beeped. "I'm sorry, okay?" Joy's head bowed down.

"You have no idea." All of the nights he'd slept on the couch. The Sundays pretending that seeing the other guy in the parking lot wasn't a big deal, when all John wanted to do was run him over with the car. Not very Christian, as Chris would point out, but at least it was the honest to goodness truth.

"How do you think it feels to me, John?"

Before John could snap back and tell her exactly how to feel, Chris pulled the phone from his hand and took a couple of steps away.

"Joy, ehm, hello. I'm Chris. We've not spoken before. John's a bit busy at the moment. He'll call you back. Or maybe he won't."

Once Chris stopped talking, John looked up. Now one other person on the planet knew. But it still didn't seem real. John drew in a deep breath. Time to put this façade to rest.

"She cheated on me."

# CHAPTER 10

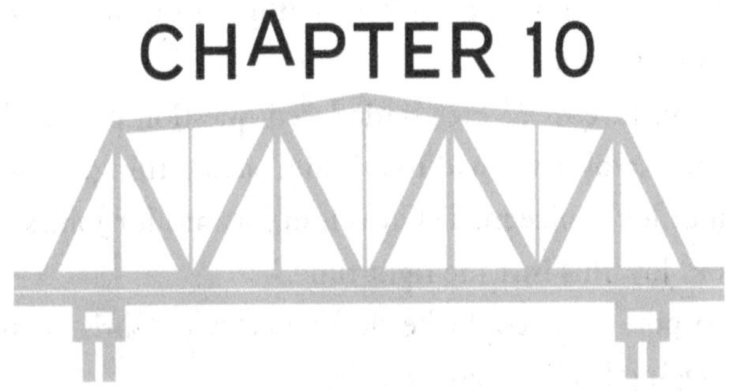

## LIAR

*Chris*

**MAYBE IT WAS THE LOOK OF SHEER DESPERATION THAT** made Chris hand over the mobile to John. The man was doing his best to patch up what was left of the shambles of his marriage. Seemed rather pointless if he was having an affair. Or had one.

Either way, when John slid the video chat to life, Chris was unwittingly now a passenger on the train headed for the end of the line. He leaned against the railing and watched John pace to the other side of the bridge. Kind of like an invisible phone booth or something.

"Hi, Joy," John breathed, relief allowing his shoulders to drop.

"Hi. How come you didn't pick up earlier?"

Wow. Straight away for his excuses. She brought a gun to the knife fight with that suspicion-laced opener.

Of course, John kowtowed and apologized profusely. He was rather proficient at apologies. He bobbed and dodged her questions like a professional boxer. Probably well-practiced. She wasn't falling for it either. Good for her! Sniffing it out like a detective that he wasn't alone.

"Do you love me?" Her static-laced question punched Chris in the gut. Carol never had to ask him such a thing. Never. And the pain in Joy's voice made Chris lean forward for John's answer.

"Look, Joy, this isn't the right time."

All to pot. How could he do that to her? Chris crossed his arms, wagging his head side to side.

"Why do you love me?" Her voice popped and garbled on the speaker.

What's that now? Bizarre thing to ask. Chris pulled his eyebrows together in thought. Why do you love someone? He loved Carol for so long that he didn't rightly know why.

"Because I choose to." John waved his free hand down in surrender.

"You choose to?" Her voice squelched like a banshee.

John sighed before he answered. Chris was sure if he could see John's face, it was as crestfallen as he sounded.

"We're married, Joy. I'm committed to you. I…I love you, I truly do."

Chris was shocked again at John's crass approach. It was torture to listen to him speak to his wife like this.

"I think I really need to call Jenny."

"Yeah, make sure you do. You know, we're losing her."

John's entire body went rigid. Even from behind, Chris could sense the anger John had talked about suddenly flare to life.

"And when did that begin?" John seethed.

They bantered back and forth like angry badgers circling one another.

"Hey," John snapped, "I'm not the bad guy here." He brought

the phone closer to his face. "Since when am I the bad guy?" Though he proclaimed to care, the fury broke the surface.

"I care about you," Joy said, sounding far away and quite whiny.

"The truth is, if not for you, everything would be fine and happy!"

John gripped the railing across the deck from Chris, his body now shaking. Chris's mouth went slack. He knew a liar, and John was not one. This was the beginning of an unraveling ball.

"You know what," Joy said all distorted, "don't be so cruel."

"I'm cruel?" John's voice lowered, his words tumbling out unfettered. "I'm the guy who's trying to fix everything." He lapsed into apologies again, much to Chris's dismay. She was the one goading him. It sounded like he was truly trying to mend what he'd broken. His wife didn't seem happy with anything he tried.

John sucked in a quick breath, his body going stiff. "You cheated on me," he said, voice catching on his own words.

Chris's blood chilled instantly. Utterly and totally unexpected.

Just like the time he sat across the desk with the church secretary, Shirley. She'd been cleaning and folding bulletins, along with depositing the tithes and paying him, for over thirty years. He'd gone over on an expenditure for new curriculum and wanted to make sure it would be deducted from his paycheck.

Shirley rummaged in her handbag. "I just need to find my throat lozenge." Her glasses slipped down her nose and she rammed them back up with a bony finger.

"No hurry," Chris said, adding a chuckle. "I'll just grab the books from your desk."

"No!" Shirley scrambled out of her chair, her purse dumping its entire contents to the worn rug. "I mean, I'll get it."

"I can do that while you pick up your things."

Shirley beat him to the doorway that separated her desk from his. "I have to unlock it anyways," she said, voice warbling.

Chris watched as she knocked around her desk, pulling the key from a hidden nail underneath it. Not high tech, but efficient for the small church. Her hands shook, and putting the key into the lock took longer than it should.

"Let me help you," Chris offered, covering her hand with his.

Shirley wilted into her threadbare chair. "I guess you should."

Chris smiled and opened her drawer. In the hand-kept ledger, numbers were crossed and moved with long arrows. "What's this?" he asked, holding the book for her to see.

"I always intended to pay it back." Though twenty years his senior, Shirley looked like a child caught nicking the last of the plum pudding before dinner started.

He hadn't expected that either.

John waved his free hand in the air. "Every time I look across the church, and there he is all 'hallelujah,' I gotta deal with that."

Oh mercy. All of the things he'd heard across his desk while counseling and this was worse. Chris watched John freefall into admission across an ocean.

"Every time you go, 'Oh honey, I'm cold. Put your arm around me,' I gotta think about his arms around you." John's voice broke, and he abruptly ended.

"I'm sorry," she said. It fell as flat as a pancake.

That was all she had to say? And she had the audacity to call *him* cruel. No, this would not do.

Chris marched across the bridge, intending to place his hand on John's shoulder. Maybe it'd help the poor bloke.

"How do you think it feels to be me, John?"

Oh, that was the cherry on the cake. No more.

Chris reached his long arm forward and plucked the mobile

from John's unsteady hand. John looked like he was ready to collapse. Chris took two steps backward and angled the shattered screen to his face.

"Joy, hello, I'm Chris. We've not spoken before. John's busy at the moment, so he'll call you back."

The picture divided her face a hundred different ways. And Chris suddenly felt protective of his American.

"Or maybe he won't. Bye." He hung up on her and stared at the black screen.

"She cheated on me."

John still faced away from Chris, looking up at the gray English sky. Chris watched John's brown jacket rise and fall with each breath. It was better to be quiet in this moment.

"She said it was only three weeks." John's chin dropped to his chest. His defeat was made more deafening by the nearby wildlife coming to a brief hush, as if they paused in grief.

Chris shook his head. He'd been so wrong. All of the signs pointed to John taking the path of infidelity. Either way, here they were.

"Well," Chris said, "it had to be one way or the other."

"Joy said she was lonely because I'm away so much."

"It's natural. A lot of marriages end that way."

Of course, the mobile vibrated and rang in Chris's palm. Joy's stitched face filled the screen. Chris slid the phone silent.

He took a breath to answer, and the mobile rang again. John turned this time, eyes on the prize. Chris silenced it without looking. It was her.

The third time it began to ring, John lifted his arm toward Chris.

"Let me answer that," John pleaded, hand outstretched.

Chris didn't even consider the request. This poor man needed to be rid of this once and for all. He swiped the phone to send her to voicemail.

John sighed and turned his back on Chris.

Chris couldn't fathom such devotion to a woman. If she'd cheated on him once, who knows how many times it'd been. And she kept him tethered to the phone, checking on him like a stray dog. Always checking in, asking who he was with. Yet John said that he loved his wife and was committed to her, when he was obviously in agony.

"John," Chris said, voice raised. John didn't react at all. "John."

When he turned, John's gaze went right for the phone. "What?" he asked, flat and defeated.

"Do you want to know what I'd do?"

"No, I don't want to know what you'd do." John turned back to the railing.

"John!" Chris yelled. He knew just the trick to hold his American's attention. When John begrudgingly turned, all mopey and dejected, Chris slowly moved the mobile back and forth in the air. The snake charmer and his cobra.

"John," Chris began more calmly, "I'd do this."

Joy's ringtone started again, her face splashing across the broken screen.

With a flick of his wrist, Chris sent the ringing mobile into the air. John bolted to Chris's side of the bridge, and they watched the blasted thing plop into the clear stream below, ripples immediately swallowed by the current. Quite satisfying, to say the least. Chris leaned onto his elbows to see if he could make out the phone at all. It was gone. Good riddance.

A small noise came from John. "Why would you do that?" He motioned to the water, anguish hanging on every word.

Chris paused before he responded. John deserved the truth. A little bit of seminary training still proved helpful.

"I really don't think you were helping each other."

John turned and put his back against the railing before sliding down and landing in the gravel on his rear end. He rested his head on both hands. Chris sat down next to him.

"We were going to make it," John said through his fingers before straightening. "I had promises from God. We were gonna work through everything."

Unfortunately, Chris had heard that line before. Mother's mantra about hard work never did pay off. He wasn't surprised when his parents divorced. Father gave him a nod once it was finalized in the courts. "Well now that's all over," he said, toasting Chris with a tumbler of whiskey. Mother, in kind, met with Chris in the lobby of a hotel. "You will receive no inheritance. My money will go to charity," she said from her plush chair.

"Marriage. So much for hard work, right Mother?" Chris never saw or heard from her again. It didn't matter much to him anyways.

What John needed now were options. A way to make a fresh start and break free from the pain. He obviously wasn't going to leave God, as evidenced by the tract in his pocket and those claims of promises. Promises usually never worked out. Chris spun his wedding ring round his finger until he caught an idea.

"Perhaps," he carefully started, tone light and bouncy like he'd learned at conferences, "you should change jobs?"

"No." John emphasized by crossing his hands and slicing them apart. He raked his fingers through his hair. His anguish saturated the air, pulling the mood down. "It runs deeper than that."

Without a doubt. Chris recalled the times he'd counseled couples and it took weeks to unbury the truth. A spur of discord carefully pushed back until it burst, husband and wife opposed like angry street cats. Those nights, he'd walk home to the parsonage with careful, slow steps while praying he and Carol never fell into strife.

And as if she knew before he arrived, Carol would greet him with longer hugs and a kiss that still stole his breath away. They'd chat over supper, asking Chloe about her day. At night, after Chloe finished her homework and closed her door, Carol would draw Chris into the bedroom and remind him of their commitment to each other.

The very thought of another night with Carol made Chris curl his toes inside the slip-ons. Bits of gravel dug into his behind. Carol would've laughed at his predicament just then, sore derriere and craving a proper snog.

John wiggled next to him. Probably having the same problem. He stared somewhere beyond the bridge, throwing bits of gravel he picked up. They watched the gravel bounce off the ledge into oblivion.

The solution to John's problems niggled the back of Chris's mind. It was painful to suggest, but then again, this man had single-handedly thwarted his day.

Chris shifted, acutely aware of every single piece of gravel through his trousers. "Why don't you admit you hate her?"

John jerked his head around, mouth drooping open. "No!" He scrambled up, wincing when he placed his hands on the ground. "I'll never say those words."

Pacing to the other side of the bridge, John slouched.

Chris stood, wiping his trouser clean. Not that it would matter by the day's end. No one would check to see if his trousers were stained when his body was recovered.

John cleared his throat and straightened. He turned, exhaling, and pulled his shoulders straight. Oh no. The onward Christian soldier was back.

"I love my wife," John said with a curt nod. "I love her."

The quick blinking gave him away, along with the way his hands curled into themselves.

No, he did not. And he knew it. Chris saw John was a wind-up toy, repeating the same line in hopes of believing it one day. Like all of those times Chris tried to make Carol appear in the kitchen when he arrived home. If he smelled her perfume, it meant she would be back from the store at any moment. Yet, his promise never happened.

Chris lifted his chin in boldness. "You're such a rubbish liar."

# CHAPTER 11

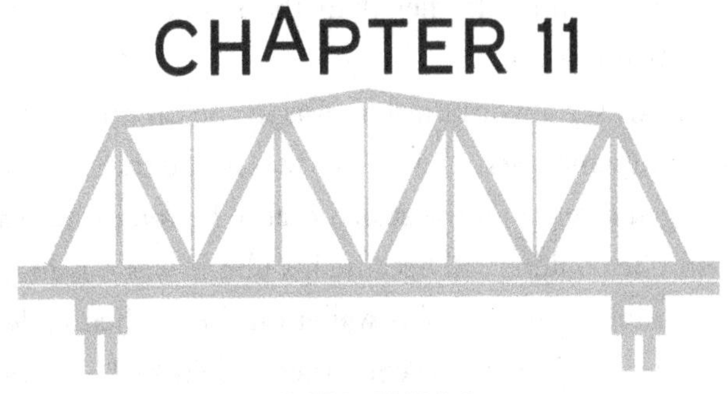

## CELERY

*John*

"JOHN!"

Behind him, Chris raised his voice, and John flinched a little. A little privacy or just time to figure it out would be nice. A second or two to think through what he'd just said out loud. Joy cheated on him. She broke their vows. Kissed another—

"John!"

John turned, smashing his lips together to keep from spouting out something very unbiblical. There in Chris's hand was his phone, his lifeline to Joy. Maybe Jenny, if she'd ever answer.

"What?" His question plopped as flat as his mood.

"Do you want to know what I'd do?"

Everything was a sick, dark joke to Chris. John turned back around. "No, I don't want to know what you'd do." Probably call Joy back and lecture her on the sanctity of marriage. It wouldn't do any good, since that part had been run over months ago. A day that crowded his mind again now.

Joy had asked him to go get celery from the grocery store about five miles away, much farther than the market he preferred. "I want the organic kind."

John didn't say a word until he was in the car and then mumbled about organic celery the entire ride. Ironic thing was that he left the organic celery in the store because he forgot his wallet at home. And he couldn't call because his phone was missing, too.

Once inside, John spied his wallet on the kitchen table. Next to his phone. He'd nearly reached them when he heard Joy sobbing down the hall, behind a closed door. The closer he crept to their bedroom, the more clearly John could make out that she wasn't only crying, but talking with someone. Though he thought to knock, instead he leaned his ear onto the door, like a cheesy television show detective.

"Tell me how to end it," Joy cried. She mumbled something else before saying, "He will hate me. He's never gonna forgive me because I'm not worth it."

John paused, perplexed. Who would hate her?

He knocked twice. "Joy? Are you okay?" Twisting the handle, John walked in on Joy swiping her phone off, mascara streaking down her face. He looked at her phone. "What's going on?"

Organic celery revealed the truth about the sanctity of their marriage.

"John!" Chris shouted again now.

He would never stop until he turned, so John again faced the man in the full cream-colored suit. Chris held the phone up in front of his body, moving it side to side. If John could only get it back and apologize to Joy for blurting out that truth, they could move another fractional step forward.

"John." Chris's voice was quieter. Soothing almost. "I'd do this."

Joy's ringtone started.

In horror, John watched his phone sail from Chris's hand into the wide-open air. John ran to the other side of the bridge just in time to see its final few feet before it splashed into the creek, Joy's ringtone still playing.

No. Oh, no.

Words stuck in his throat. What a jerk! He looked up at Chris, dread wrapping its tendrils around the hope in repairing his marriage.

"Why would you do that?"

Chris crossed his arms and leaned onto the railing. "I really don't think you were helping each other."

Great. Another unwanted opinion from the guy whose life he just saved. He should've taken the picture and left. Or just left. Hindsight always showed up too late.

John sat down on the bridge, back against the solid railing. They didn't make bridges like this anymore. Oldest wooden bridge in England, built by an American, and still standing after all of these decades. Now, it was about engineering and the right chemicals to add into the cement mixes. There was a massive layer of tar underneath the gravel somewhere. The same gravel digging into his butt. This bridge was more solid than his marriage.

He really did try. The counseling. The dates. It seemed to be going...okay. He didn't flinch when she reached to hold his hand.

"We were going to make it," John said softly. "I had promises from God. We were gonna work through everything."

Holidays were already planned out. A vacation, too. Those promises from the Bible helped. Claiming those really helped when he worried about her leaving the house. Was she going to see *him*? Someone else?

*Be anxious for nothing*. It became his daily internal chant. Why wasn't it working now?

Chris folded his long legs next to John on the bridge's deck.

"Perhaps you should change jobs," Chris suggested in that "let's-be-nice" tone.

"No," John shot back, slicing his hands in an X in front of him. This job paid for the mortgage, Jenny's college tuition for her law degree, and the health insurance. Heaven forbid one of his girls needed to go to the hospital and the insurance had been dropped. They'd lose the house.

Besides, his boss Bob was the owner of the company and a really terrific guy. When John asked for an extra two weeks off, Bob didn't pry. One text confirming it was done and to call him for the next job assignment. There probably wasn't another boss like Bob.

And it wasn't about the job.

Beneath the pain of Joy's affair and the fear that she'd do it again, John really wanted to at least try and repair their marriage. She was the girl who showed up with melting ice cream cones to his college soccer practices. Or drove to the airport to hand over a package wrapped with Christmas paper when he forgot his underwear.

"It runs deeper than that." John scooped up bits of gravel and tossed them across the bridge, where they bounced off and landed downstream from his phone.

For a few blessed moments, Chris's jabbering ceased. Just the birds and the damp breeze. John wiggled his toes. They were freezing!

Chris pulled in a long breath. John braced himself.

"Why don't you just admit that you hate her?"

For a moment, John thought he must've heard wrong. What kind of psychopath would suggest that? His mouth went slack, and he turned toward Chris, who stared back, no trace of malice or humor on his face.

John clambered up, invisible thorns igniting in his palms again. "No!" he shouted. He stumbled back a step as he righted. His lungs burned and his mind spun.

He'd never say that. Hatred ate at a person. He'd watched it when he was a kid. There's no way he actually hated her. Strong dislike, of course, at times.

"I'll never say those words," he breathed, chest tightening. Feet made of lead, John walked to the other side of the bridge. He grasped the railing and looked down. If only he had the guts…to jump, to scream, to admit everything. But like most things with Joy, he didn't. Life went more smoothly when she was happy. It added to the invisible millstone around his neck.

It seemed the Lord had destined John to be marooned on a remote bridge with a jaded man whose mission was to cause John to question every single thing he knew was true. He loved Joy. It wasn't gushing or overwhelming at the moment. It took practice and dedication to live with her after that. To commit to work through his pain. He'd made the vow of marriage and it included, "for better or for worse." This was most definitely the worst part.

And Jenny. He'd never leave her without a dad. She was a smart cookie who could tell something was off between her parents. And Joy didn't help by perpetually being defensive. It made Jenny angry with John, like whatever happened had been his fault.

Maybe that's when he started apologizing.

But for Chris to even suggest that he hated Joy? Preposterous. It went against every prayer he desperately threw toward God when she reached for his hand and he held it instead of pulling away. Strong dislike at times. Sure. That was it. Nothing more.

Chris could take his cockeyed counseling and toss it into the creek. Right next to the phone. John wished he could call Joy and at least tell her he'd call her later. Now, he couldn't even call Jenny. And that made his heart ache. She'd have another arrow of anger to shoot at him.

John exhaled his resolve through pursed lips and straightened his slouched shoulders. Time to face the resentful man. John turned and looked at Chris, who was now standing across from him.

"I love my wife." He bobbed his head to agree with his words. "I love her."

It tasted bitter and artificial. But the more he said it, the easier it would get. Eventually. Right?

Chris tilted his chin up. "You're such a rubbish liar."

John worked his jaw before answering. "I don't hate my wife." He looked beyond Chris and focused on the lush forest. "All I ever do is try hard, try to do the right thing. You know, make sacrifices. I have to work long hours and for weeks away at a time. I hate living in hotels. I missed so many birthday parties and soccer games."

Most nights, he curled up to videos he'd saved on his internet storage site rather than read a book. He'd watch Jenny defend the goal. Their old dog twisting in circles for a treat. Jenny yelling when she'd been caught dancing in her bedroom.

"And she did this to me."

Joy took everything sacred and threw it out of the window. Then lit it on fire.

"So," Chris started, folding his arms together, "you must hate her a little."

"No. There…I admit there are times when I struggle."

"Hmrm. Struggle. There's another *great* Christian word."

"There are days when I'm angry, that's for sure."

Chris's eyebrows flagged upward. He nodded his chin at the sky. "What? At *him*?"

John shook his head and dropped his gaze to the bridge deck. Chris could never understand the betrayal that seeped into his bones. A hefty sigh blew past his lips as he kicked a piece of gravel. "Especially at him."

"You mean the other guy?" Chris sounded so…disappointed.

That anger John just described flared. "Is there another him? Don't tell me there's another him."

A long, steady breath whistled out of Chris's nostrils. "Finally. Some honesty."

John had a desire to knock honesty into Chris's teeth right then. Instead, he counted to three before answering.

"I'm not perfect, but I sure didn't deserve that."

He should just leave. What good would rehashing this with Chris do? Chris seemed bound and determined to tear what was left of his marriage apart. But if John could find an inkling of hope after all he and Joy had gone through, Chris could find it too. As long as John didn't haul off and punch him first. Jesus would frown if it came to that.

"So why don't you divorce her?"

Would he ever stop? "You know as well as I do that God hates divorce. I'm sure you can quote the scripture."

"But he tolerates fools?" Chris's voice was low and flat. He was the one staring past John now, lost in thought.

John scratched his head. He wasn't a fool. He was a Christian and trying to do the right thing. "I have to love my wife."

That brought Chris back to focus.

"I have to forgive her and love her."

"Oh, you have to. Why? Because some pastor told you to?"

Chris narrowed his gaze. Probably counseled couples the same way, so of course he knew what John had been through.

And like the blind man from the Bible, John could see Chris's point. He dropped his head, toeing the gravel. Chris might've even used the same counseling book Pastor Ryan talked them through day after day for a week. A very long and painful week.

Despite Joy's tears, John never cried. Not once. He dutifully worked at softening his heart to her persepctive. He echoed her loneliness and made her see his absence was worse without family. At least she got to be with their daughter!

He memorized the verses and answered every blank on the worksheets. The first "date" flopped miserably. Joy couldn't keep from asking if he was okay, and it shut him up until the next day. Better to be quiet than to erupt in a full restaurant that his wife had slept with his friend. Oh, and that they all still went to church together.

Prayer worked. Sometimes. He prayed for *him* to feel guilty enough to go to another church. But that was far-fetched, as he was the son of a deacon. John watched the back of the *other* wife's head for more than one sermon, wondering if she felt as adrift as he did. The vortex of uncertainty. Ever-present "what-ifs" of a phone call. Did she drive by his work now? Or did her compulsive mind spin elaborate tales if he didn't answer her calls?

Everything upended by organic celery.

And he hated celery anyways.

"Okay, you're right." John shoved both hands into his pants pockets. The burning thorns had nothing on the pain in his chest. "Sometimes I feel like I hate her. You know, there's pretty much no one I can turn to."

He paused and looked up, expecting Chris's smug grin. Instead, it almost looked like the man was heartbroken.

Something deep inside told John to talk. This was his one and only chance to admit everything out loud, in an English forest to a suicidal ex-pastor. Everything would be forgotten.

"It's like, if I told people that I'm angry, they'd just scatter because I'm not that guy. But as long as I keep that 'hallelujah smile' going, everything's okay."

# CHAPTER 12

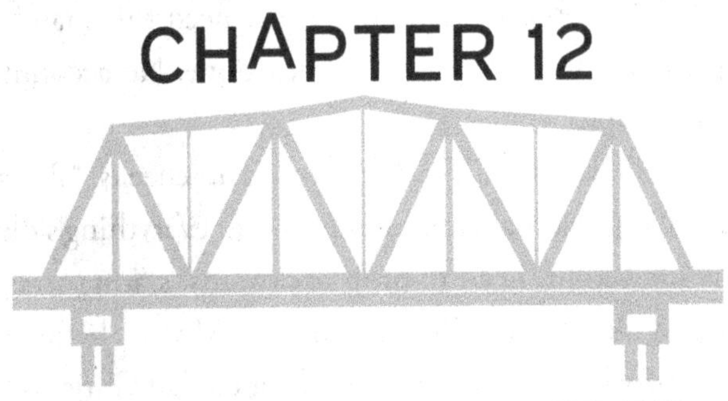

## LIVE LIFE AND BE FREE

*Chris*

"I HAVE TO FORGIVE HER AND LOVE HER."

John's forced words laced around what was left of Chris's heart and dragged it down into murky depths. It physically hurt to hear. Chris would give anything to tell Carol he loved her again. This part of counseling had always been the worst. Now, he could see it smacked the face of reason. Forcing someone to declare their love to patch up a shoddy marriage?

"Oh, you have to," he spat. "Why? Because some pastor told you to?"

The sigh that escaped John was hung with grief, sorrow, and something else dreadful—the same nameless monster that chased Chris once Carol quietly passed. She said she was running home to Jesus. That meant she was running away from Chris and Chloe. With Carol gone, and Chloe having stormed out weeks before, Chris was left with a gaping hole.

"You know," John continued, "there's pretty much no one I can turn to."

Chris held his breath. No, he did *not* need this man to mess up his plans any more than he'd already done. No accountability or venting. Nope.

John's small, weak smile didn't even lift his cheeks. "But as long as I keep giving that hallelujah smile going, everything's okay."

Chris allowed his head to drop backwards, staring straight up into the grey sky. His hallelujah smile started years before Carol's diagnosis. Way back when the elders decided that Chris also needed to reach people online. And then as members left or died and the finances changed, Chris wasn't sure that they'd keep him on at all or ask him to give up part of his salary. When he'd sobbed his way through the leadership meeting revealing Carol's grim timetable, not one of them offered to help. How was he supposed to take care of her and work more than sixty hours a week for a dwindling congregation?

Carol threaded her fingers into his when he came home and sat next to her on the sofa. She listened as he vented to her.

Tucking his hair behind his ear, she cleared her throat. "My love, you didn't go into the ministry to be served."

"But I have to take care of you now," he said, a tear spilling out. "I need to be able to cook you a good meal without burning it to bits."

She chuckled. "That's true. I don't like burnt dinner." Her easy smile made his worries ease for a moment. She always had a way of doing that.

"You know," John suddenly said, loud enough that a couple of birds fluttered from the nearby branches. "I never told anyone this…" His voice dropped off as quickly as it had erupted.

Chris narrowed his eyes. This was never a good way for a conversation to go. It usually ended poorly.

"My father cheated on my mother." John gritted his teeth together, jaw muscles flexing. And now Chris understood why John tried to hold everything together with duct tape and prayer. He had to make it work so that he wouldn't be like his father.

"I'll never forget the day he left us. I'm just this little boy." John talked with his hands swinging back and forth. "He bent down and said, 'Someday, you'll understand.' And I don't understand even to this day."

Chris stood as still as possible while John started to pace. Let the man get it all out and then leave. Don't get involved. Stay quiet.

"He was selfish," John said, chopping the air with an open palm, anger creasing his forehead. "He left me and my mother. She lost her job. We lived in a motel, our car. Kids at school figured it out, and kids are just plain mean sometimes."

The more he revealed, the more Chris had to remind himself not to care. It wouldn't do either of them any good if he remembered how lonely it felt at his own home. Or how much he resented his distant and unloving father. John needed to just get it out of his system.

"I'd never do that to my family." John's voice was husky with emotion. Chris knew if he looked up, there'd be tears in John's eyes. "I wish I could erase her pain."

Chris glanced up then, not sure if John meant his mum or his wife. How could this man still be worried about a woman who nearly tore apart their marriage? His commitment was astounding.

"Divorce her."

There. He once again laid the option out that no one else seemed to give John.

John spun on the gravel to face him, mouth open. "What?"

"Get rid of her." He pronounced each word with emphasis,

to try and drive home the point. Surprisingly, John didn't yell or react, other than to scrub his face with both hands and moan.

"What about my daughter?"

Well. That was unexpected.

"She'll get over it." If she was anything like Chloe, it'd be fairly quick and decisive.

John snorted. "You don't know my daughter." He shook his head and jammed both hands into his jacket pockets. "If she had any idea what her mom did…oh, it would just kill her." His eyes rolled closed, and he tilted his chin up. "Jenny's been avoiding me for weeks."

Ah. *That* Chris could understand. The last time they'd been together as a family, Chloe held a bag in each hand in the passageway of their house. Gone was the girl who'd sung beautiful solos to the congregation. Instead, Chloe's black-rimmed eyes and glaring red lipstick screamed disdain to the rules they'd raised her with.

"I can't stay, Mum." Chloe ignored Chris altogether after their row when she refused to go to church that morning.

Carol placed her teacup onto the table. "Why not, Chloe?" she'd asked, knowing full well that their daughter intended to leave.

"I can't live like this." Chloe lifted her chin around to the room. "We're different."

Chris took a deep breath to respond, but Carol laid her hand across his. "I know we're different but—"

"Look, Mum," Chloe said, contempt weaving through each word, "I understand what you believe, but I am not a Christian."

"Perhaps not now, but give it time and you might change your mind."

"Don't, Mum."

Chris wouldn't stand for rudeness. "Chloe, listen—"

"No." She shifted on her feet, bags weighing down both arms. "You don't listen to anyone. At least anyone who thinks differently than you."

Carol squeezed Chris's hand on the table. "Will you sit and talk to us for five minutes?" she asked.

Chloe's jaw jutted forward. "There's nothing left to say."

"Wait," Chris said, eyes darting from Chloe to Carol, "I need to tell you something."

Carol shook her head, eyes immediately laden with tears. "No, Chris, don't."

"What?" Chloe's impatient reply came just before a car horn sounded outside.

She had the right to know. She needed to know.

"Your mum has cancer."

Chloe's eyebrows lifted, and she nodded. Then she turned on her heels and left, door slamming against the frame.

On a different but oddly same level, he could understand John about his daughter's pain. He still believed, deep down, that Chloe left to save face instead of crying.

"One day she walked in on her mom and me arguing. Joy kept going at me, picking at the same thing." John cleared his throat and moved his voice up and octave. "'Can't you show me a little affection?' Like I should be kissing her all of the time and holding her hand after I found it out. So, I reminded her that I was still there. Right? That should be enough, but not for Joy."

Chris smashed his lips together.

"I was a scab she couldn't stop picking at. So I offered to go, and by then, we were really yelling. Neither of us heard the back door. Jenny looked at me like…well, like I'd been the one to have an affair. And I'll never forget what she said. 'Dad! Just stop! You act like you hate her.' When I tried to tell her that there were things she didn't know, she stormed off to her bedroom. Because Joy and I had agreed to never tell her."

John stopped his walk and leaned against the railing opposite Chris. He shrugged. "The truth is, my life is a lie." For a brief moment, sheer confusion streaked across his face. Ear to ear uncertainty until his muscles relaxed and his mouth twisted into a mocking grin. "Some witness for Christ I am, right?"

Chris remained silent as John pulled out his hands and unconsciously spun his wedding band round and round with his left thumb. Chris mirrored the American just to make sure his own ring was still there because that was the only part of his life that wasn't a lie. No one in the church knew Chloe had left because she didn't want to be a Christian. Chris didn't want their opinions. They were given an edited version: she moved. Not a whole lie, not a whole truth.

A cool breeze made Chris buck his shoulders inward. Something scratched his chest. No, it wasn't God. Certainly, that explanation was overused and long gone in his mind. It most definitely was the wind that made the note in his inner jacket pocket remind him of its existence. A ridiculous note he'd typed out on the computer and printed long ago. It went with him everywhere—the grocery store, pub, pharmacy. It was one of three things always present on his person: wallet, ring, note.

Chris fished the tattered page from his pocket and flipped it over a few times. Across from him, John sat down again, head in hands, as if his life were over. Chris crossed the deck and sat next to John. He held the note between two fingers and extended it to John, who looked at the paper like it was on fire.

"Read this."

Behind his rib cage, Chris's heart raced. No one had read it.

He had half a mind to tuck it back into the safety of his pocket even now.

"What is it?" John still eyed the note, eyes shifting between it and Chris.

Chris leaned the note further toward John. "Read it."

John nabbed the note so quickly that Chris had no time to change his mind. Finally, John wasn't being all higgledy-piggledy and unfolded the paper. Chris looked to the left so that he didn't read along with John after he cleared his throat.

"Dear Chloe, I'm sorry I've let you down."

John paused. From the corner of his eye, Chris could see the man look at him. Tension pulled taut for a moment before John held the note up.

"I hope one day that you…you'll be able to forgive me. I'm sure in time, you'll learn to cope."

Chris wrote that line remembering the look on her face when he told her about Carol's cancer. She'd be fine.

"I miss you."

Every part of his being missed his little girl. Even the arguments and disagreements. He missed the way her smile made him feel better. The subtle way her eyes looked like Carol. Her laughter that tilted up at the end.

"You are a wonderful daughter and I'm sorry we've moved apart."

That was more his fault. Never really tried to pursue her once she left. And that's not the way a proper father should've acted.

"I should've spent more time with you, more time listening—yes, I really should have listened."

Not to the bitterness when they'd have a row, but her point of view. And when they would chat at the dinner table. He'd steer the conversation when Chloe brought up something he didn't like or approve. He'd turned into his mother after all.

"I'm sorry I haven't been there for you, and I do understand how I upset you deeply."

He'd lost control when she blasphemed God. It went against how they'd raised her. Ironically, her stance also laid down his exit path. But he should've talked instead of yelled.

"I miss your mom so much."

Chris pursed his lips when John read that line aloud. His chest hurt. Ached, really. Nothing took away the pain. Not ignoring the phone, not whisky, and certainly not hearing his own admission from another man's mouth. Loneliness slithered around his mind, slinging off of happy memories and broken future dreams.

"I hope you find happiness."

With every breath he had left, Chris dreamed for Chloe's happiness. A husband and children, if that's what she wanted. A good job. A home or lovely vacations that brought her joy. Memories full of her mother that would bring only delight. Everything good and lovely for Chloe Marie.

"Live life and be free."

Cocking his head a tad to the side, Chris thought that particular line sounded a bit more hippy than he intended. But those kinds of things helped, in his experience over the years.

"Enjoy what you've got, every second of the day."

In his mind's eye, Chris saw Carol's head against her favorite pillow, saying the same thing to him. "We've had lots of seconds together, my love. You need to keep enjoying the ones you have and the ones with Chloe." She'd be gutted to see him now.

"I am truly sorry."

No one wants their child to be alone. That was the hardest part of his decision. Even if they didn't talk, Chloe wasn't by herself.

This plan would leave her deserted, the only part that weighed his heart.

"Goodbye."

Chris kept his gaze down the abandoned road, blinking away his tears. His words sounded odd from another man's mouth. Still, the note read true.

"With love always, Dad."

# CHAPTER 13

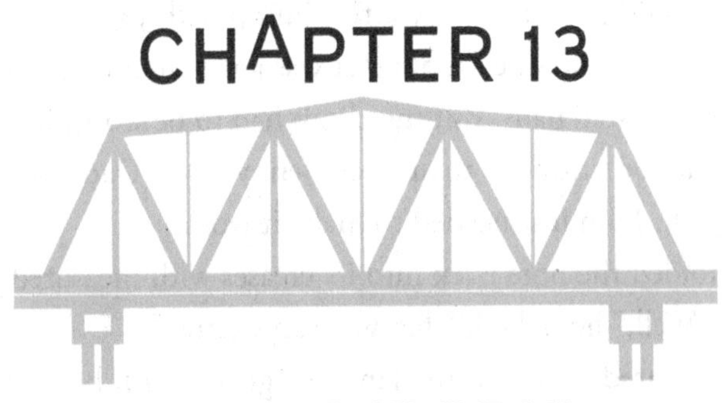

## POKE THE BEAR

*John*

**WHEN CHRIS FLAGGED A FOLDED PIECE OF PAPER IN HIS** direction, John didn't expect what he read out loud. Maybe a sarcastic letter to whoever found his body. Or a bitter send off to the world. The more he read, the more his mouth felt full of rocks and his heart burdened with Chris's hopelessness. And yet, he could see how much Chris loved his wife and daughter. It was right there, between the apologies and wishes for Chloe's future.

Sure, John had just blabbed about his dad abandoning them. And hating Joy. Boy, what a revelation that was to admit out loud. Talk about ripping off a bandage. That was like yanking off a roll of duct tape from both legs.

A shudder worked through his body when he thought about divorcing Joy. Jenny would never, ever forgive him. She already thought the whole rift was his fault to begin with. It'd cut her off from him entirely. And he couldn't even wish her a happy birthday with his phone underwater, so his footing already teetered on the edge.

If he could just make it past this bump with Joy...

Bump? Who was he kidding? It was a mountain made of glass shards and rusted nails. But the climb had to be worth it. He and Joy would be stronger than ever. Jenny, too. Daddy-daughter dates again. John just needed to make it work.

He folded the note back into its creases with measured movements. "Well," he sighed, "that was some letter."

Chris stared far down the lane overgrown with brambles and saplings. Maybe he was remembering a sweeter time. John held onto the letter until Chris swiveled his gaze back. With the expediency of a prisoner to their cell, Chris reached over and plucked the note between two fingers.

"You know," Chris said, tucking it against his breast again, "Chloe didn't come to her mother's funeral."

His despair hung between them. Chris had no one.

John rolled his sore shoulders. "Well, we all make bad decisions."

Chris groaned.

"You can't blame God for her bad decision." John couldn't believe he had to point that out.

"Cancer is hardly a bad decision!" Chris threw his hands up, stood, and walked away, scrubbing his face with both hands.

John tried to blame God for bad decisions. It seemed easier to blame the Big Guy than to think that his wife, the love of his life, mother of his child, and best friend could have done the unthinkable. The blame game was easy as long as none of it fell on his shoulders.

Like the third day of counseling. John sat out of reach from Joy. Pastor Ryan smiled and shook their hands. "John, how was your trip?"

"Yeah, it went well."

No, it hadn't. He didn't sleep because he was sure she'd be unfaithful again. One employee had to be walked off the job site. The flight home was late. So, while it hadn't been great, it could've been construed as having gone "well." He'd been avoiding her at the house for two days before their appointment.

Pastor Ryan looked to Joy. "Did you miss him?"

John stared at his shoes.

"It wasn't so bad," she said, voice quaking. "But I'm glad he's home." Joy shifted in her chair. "It's like he's avoiding me, though. He's...he's always focused on something other than me."

A cork popped behind John's rib cage. "Oh, and I suppose you were focused on me when you were with freckle face?" He leveled a finger and pointed at her, fury rolling over him in waves. How dare she? She was the one who'd led them to the counseling session in the first place.

Tears streaked down both of Joy's cheeks. "See?" She pulled a tissue from her purse, hand shaking. "He always does that."

John wagged his head side to side, trying to shed her words and the rage.

"You keep coming back to the same place every single time, John," she wept.

He gritted his teeth, ready to unload in response to her nonsense. And what he saw was his broken soulmate. The one who clung to his arm when their son was stillborn. His anguished wife who took the phone call when his mother died and had to tell him the news. It melted his hardened heart. For the first time in weeks, he stretched out his hand and laid it on her knee.

Joy placed her hand on top of his. "John, I love you."

"I love you, too," he whispered.

And he still did. That's why it hurt to admit that part of him loathed her. That affair drove a rift between them. No, a canyon.

And even though he was an engineer, the bridge back to being together was more difficult than any design he could've ever imagined.

The lines on the vertical and diagonal members of this English bridge were simple and functional. John looked up through the open design, unhindered by struts or bilateral lacing. The gray sky darkened, wisps of rain pulling the underside of nearby clouds.

"You were right," John said, fiddling with the zipper on his jacket.

"Yay. Finally." Chris stood only a couple of railings down, eyebrows knitted down.

"No, I'm talking about the weather." John pointed to the sky. "You said earlier it was going to start raining."

"Yeah. I live here. I know when the rain is coming."

"Well, I didn't check my weather app. And I can't now because—" John swept an arm over the creek, ignoring the queasiness in the pit of his stomach. Beyond the creek was the field where his— "Oh wow." He slapped both palms to his forehead. "My camera."

Twelve hundred dollars was about to be as useful as his phone in about a half an hour.

"Oh," Chris intoned, lazily wagging a finger in the same direction. "go get it quick, before it gets ruined."

John took two steps and stopped. Chris would jump. He had nothing to lose. He'd just proven that by allowing John to read the note. Chloe, on the other hand, would never be the same.

He folded his arms across his chest. "I'm not that stupid."

"You cover it so well." Chris groaned.

The men were at an impasse. They stared at one another until Chris grunted and turned away. Maybe John's travel insurance would cover the camera. He'd only used it once, to replace a suitcase that came out of the luggage tunnel looking like it'd been in a fight with a woodchipper.

"You know," Chris said from the opposite side of the deck, "I don't blame God for my pain."

Oh good. At least something was going in the right direction.

"I can't blame God. I don't believe in God."

Great.

How does one preach to an acidic ex-pastor about hope when said man is impossible? It was like trying to talk with an angry teenager.

John swallowed his chuckle. If Chris wanted to be treated like a child, then by golly, that could happen. It only took a spark to get a fire going, so the song went. John just needed to find Chris's flashpoint.

And all of his roads led to one place.

"God gets us through our pain."

It was solid. John believed every word. Lived them, too. The pain of betrayal infected his life for too long. After this day, John wanted nothing more than to rely on God to get him over the ugly parts.

"Fairytales get us through our pain." Chris's face set like an opposing lawyer readying for the argument of his life. "Drugs get us through our pain. The occasional large whisky has often helped me get through my pain." His chapped lips tipped down as his shoulders rose. "Pleasurable ladies have often kept—"

"Oh!" John held up both hands in front of his body to ward off the image. Disgusting. "Okay. Enough, enough."

This was obviously going to be harder than a teenager. More like a toddler but without a flannel board or songs with hand motions. Basics. He needed basics.

John took a deep breath. "Jesus said—"

"Jesus was a cult leader."

"Excuse me?"

"It's a cult." Chris talked through his nose. "You have one enigmatic guy with twelve followers who bamboozled people with so-called miracles into following what he claimed. No different than the people who thought they were aliens and going back to heaven's gate. And what Jesus said was that he was the son of god."

John shook his head. Was this really happening? "Wait."

Chris pointed his bony finger. "No, you wait. Others have come along and also claimed to be a son of god or to hear what god tells them. So, you tell me the difference. Why should I believe in this particular fairytale? What makes this god so amazing?"

"Well," John fumbled. Then a blip of an idea. "You were a pastor. You already know the answer."

"I want you to tell me why."

John felt like he was in the middle of an argument with Jenny, where the rules were fluid and the reasons for the argument were vague. "Look, I can't force you to admit God gets you through pain or that He gives peace. But I know you've experienced God. When you relied on His grace, you saw hope and mercy when you didn't expect it."

"That's just a fluke. Miracles happen in every religion." He raised a hand and started counting on each finger. "The Catholic saints. Joseph Smith and his vision about Mormonism. Even the Quran mentions miracles."

"It's not a fluke. It's true. You can argue with me, but I know you saw it. Your wife, she saw it."

Pink bled into Chris's cheeks, and his nostrils flared. "Don't you dare bring my wife into this."

*Poke the bear for the sweetest prize*, John's grandpa used to say during their summer trips to the mountain cabin. It never made much sense until this moment. "Why not? You seem to have blamed her for losing sight of God. You blame God for ultimately easing her pain. You blame God for giving her a perfect body in heaven. So yeah, you are basically telling everyone that because she died and you didn't like it, you're gonna have a temper tantrum and demote God to a fairytale."

"And you have so much room to talk!" Chris exploded, both hands flailing. "You leave your wife for weeks at a time and then grovel and beg to fix it."

The bear had claws. John nodded slowly. Chris wasn't wrong. "You're right. We messed up and are trying to make it right." Chris tried to interrupt, but John raised his voice. "You're not even trying. You still have a daughter and you've given up. That's… that's pathetic."

Chris showed exactly what he thought with a finger gesture before turning and strangling the rails until his knuckles turned pale.

Poking the bear didn't work. Maybe it was time to try the honey.

John took a step toward Chris. "Don't you think Chloe has pain? Her mom died. Her dad is about to leave her all alone in the world. That pain you're talking about removing? You're about to unload every ounce of it on Chloe. Your loneliness will get dumped on her lap."

From behind, John could see Chris's shoulders bow further in. His head dropped.

"So, she made a mistake not coming to her mom's funeral. I bet you've made horrible mistakes, too. Ones she doesn't even know about. Don't give up, Chris. God is there. We both know it. But you need to climb out of that pit you're in."

Chris scoffed and straightened. When he turned, it looked like he'd swallowed vinegar. "Pit. Yeah, I'm in a pit. It's better than being deluded by a god who took away my joy."

Honey. No more poking. Like a toddler wanting a candy for a reward, John would lead Chris there. "There was a thing I learned in counseling—"

"Shocking."

John ignored the barb. "I have to choose to find joy. It's my decision. I can't rely on anyone or any situation."

"You sound like a seminary class."

"Good. Then you already know what I'm saying. You are just choosing to be stubborn and ignore what is right because you don't like that your wife is gone."

Birds flew through the trees during the long pause before Chris spoke. It stretched on for minutes. John shifted from one foot to the next. He felt the back pocket of his blue jeans and came up empty. Joy was probably worried sick by now.

"You have no idea what I've gone through."

"You're right. I don't. But there's got to be something you can find joy and hope in."

"God isn't one of them."

"Fine. Don't. Don't find joy in God. Is there somewhere you'd like to go to have lunch?"

"Not with you."

A gaping hole was in the place of Chris's heart. John guessed that he'd been shunned from love for so long that he'd given up entirely.

"Look," he said, both palms up, "I know that God loves me. And He loves you too."

"How do you know?"

"How do I know what?"

"How do you know that God loves you? Or me, for that matter."

# CHAPTER 14

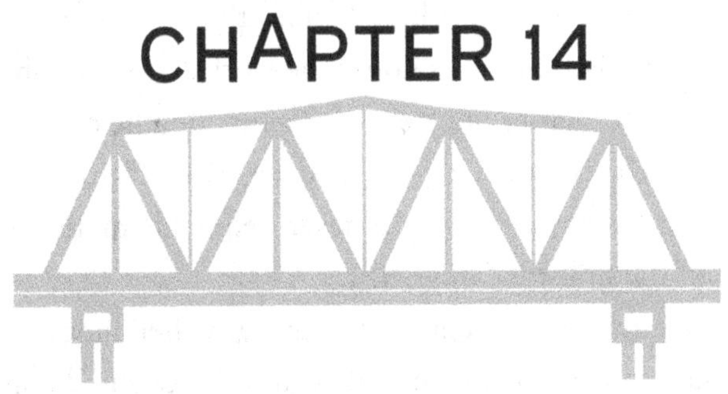

## HEBREWS IT

*Chris*

"YOU'RE NOT EVEN TRYING. YOU STILL HAVE A DAUGHTER and you've given up. That's…that's pathetic."

Chris gritted his teeth, every bit of learned English countenance worked to keep his facial muscles relaxed, even in the rain. *That's right. Pretend not to care.* Those words didn't raze him to the quick. Soon, it all wouldn't matter.

But it did.

He flew the most un-Christian finger in front of John's nose before turning on his heels and grabbing the railing. When Chloe said she didn't believe in God, that she wasn't a Christian before Carol died, it made his decision to walk away that much easier.

Behind Chris, gravel crunched underfoot. Why wouldn't John just go away?

"Don't you think Chloe has pain? Her mom died. Her dad is about to leave her all alone in the world. That pain you're talking about removing? You're about to unload every ounce of it on Chloe. Your loneliness will get dumped on her lap."

Chris knew this would hurt Chloe. But she'd eventually get over it. He'd raised her to conquer the world. The least she could do would be to master her feelings—something he couldn't seem to accomplish. No matter how hard he tried, Carol still flitted throughout his days. He would never defeat his monsters or rid himself of the millstone of grief.

"So, she made a mistake not coming to her mom's funeral. I bet you've made horrible mistakes, too. Ones she doesn't even know about. Don't give up, Chris. God is there. We both know it. But you need to climb out of that pit you're in."

This "bro" couldn't fathom that it wasn't a pit. It was a bottomless hole. Chris turned and narrowed his eyes at his intended target.

"Pit. Yeah, I'm in a pit. It's better than being deluded by a god who took away my joy."

John's face relaxed and his mouth dropped open a bit. Then Chris watched the man's internal "never-give-up" rekindle as John nodded once and straightened his shoulders.

"There was a thing I learned in counseling—"

Chris pounced. "Shocking." He had years of counseling parishioners. This guy had a wrecked marriage and a tract in his pocket that he couldn't even read correctly.

"I have to choose to find joy. It's my decision. I can't rely on anyone or any situation." John talked with his hands, first pointing at himself, then slicing through the raindrops.

A chill settled into Chris's shoulders as his suit absorbed the wetness. Crossing his arms not only helped warm his hands, but made him look snobbish. And that was exactly what he wanted. "You sound like a seminary class."

"Good. Then you already know what I'm saying. You are just

choosing to be stubborn and ignore what is right because you don't like that your wife is gone."

"Obstinate man with obstinate hair," Carol whispered on Sunday mornings, trying to brush the cowlick from his hair while he ignored her and fastened his tie. She'd catch his eye in the mirror and wink. Oh, to see that gleam in her eye one more time.

"You have no idea what I've gone through." Chris barely recognized his own voice, low and laden.

"You're right." John's eyebrows arched high below his wet matted hair. "I don't. But there's got to be something you can find joy and hope in."

"God isn't one of them."

"Fine. Don't. Don't find joy in God. Is there somewhere you'd like to go to have lunch?"

"Not with you." Chris would rather get back to the task at hand than spend time across a table having a kumbaya moment over a meat pie.

John sighed. If it were any colder, it would've curled into a mist. "Look," he said, both palms up, "I know that God loves me. And He loves you too."

"How do you know?"

"How do I know what?"

"How do you know that God loves you? Or me, for that matter."

Nothing could convince Chris of that. Not after the drinking and other things Carol would've been disappointed in. God could love everyone else in the world. But there wasn't a speck of anything left for a pastor who wanted to jump from a bridge to find peace.

"How'd you and Carol meet?" John shoved both hands into his coat pockets. He flinched. The thorns must've dug in deep.

John's question put Chris back in the academy, before he'd even met her. Back when some of the other cadets discovered his dad was titled and that he'd attended a school they'd never be able to afford. Every barbed question had an agenda, so he gained the reputation of being as aloof as his ancestral name.

"I see what you're trying to do," Chris said, shaking the hair from his eyes, "and it won't work."

John's face morphed into confusion. "No, really." He shrugged. "I'm genuinely interested in how it happened. She seems like such an amazing woman." He smiled, all teeth and truth.

Fine. Chris would play along because if another person could remember Carol, then the world would be better off. "Through a mutual friend."

"That's cool! Ours was completely a coincidence. Right place, right time."

John's anecdote was fine and dandy, but he still had his wife.

"Love," Chris started, before clearing his throat, "love is a wonderful thing, if you can find it." For half a heartbeat, he wondered how utterly horrendous life would've been without Carol. "But when it's over, it's over. You see people die," he said, before swiveling to look John straight in the eye, "or betray you, and then what? You're left alone."

Rainfall blanketed all other sounds. Even the birds let Chris's accusation fall heavy.

Still, John didn't look away. "You'd have me abandon all hope?"

"All false hope." The more the cold seeped into Chris's bones, the easier to convey his misery. "So, how can you really *know* God? You've never heard him, have you?"

John screwed his face muscles tight. "No, not directly."

A chuckle escaped Chris. This was all too easy. "Good, because if you start telling people you're hearing voices, they'll lock you up."

John weakly laughed the polite kind of laugh that you make after a lame joke at the office. Or when a kid asked Chris for the umpteenth time how Moses made his tea.

*He brews it.* Chris made sure to laugh loud and long when Chloe picked that one up and brought it home.

And though he joked about it with John, Chris saw the anguish that mental health problems brought to those involved in it, from patient to family to friends. There were moments of pure brilliance and joy tempered with days upon days of turmoil and frustration. Joking about it with his own "goodbye note" tucked against his breast? The epitome of irony.

"If they see me standing on this bridge in the rain, they'll lock me up," John mumbled behind him.

"If Jesus was God, was he truly human? Wouldn't it have been sacrilege for God to take a fallible body?" Chris set out the breadcrumbs for his ignorant Christian and shrugged one indifferent shoulder. "Must've been an illusion."

"No, no," John said. A smile ripped across his face, lighting up. "'The Word became flesh. And the Word was God.'"

Chris dipped his chin. "At least you know that much."

John hooted in triumph, throwing a fist into the air before stuffing it back into his jacket. His grin even lifted his ears. "I thought you'd at least argue with me or something."

"I'm tired of arguing now."

"So, you agree God is real."

"I didn't say that at all."

"But you didn't deny it either."

"Give the man a biscuit."

John shivered, but Chris refused. A nice cuppa would hit the spot, though. He'd already had his last one this morning and thinking about another didn't help. Still, some of that fancy raspberry would be nice, though he'd used the last of it months ago and set these plans in motion.

Carol searched the internet high and low after her doctor faced her across the desk. She'd said that the doctor had never looked so sad before, face etched in sorrow. "I'm so sorry to tell you, Mrs. Arnold, but it is advanced and the metastasis too great to attempt treatment." The more Carol recounted the appointment, the only thing Chris found he could focus on was the way their fingers were intertwined on his knee, Carol's knuckles white from squeezing his. Underneath the skin on the back of her hand, veins looked like blue rivers. He'd find a way to stop this, to keep her here with him.

"Christopher," she whispered, shocking him back into the kitchen.

For two days, she hunched over the laptop, clicking and scrolling. He cycled out her cold tea for warm mugs with sandwiches she never ate. On the third morning, she made it to the kitchen before him and had breakfast laid out when he emerged from the bedroom.

"I thought we'd head to the farmers market today. I'd like to try to find some herbs."

So began their weekly adventures to the open-air stalls to hunt for the best dried leaves and blossoms. When Carol discovered the young couple who sold the raspberry tea mixture, she declared her searches were over.

Chloe begrudgingly admitted it tasted good one morning, when she graced them with her mascara-streaked and stale-alcohol-smelling presence.

Chris drew in a breath to rail her about her choices. He pushed all of the air out through his nose when he saw Carol shake her head side to side. Carol begged him not to say a word about her diagnosis just yet.

"Let her enjoy this time in her life," Carol said, once Chloe stumbled to her room.

"I think she's enjoying it a bit too much," Chris replied, emphasizing with air quotes.

Now John stretched and groaned. He began to jog in place. "Brrr!"

Chris rolled his eyes. It really wasn't that hard to stay warm. But when John eyed the edge of the bridge, his forehead wrinkled, and he stilled.

"Prepare yourself," John whispered. "Take it slow. Visualize success. Breathe. Take it easy on yourself." He closed his eyes and nodded to no one in particular.

"How can you be a bridge engineer and be afraid of heights?"

"It's not heights that I fear," John said. He inclined his chin toward the railing. "Falling off of a bridge is another issue altogether."

"And when you bolted over when your phone fell?"

John's face fell flat. "You mean when you threw it over? That was different."

"How so?"

"I was only thinking about the phone and that Joy was calling. You heard her ringtone."

"Yes."

"I was thinking my wife was more important than my safety."

Chris hummed instead of answering. Fair point. If Carol had needed him to brave a snake or two for a cure, he would've done it. A pit of snakes would've been vile, but he could've talked himself into it.

"And I was thinking of not being able to call Jenny for her birthday," John added. "I mean, I'm not going to get any father of the year award for it, but I should've called."

Chris didn't respond, although he agreed. It did no good since he had chucked the blasted phone into the stream.

Chloe had been so angry when they disconnected her mobile service after missing curfew for more than a week.

"You're ruining my life," she screamed, slapping her open palm onto the wall for emphasis. She didn't even flinch when a photograph fell to the floor and the glass shattered. "Why are you like this?" Chris recognized the spite and lack of sadness in her tears.

"As long as you live here, there is a curfew." He tamped down his anger, though it simmered just below the surface, ready to pop. "Because you have no regard for our rules, there are consequences. Since your mum and I pay for your mobile, this is the punishment."

"Punishment?" Chloe's cheeks flushed pink. "I'm not seven years old, dad!"

"Then you're old enough to remember curfew."

"Darling," Carol said from her seat at the table. "Your dad has a work schedule, so you need to understand why you can't be traipsing in at all hours of the night."

Chloe glared, hot tears spilling over.

It was a standoff. Chris wanted to blow up. Chloe, too. Yet they both loved Carol so much—Carol, always the peacemaker between the two—that the pair remained mute.

"We will turn on your mobile once you make curfew this week." Carol coughed daintily, pulling her kerchief to her mouth. "There's some leftovers in the fridge."

"I'm not hungry." Chloe turned to leave, stepping on the glass.

"Clean that up," Chris snapped. How could she even think of making them clean up her mess?

Chloe looked back over her shoulder, eyes hard. "I've got to get the broom and dustpan from the broom closet." She pronounced each word for emphasis so that he'd understand that her will to have the last word was as strong as his.

"I miss Jenny when she was a little girl with ponytails and held my hand." John sighed. "We had a fort in the backyard that I built. It was a castle with flags on each corner. The last time I was home, it was gone."

Chris grunted. They'd never had room for a fort in the church-owned manse garden. But he and Chloe built a bookshelf and filled it with their favorite books. She'd taken several when she'd left. And he'd left the rest behind when he moved, reasoning that the flat was much too small for so many books.

"I'll call Jenny when I get back to my apartment." John chuckled. "I mean, back to my flat."

The rain slowed. Chris shook his head to get the lingering drops from his hair. He didn't want to hear about John mending relationships.

"Hey," John said, extending one palm out. "Why don't you try calling Chloe?"

"[illegible]," Chari snapped. "How could she ever think of [illegible] up in [illegible]?"

[illegible] looked back over her [illegible]. [illegible] emphasis [illegible] understand [illegible] last word was [illegible].

[illegible] my [illegible] hard [illegible] with [illegible]

[illegible]

[illegible]

[illegible]

[illegible]

# CHAPTER 15

## HAND PHONE

*John*

"LOVE...LOVE IS A WONDERFUL THING, IF YOU CAN FIND it." Chris stilled. "But when it's over, it's over. You see people die or betray you and then what? We're left alone."

John crinkled his nose. Neither of them was alone. He had Joy and Jenny and Chris had Chloe. If only Chris would let go of the stupid notion of being alone.

"So," John said, leaning forward, "You'd have me abandon all hope?"

He left the rest of his sentence unsaid: *hope in God, my family, and love.*

"All false hope." Chris's snobbish tone returned. "So, how can you really *know* God? You've never heard him, have you?"

"No, not directly." Hey, if that happened, John would've written a book by now.

Chris scoffed. Or kind of laughed. It was hard to tell the intent. "Good, because if you start telling people you're hearing voices, they'll lock you up."

John smiled, lips pressed together. Rude. Even Chris's sense of humor was warped. But it was better to smile politely than to chastise the man with a death wish. And it would be even better to try and play along to gain his trust.

But when he looked up, Chris was staring into the distance.

"If they see me standing on this bridge in the rain, they'll lock me up," John muttered.

"If Jesus was God, was He truly human? Wouldn't it have been sacrilege for God to take a fallible body?" Chris set his jaw, eyebrows sinking. "Must've been an illusion."

Wait, what? There was that verse, John remembered. From a sermon.

"No, no," John said, remembering the first verse in the book of John. Pastor Ryan led a Bible study on it once, and John still had his book. "'The Word became flesh. And the Word was God.'"

"At least you know that much."

John fist pumped the air. It was freezing! He stuffed it back into his jacket. But a smile worked its way up from his soul. So cool to remember that! And even better that Chris didn't rip him apart. "I thought you'd at least argue with me or something."

"I'm tired of arguing now."

Ah! John saw an opening. "So, you agree God is real."

"I didn't say that at all."

"But you didn't deny it either."

"Give the man a biscuit." Surely Chris didn't clap because of the chilly air, but John felt it in his flat response.

John's body shivered from the cold. Couldn't catch a break today. Joy was probably worried. Jenny hated him for missing another birthday. His camera was toast. Or rather, mush. And he'd likely catch pneumonia or bronchitis from being out here.

But it was worth it. Chris needed a friend so he didn't feel lonely. What he really needed was Jesus and a kick in the butt. Another shudder worked from John's chest to his legs. He stretched, then groaned when his thigh muscles complained. Climbing that path to the bridge must've been harder on his body than he thought.

John stamped his feet rapidly. Up in the Dakotas, it was the only thing that made him feel his toes again.

The Dakota trip was when he came home and found out Joy had…

He wouldn't give up. He wouldn't be his dad and walk away. He and Joy would make it. If only he could call her and tell her not to worry.

John looked toward the railing where his phone had departed this earth. His stomach began to squeeze. Feeling light-headed, John realized he was panting. There's no way he'd pass out in front of Chris.

"Prepare yourself." John focused on the railing, recalling the way he approached every bridge on every project. "Take it slow. Visualize success. Breathe. Take it easy on yourself." He closed his eyes, wishing for a harness or at least a safety rope. Not that it would help with these old timbers.

"How can you be a bridge engineer and be afraid of heights?"

John opened his eyes to find Chris adjusting his crossed arms.

"It's not heights that I fear. Falling off of a bridge is another issue altogether." Even that sentence made his insides lurch. He swallowed hard to keep from vomiting.

"And when you bolted over when your phone fell?"

"You mean when you threw it over?" Chris needed a slap to the back of the head. "That was different."

"How so?"

John could only imagine Joy's panic. "I was only thinking

about the phone and that Joy was calling. You heard her ringtone." He swept his arm toward that fateful drop area.

"Yes."

"I was thinking my wife was more important than my safety."

Instead of answering, Chris hummed an arrogant sound. Fine. Be that way.

"And I was thinking of not being able to call Jenny for her birthday," John added. "I mean, I'm not going to get any father of the year award for it, but I should've called."

Jenny was already asleep by now. He hoped she was safely tucked in her bed and home from the club or wherever she went. As long as she was safe. As she grew, John would tuck her into bed on the nights he was home. Even after she fell asleep, he'd make one more trip into her bedroom to kiss her tangled hair and whisper, "Goodnight."

"I miss Jenny when she was a little girl with ponytails and held my hand." John sighed. "We had a fort in the backyard that I built. It was a castle with flags on each corner. The last time I was home, it was gone."

He'd dropped his bag in the laundry room and made his way to the kitchen, passing the sliding glass door. And stopped dead in his tracks. The bare dirt shocked him. Their fort had disappeared. Not even a scrap of wood remained.

Joy walked past him and opened the fridge. "There's some lunch meat in here. Or I can cook up some mac and cheese."

John remained rooted at the door. He glanced at Joy and then the vacant dirt again. "Where's the fort?"

"Oh, that thing?" Joy closed the fridge and opened the bread cupboard. "Jenny tore it down, and I had some kids from the youth group haul it to the dump."

"But it was our fort." John's heart ached under the weight of Jenny's decision. She tore it down?

"It was rotten, John. Part of it fell in the last storm. So she knocked the rest of it down." Joy chuckled in the kitchen. "It's not like you two played in it anymore."

"And the flags?" Maybe he could save those. Tuck them away in his dresser drawer.

"Um, I think those went to the trash."

John nearly ran to the cans on the side of their garage. Empty.

Even now, it hurt.

"I'll call Jenny when I get back to my apartment." John laughed at little and spoke again before he was corrected. "I mean, back to my flat."

Finally, the rain slowed to sprinkles. Chris shook out his drippy hair, flinging water and looking miserable.

"Hey," John said, an idea forming in his mind. If he could do it, Chris certainly could. "Why don't you try calling Chloe?"

Chris stared daggers at him. "Do you really think I'd be standing here, waiting for you to leave, if I hadn't tried that already?"

His admission stole John's breath. "You really love her, don't you?"

"She has no interest in me." Chris turned away. "She's just as selfish and obstinate as I am."

A snort escaped John. "You're not, well, selfish."

Chris suddenly spun and grabbed John's jacket with both hands. "She hates me." He pushed, and John stumbled backwards.

"You must be one of those promised trials in First Peter. The fiery ones." John gave Chris a look from the top of his shaggy hair to his scuffed loafers.

"Possibly," Chris said. "What's even more strange is that you are living out the entire verse even though you only remember part of it."

"Oh yeah?"

"'Beloved, do not think it strange concerning the fiery trial which is to try you, as though some strange thing happened to you; but rejoice to the extent that you partake of Christ's sufferings, that when His glory is revealed, you may also be glad with exceeding joy.'" Chris sniffed and lifted his chin. "You've certainly got the 'be glad' part down. Doesn't seem to matter what's thrown at you."

John shook his head. "Well, you're just seeing me now. I wasn't all happy clappy, as you called it. I was really more like, um, mad Chad."

"What?" Chris's face bunched into confusion.

"It's the best I could do," John said with a shrug. "I'm an engineer, not a poet."

"That's obvious."

"I mean, I wrestle with my anger. It's always there." John motioned to the creek below. "It's why my phone was all broken and needed to be replaced."

"Ah, 'don't let the sun go down on your anger' and all."

"Hey. You're still good at this pastor stuff, ya know?"

Chris's shoulders bowed forward. "It doesn't change the fact that Chloe hates me."

No. Chloe couldn't hate Chris. Because that meant that Jenny probably hated John, too.

"You're her daddy. She loves you."

When Chris lifted his head, the shimmer of tears showed before he blinked them away. "We haven't spoken in two years."

Holy smokes! John would want to cry too if he hadn't talked to

Jenny in that long. Chris needed some soft prompting. And not the kind from the Holy Spirit, either.

"There's no time like the present."

"No."

Obstinate was right.

John reverted back to toddler-time teaching. He held up a fist, pinkie and thumb extended. The hand phone. Back when Jenny was in first and second grade, they'd have phone calls across the living room, she on an old and broken cell phone and he on the "hand phone." They'd talk about school and her new clothes. Or when they were going to build a canopy for her bed so that she could have a princess bed. He never did that. And she probably wouldn't like it now anyways.

John shoved his hand phone to his ear and made sure Chris saw him. "Hello, Chloe. It's your daddy calling."

He imagined Jenny's silence on the other end of the line. Her bitterness from forced perception because she didn't know what ate him alive from the inside out for the last year. It clawed at his throat.

"I've missed you so much," John continued, choking on the words, and leaning onto his hand as if he could hear Jenny breathing. He missed a lot of things as she grew and he worked. Trumpet recitals. Proms. Tearing down the fort. What was the saying about regrets? Something about learning from the mistakes of yesterday and moving on. Well, he was going to fix everything with Jenny, and Chris should at least try.

"I know I haven't handled everything very well, but you're a wonderful daughter."

Chris stared, face devoid of emotion, but his unshaven jaw worked back and forth.

"I love you."

John hadn't told Jenny that in such a long time. So long ago that he couldn't remember. He'd tell her the next time they were on the phone, even if she didn't say it back.

"I know I need to listen more—"

"Okay," Chris interrupted. "Enough."

John took a step back, dropping his hand phone. Across the bridge, deep in the lush canopy, two birds argued. Their angry chatter made John think of an argument with Joy—that one where Jenny nearly discovered the truth.

He hadn't been able to tell if his mood was off because the air conditioner was broken and the house was sweltering or because of his aching back from sleeping on the couch. Everything Joy said that day hit him like flint sparking. It was only a matter of time before he burst into flames.

When Joy yelled, he yelled right back. Neither of them had an inkling that Jenny'd come home until she came flying into the kitchen, a banshee on the warpath to defend her mother.

Jenny stepped in front of Joy, both hands balled into fists. "Dad! Just stop! You act like you hate her."

John felt his mouth open and close before he came up with a sensible answer. "Jenny," he started, taking a half step forward, "there are things that—"

"John!" Joy slapped a hand over her mouth.

Looking at both parents, Jenny burst into tears and fled.

"Are you going to help me with her?" John asked, torn between anger at Joy and the chance to comfort Jenny. "You've made her hate me."

"I didn't," Joy cried, tears tracking down her cheeks. "I just didn't want you to say anything, John. We agreed."

"I know we agreed. Believe me, I feel every part of the agreement."

Jenny would never know the truth unless she somehow unearthed it on her own. There would never be the right time to explain the depth of his pain to her. All John could do now was look forward and build a new future.

Chris had the chance to do the same.

"The time is now, Chris." John smiled and showed double thumbs up. "Now is the time."

Chris nodded. "You're right. Now is the time." He looked up to the top chord above the handrails and diagonals. "I need to get higher."

# CHAPTER 16

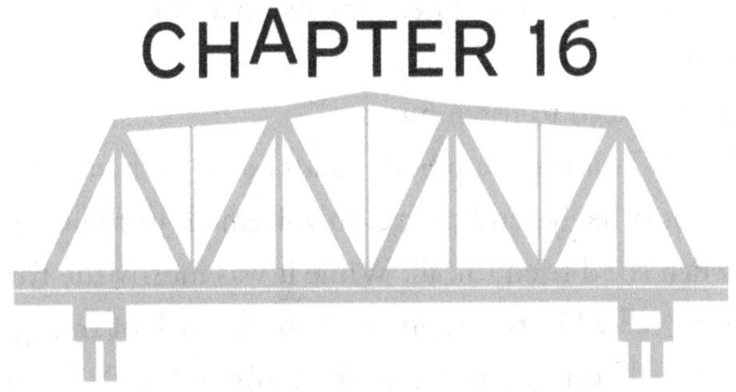

## THE FLY

*Chris*

"HELLO, CHLOE. IT'S YOUR DADDY CALLING."

Chris held his breath. He wanted to simultaneously punch John in the face and admit he was correct. Every fiber of his being wanted it to be right between him and Chloe. He wanted to cradle the mobile to his cheek just to hear her answer his call. He might even promise to go back to the pulpit if he heard her laugh again.

"I've missed you so much. I know I haven't handled everything very well, but you're a wonderful daughter."

The loss of Carol devastated him. But Chloe's departure gutted him. Left him nursing a bottle of whisky, which was how a deacon found him.

"I love you."

Chris's lungs burned with the need to inhale. He should've said it more often. It was a right shame that he couldn't even remember the last time he told his daughter that he loved her.

Usually, toward the end of her time living at home, it was shouting matches.

"I know I need to listen more—"

"Okay!" Chris threw up both hands between them. "Enough."

She'd most likely send his call to voicemail. Just like he'd done to her when she'd tried to call. While it was mostly the truth that they hadn't talked in two years, it wasn't for lack of trying on her part. And he'd been so upset that she'd missed Carol's funeral that he didn't exactly want to talk to her ever again.

Funny how time changed a heart. He'd answer the phone if she called.

"The time is now, Chris." John smiled and gave a cheerful double thumbs up. "Now is the time."

No truer words had John ever spoken throughout the entire morning. "You're right. Now is the time." He looked up to the highest parts above the railing. "I need to get higher."

"What?" John's flabbergasted question bounced into the trees. "Wait."

His words fell on deaf ears as Chris grabbed hold of the crossbar and swung one long leg up onto the handrail. "Spider Monkey" was his nickname as school, all lanky. But he could climb faster than anyone, shifting and adjusting his limbs. He'd learned as a boy, sprinting from his mother's grasp and shimmying up a pine tree in the backyard.

*"Christopher. Come down at once."*

He would shield his body with a bough, peeking between the needles at her wooden spoon as it slapped her open palm.

"Obey me, child."

Keeping watch until she left, he only climbed down well after dark. Supper was obviously out of the question, so he crept straight into his room and under the bed.

Climbing a bridge wasn't much different than a tree or obstacle course wall. It just took a bit of momentum and keeping an eye on where his hand landed.

"Chris," John called out behind him on the bridge deck. "Chloe needs you."

"She's done all right on her own." One turn of his foot for a better hold and he nearly had a clear path to the top.

"I know she's angry, but she needs you."

The genuine tone John used nearly made Chris stop. But he pushed on.

"Come on, I know Chloe needs you."

Chris stretched his left arm out as far as it would go to clasp the top wooden board. It creaked so deeply that he thought it might break and he'd end up back down next to John. That wasn't an option. Every muscle screamed as he clamored up, shoving with both feet and pulling with both arms until he straddled the beam like a horse. He could see all the way down to the bend in the stream from this vantage point. He could almost imagine Chloe in her striped bathing suit wandering that way until he yelled, "Not that far!"

A quick glance down made Chris's grip tighten. "Not that far, indeed," he mumbled.

"Chris—"

"Oh, what do you know?" He was sick and tired of John's belief that everything needed to be saved. "Go back home!" Chris motioned wide with his hand and then grabbed tightly again as the entire thing wobbled. "Go…go save your marriage."

John took a tentative step toward Chris's dangling feet. "I bet she cries herself to sleep every night because of her mom. And because of you."

Weak. "I see what you're trying to do. You're trying to distract me, and it won't work." It was true. Chris would study for a sermon while Chloe blared her music in the next room, and it didn't faze him. Even when the workmen jackhammered out the old lavatory at the church, he paid them no mind. Putting his mind to a task came naturally. Swinging both legs to face the stream was the next step, so he did that.

"Wait!" From his peripheral vision, Chris saw both of John's arms extend forward, as if to catch him. "We were doing so good down here."

It'd almost worked. Chris nearly gave up for a chance to talk with Chloe until he came to his senses.

"When Chloe told her mum and I that she didn't believe like we did, that she wasn't a Christian, it wounded Carol. I think she thought she'd failed Chloe." Chris looked out into the forest, teeming with all sorts of sounds and movement coming out after the rain. A breeze made him shiver beneath his coat. "For as long as she was able, Carol would literally pray on her knees for Chloe to come back round."

"My mom did, too." John still wasn't any closer to the railing, and one arm had dropped. "I had some wild years in college until I met Joy."

"Oh, she tamed you into those…" Chris cast his eyes down, "…flannel shirts?"

John chuckled, examining the shirt in question under his jacket. "Nah. Those just came with the job when I'm out in the weather. Joy also made me start going to church again."

"Carol never lived to see that."

She didn't live to see a lot of things: their thirtieth anniversary that he spent in a drunken stupor. Or her great-niece's baby announcement. The horrific bombings that flooded the news. Another brilliant bonfire for Guy Fawkes. The beautiful sunrise after she passed that broke his heart into tiny inconsolable pieces because she was gone.

"I bet it was one of the last things on her mind."

"No. She said she was scared. And then she sang."

"What'd she sing?"

"It doesn't matter."

If Chris never heard the words to that beloved song again, he'd be all right with that.

"Can't you come down here with me again?" John sounded despondent.

Chris snorted. "I'm more likely to die up here. You told me that yourself."

"Okay," John said. "Okay. You're in control here. So, just a few more minutes."

It'd grown tedious. Repetitive. The snake eating its own tail.

"No." He took a moment to look up at a break in the clouds. Would he feel anything? Would Chloe forgive him? "No, John. I'm done."

Chris scooted as far forward as he could, perched on the edge, wood digging into the backs of his thighs. His eyes slipped closed, and he thought of Carol.

Until the entire structure nearly jerked out from underneath him.

"Are you kidding me?"

John clung to the diagonal beams above the railing, grunting and groaning. "I'm not gonna die. I'm not gonna die," he chanted, robotically moving from one upward piece to the next in his pursuit. "Visualize success. Breathe."

The entire beam lurched. Chris adjusted his body position to keep from falling backwards or sideways. A lot of good that'd do him to end up being injured with this dimwit who looked like a baby just learning to walk instead of a man who worked on bridges and couldn't even scale the side of one.

"Are you quite finished?" he asked while John groaned and laughed nervously when he reached the top. "It's like watching an exponential augmentation of a spore patch."

John screwed his face together. "You're one of those people who think you're superior to others." His knuckles were pale, and he had a leg wrapped around the closest diagonal timber. "You use big words like 'galvanize' instead of 'strengthen.' Your decision is always right. No one should have different opinions, and if they do, they're wrong."

"That's what Chloe said when she left."

"Well, I can only imagine how many times you talked her into a corner."

Chris swung his head to face John's pallor. "What do you mean by that?" How dare he assume.

"Exactly what I said!" John nodded and pitched forward a bit. He quickly righted himself. "I'd even wager that the only other opinion you listened to, barely, was Carol's. Even then, it was begrudgingly."

A huff of sarcastic air escaped Chris. "Now who's using big words?"

"You're a pro at turning the argument to your favor. Not with me." John shook his head in quick tiny increments. "I've got nothing to lose by standing up to you."

Chris twitched his eyebrow up. Standing up? More like barely sitting there. If John would only give up on this crusade, it'd be over. Finally.

"And if you eventually get it through your thick head that the world doesn't revolve around you," John continued, letting go just for a moment to point and then grabbing the wood again, "maybe you can fix your relationship with Chloe. I bet all she wanted was a dad and not a preacher."

"Chris," Carol whispered into his mind, from years ago. "Darling. You have to let go of the fact that the world doesn't stop for you."

His gallbladder surgery had complications, and no one had stopped by the parsonage to visit. Not even to drop off a meal.

"I'm the shepherd of the congregation," he'd pouted from the sofa, playing with the frayed ends of his favorite lap throw. "Chloe burnt the toast this morning while you were out."

"Yes, you've already told me."

"Well, I feel better saying it again."

"You sound like a spoilt brat."

"Am not."

Carol's laughter spilled from the kitchen and into the living room. It made him smile then, and he never complained during the rest of his recovery.

His smile disappeared as the memory retreated. "I don't want to talk about it," Chris said, turning away from John, hoping the fear of falling would terrify the man to retreat.

"Chris." John's tone softened. Like he was talking to a baby. Or a man about to jump from a bridge. "If only you'd see how much you have. Sure, there's going to be some fence mending with Chloe. I mean, I have my own to do with Joy and Jenny."

Still, Chris refused to look at the man whose face was probably teeming with hope. He rolled his eyes at the sky.

"Hey, we're like brothers in repair work!" John laughed politely. Chris turned to tell him to go away, but John held his bottom lip between his teeth and extended his fist. He sucked in a quick breath. "Fist bump, bro. Come on, give me a good one."

Irksome. Like a fly on a hot, humid day, buzzing around and refusing to leave.

Chris looked away again. Had he just rung up the driver fifteen minutes earlier, this wouldn't have been an issue. But he had to go back through the house, double-checking. This was his penance.

Except that he didn't believe in penance. Because that was punishment from God. And Chris made it well known to everyone from this American to the landlady that God, in fact, was a children's story.

Maybe this was what karma felt like. But who had he offended so deeply to deserve such torture? All he wanted was to leave this world in peace.

His only way of escaping was off of the side with an audience or to climb down and try again. The latter, though the better of the two, was thwarted by John to his left, blocking the way down. Chris tilted his chin to the sky. He rubbed some warmth into his thighs with both hands.

Suddenly, something wrapped around his wrist. Most decidedly not a human hand. Chris glanced down to see John wind a thin black strap around his wrist before mirroring the same. Thus, the men were attached. Shackled. No chance of fleeing John now.

"Ha!" John yelled, his free hand clutching the rail between them. "Gotcha."

Chris looked at their wrists. Hobbled together by some flimsy plastic strap. As if the day couldn't get any worse.

John triumphantly laughed again, his right hand pulling Chris's back to the beam so that he could hold them both in place. "Betcha didn't see that one coming, bro. Where are you gonna go now?"

Telling John where he could go would have little effect. Every time Chris tried to shed the man, he came back even worse. Like a bad rash. A bubble of anger popped below Chris's ribcage. He hated God. He hated that Carol left him. And he most certainly hated John, who thought that everything could be solved with God, bubble gum, and prayer. Even his miserable marriage to a terrible woman. If Carol had cheated on him, Chris would've left her behind. But she never would have.

Good riddance to this terrible existence with people like John. It wasn't as if Chris couldn't cause them both to fall. Fury boiled up to his chest.

And what right did John have to lash them together, like a nanny to a child who likes to run into the roadway? Chris knew exactly what he was doing. His life, his choice. John had no idea what it felt like to waste away, watch life disappear in incremental doses. A dandelion blown to bits in a storm. Rage bounced in Chris's throat and vibrated down his free arm.

"Well, how about this for a fist bump?"

Chris slouched down for balance, balled his right fist, and swung hard.

# CHAPTER 17

## FIST BUMP, BRO

*John*

**"WAIT! WE WERE DOING SO GOOD DOWN HERE." JOHN** held up both arms. Maybe it'd break Chris's fall if he happened to tumble backwards. It'd been horrifying to watch Chris shimmy up the diagonal with ease. John's stomach lurched. He swallowed hard. But if John needed to be up there beside Chris, Jesus would somehow make that happen. John just wished there was a safety harness around. He dropped one arm and patted his jacket. Only the extra camera strap to the now useless camera that was probably covered in mud. And he hadn't downloaded the pictures from the card yet, either.

"When Chloe told her mum and I that she didn't believe like we did, that she wasn't a Christian, it wounded Carol. I think she thought she'd failed Chloe." Oddly enough, Chris stared into the distance and resembled a model, linen suit still looking clean and pressed. Strange. "For as long as she was able, Carol would literally pray on her knees for Carol to come back round."

That caught John's attention like a slap to the cheek.

"Will you be coming to church on Sunday?" his mom had asked, moving cookies from the baking sheet to a wire rack while Christmas music played.

"Mom," John said, ramming his heel into a shoe, "I'm only home for a week and a half. I have plans." Which most definitely did *not* include church or seeing an old girlfriend across the aisle.

"Okay, honey." When John looked up, Mom stared at him, eyes soft and smiling. "I love you, you know."

"Yeah, I know." His shoes were on, and he swiped the keys from the coffee table.

"Jesus loves you, too," she called as the door slammed behind him.

"My mom did, too." John kept one arm up in the middle of the bridge. "I had some wild years in college until I met Joy."

Chris turned, all scornful and judging. "Oh, she tamed you into those flannel shirts?"

Let the man have a laugh. He was the one wanting to jump.

"Nah." John dropped his other arm and parted his jacket. He got this one last year from Jenny. It was wrapped in plastic cling, inside of a duct taped box. He wasn't sure by her expression whether it was done in spite because he had arrived a day late or in humor. "Those just came with the job when I'm out in the weather." Anything under twenty degrees was too cold for him. John straightened and smiled, knowing he was wearing Jenny's flannel. "Joy also made me start going to church again."

It was only two blocks from the college, but John thought he'd spontaneously burst into flames when he sat down next to her and a couple of her friends. The church he grew up in had girls sit on one side of the room and boys on the other during youth group. This one, though, was warm and inviting. They actually opened their Bibles and read from them.

"Carol never lived to see that." Chris sounded utterly heartbroken. He sounded like John felt when he discovered Joy's affair. He needed a thought to make him happy.

"I bet it was one of the last things on her mind." That'd be enough to cheer him.

"No." Chris sighed. "She said she was scared. And then she sang."

Well. That didn't work out so well. *Positive. Say something positive.* "What'd she sing?"

"It doesn't matter."

It did matter. Chris knew it as well as John. He was just so stubborn that he wouldn't admit anything.

John raked a hand through his hair to try and shake some of the dampness. Moist. If there was one word to describe England, that was it.

Above him, Chris adjusted the way he sat on the top chord. It was ten, maybe twelve feet up in the air. Hundred-year-old timbers. Fasteners that had been exposed to the humidity for just as long. A recipe for disaster. Rapture would be better than having to climb up there to stop Chris.

"Can't you come down here with me again?"

Chris snorted. "I'm more likely to die up here. You told me that yourself."

"Okay," John said. "Okay. You're in control here. So, just a few more minutes."

"No." Chris looked up to the clouds. Maybe rapture was coming. "No, John. I'm done." He scootched forward, rocking his rear end side to side, until he barely teetered on the edge of the beam.

That was it.

Jesus' clear and flashing sign.

John had to climb up there to stop him.

His stomach tumbled when he stepped forward and grabbed the diagonal brace. John forced himself to move instead of think. Put a foot on the handrail. Pull up. He kept his eye on Chris, dismissing the imminent death that awaited him if he fell. Because on a day like today, he'd land headfirst and break his neck.

John nearly heaved. It'd be okay. He had both feet on the railing now. "I'm not gonna die. I'm not gonna die," he recited, taking quick breaths through his nose and pushing them out of his mouth. He'd climb through a thousand blackberry bushes—in his shorts—rather than scale this bridge.

But Chris needed to be stopped. How would he explain it to the police? He stayed there and talked while the guy fell to his death? The entire United Kingdom would flog him.

"Visualize success," John whispered, pulling himself up higher, trying to ignore the wobbling wood. Little pinkish red dots appeared on his peripheral vision. "Breathe."

John shuffled his feet along the diagonal until the top chord was chest high and Chris's suit was the only thing he could see. If he could survive getting up to the top and sit there without losing his balance, John promised himself that he'd to go buy a lotto ticket upon return to his flat. Maybe even one for Mrs. Pottifer.

A groan escaped as John pushed his torso higher. He really needed to work out. Just a little bit more and there! He threw his left leg over the beam and straddled it like a horse, laughing nervously. His hands clung to the wood in front of him until the bridge settled again.

"Are you quite finished?" Chris twisted his head to judge John's precarious position. "It's like watching an exponential augmentation of a spore patch," he said, all stuck-up and judgmental.

John wrapped a free foot around the diagonal beam. "You're one of those people who think you're superior to others." He nodded to the ridiculous linen suit. "You use big words like 'galvanize' instead of 'strengthen.' Your decision is always right. No one should have different opinions, and if they do, they're wrong."

"That's what Chloe said when she left." Chris looked away.

"Well, I can only imagine how many times you talked her into a corner."

Chris scrutinized John when he looked back again. "What do you mean by that?"

John nodded and felt his balance waver. He dug in his fingers and pressed his thighs against the wood. "Exactly what I said. I'd even wager that the only other opinion you listened to, barely, was Carol's. Even then, it was begrudgingly."

Chris scoffed the most British sounding scoff that ever was scoffed. "Now who's using big words?"

"You're a pro at turning the argument to your favor. Not with me." John barely shook his head side to side so that he didn't lose his balance again. "I've got nothing to lose by standing up to you." Well, technically, sitting, but no one was counting.

Chris's bushy eyebrow twitched. It looked like he wanted to spout a million insults. But since he didn't, John took it as a sign to keep talking.

"And if you eventually get it through your thick head that the world doesn't revolve around you, maybe you can fix your relationship with Chloe. I bet all she wanted was a dad and not a preacher."

Without a snappish response, Chris stared off again. The lines in his face relaxed. Probably drifting down a memory. Good. He needed to remember the bad and the good.

He cleared his throat. "I don't want to talk about it."

John needed to come alongside Chris to put a spotlight on the positive. "Chris, if only you'd see how much you have. Sure, there's going to be some fence mending with Chloe." John pulled up short, struggling with the next sentence, but knowing it had to be said. "I mean, I have my own to do with Joy and Jenny."

So much mending.

He had forgiven Joy. In theory. Now he needed to start acting that way. Sure, it wouldn't be perfect or even pretty, but struggling was better than giving up. Even after the affair. And admitting that he hated her for it. It was time to move forward. Just like he told Chris.

Jenny.

That…that was a different ballgame altogether. It would be a dance to gain her trust again. If she saw him trying with Joy, it'd help, that's for sure. But he needed to keep Jenny out of their marital mess and treat her with love and respect. Except for the going to the club thing. That needed to stop. It would be a slower, more methodical mending with his daughter.

John laughed a little at the thought of being a handyman. "Hey, we're like brothers in repair work!" Use humor. John swallowed hard when he let go of the bridge and extended a closed fist. He bit his bottom lip to concentrate on balancing and not vomiting. Chris slowly turned, looking at John's fist, then face. John reached back into their first interaction on the bridge. "Fist bump, bro. Come on, give me a good one."

All of the fight in Chris's eyes faded. He glanced at John's fist again and sighed before staring back into the trees.

John latched onto the bridge again with both hands. Oh, no. Chris was going to jump. Right in front of him, and there was nothing he could do about it. If John tried to stop him, they'd both fall. With the added height and the variable of his weight added to the mix, even landing in the creek, one of them wouldn't make it. Chris needed to talk with Chloe, and John had to get back to his girls.

The way he sat made John's rear end tingle as it started to numb. He shifted, ever so slightly, to relieve the pressure. Something firm underneath his jacket rubbed against his chest.

The camera strap.

Chris definitely wouldn't commit murder by pulling John down if they were, say, tied together. With as little movement as possible, John snaked his hand to the pocket on his flannel and removed the tightly wound strap. He never understood why it'd come with the camera, but apparently Jesus knew there was a time that he'd need it.

Pinning the strap to the beam, John unwound the plastic, glancing up at Chris, who still was lost in his own thoughts. John needed to hurry before Chris made the wrong choice. First, he'd wrap the strap around Chris's left wrist because it was closest. A quick double knot would work.

John darted both hands around Chris's wrist, fingers winding the strap and securing the first knot before Chris registered what was happening. Finishing the second knot, John left a small tether and wrapped the remainder of the strap around his right hand and held onto the beam. This would work!

"Ha!" John crowed. He felt his smile lift his spirit. He saved Chris! "Gotcha!"

Chris's blank expression cemented into place as he surveyed their hands.

"Betcha didn't see that one coming, bro." John's excitement bubbled at Chris's new lease on life. "Where are you gonna go now?"

John's mind raced ahead. They could agree to climb down and go get something to eat. Probably somewhere private in case

Mr. Hot Head wanted to get all hoity-toity. Maybe he could call Chloe and have the two of them meet to talk somewhere. Offer to stay nearby in case Chris wanted to talk afterwards.

However, Chris's stern expression didn't look pleased. In fact, it morphed from frigid blankness into hardened anger.

Oh. This wasn't good. Now John was tied up with a guy who *did* look like he might throw the both of them from the side of the bridge.

John gripped the bridge tighter. Nothing good could come from—

"How about this for a fist bump?"

John saw a flash from next to Chris before something smashed into his nose. In blinding pain, John crumpled to the narrow beam, wrapping his left arm around it to keep from falling.

The pain danced circles around any clear thoughts. Tangy metallic blood dripped down the back of his throat, and the throbbing agony indicated that it was probably trailing across his cheek pressed against the wood.

As his mind grappled with the pain and circumstances, two things became crystal clear: Chris punched him! In the face!

The taste of blood and the lurch of the bridge made John's stomach roll. He needed to stop the bleeding or he'd throw up all over Chris. Not that he didn't deserve that, but it would stink.

John used both arms to right himself. He didn't look at his hands because he didn't want to see the blood. Not that he'd pass out from the sight, but looking at that meant that he'd have to see how high up they were and—

He dry-heaved to the side before mumbling to breathe. He needed to focus.

Chris waved a white handkerchief in front of John's face like a flag of truce.

With slow motions to keep his balance, John took the cloth and mopped up his face, knowing it looked like he'd been, you know, punched in the face. But it seemed that the more he wiped, the harder it bled.

This guy must've been a boxer at some point.

John's stomach protested loudly. He sighed, shoving a corner of the handkerchief up his right nostril.

"It's like the worst day of my life."

Chris snorted. "*Like* the worst day?"

# CHAPTER 18

# IT'S NOT FLORIDA

*Chris*

WHEN JOHN NEARLY VOMITED, CHRIS FELT...BAD.

Sure, the punch was warranted, but John was trying to help in his annoying and unwanted way. A different tactic would've been more effective. The poor guy gushed blood from his nose now.

Chris retrieved the handkerchief from his suit pocket. It was tucked in there out of habit. Carol's allergies and habitual tears made it a necessary practice.

Beneath his blood-streaked face, John's skin paled as he sat up straight, clutching the bridge for dear life. Chris flagged the handkerchief in the air between them. As long as John didn't ask him how bad it was.

It was awful.

John timidly took the white cloth. Chris watched blood seep into the folds, even after it was jammed into John's nostril.

"It's like the worst day of my life."

Chris pulled back the apology he almost offered. "*Like* the worst day?" He watched John struggle to keep up with the bleeding. "Put your head back." He motioned to John, and his watch caught his eye. He checked the time. Still a bit longer.

John obeyed, tilting his chin toward the horizon. His eyes slid closed. His Adam's apple bobbed up and down, and he started to hum a song.

Blasted man. Couldn't even take a punch to the face in the right way. Chris was about to snap off an insult when John quieted, and his brows knitted together. It couldn't be comfortable in that position. But Chris was sure the way John's lips tightened together wasn't about being relaxed or how to spout Jesus in the next breath.

"Are you quite done reminiscing?" Chris made sure he wasn't looking at his American captor when the man straightened.

"Yeah…yeah. Just remembering a time I'd rather forget." John plucked the handkerchief and swapped it for a clean corner to replace into his nose. "I don't suppose you have any of those?"

"None that I'd ever share with you." Ever. In a million years, he'd never share the deepest darkest secrets with a man who'd turn it into some mini sermon on God's sufficient grace. Not that he believed in that anymore.

No God. Or god. Or grace, for that matter. And show-and-tell time could just jump off the bridge. Chris guffawed at his own private joke.

The impressive rumble from John's abdomen made Chris long for a hot plate of black pudding, baked beans, and bacon.

John moaned as his stomach sounded off again. "You'd think a guy would be entitled to breakfast on the worst day of his life." He rolled his head forward, handkerchief hanging from his nose, and shook his head. "But no."

Drama must be something inherently American, Chris decided before extending his arm and checking his wristwatch again.

It was a lot closer than he thought. Surprisingly, it made him a smidge nervous. Perhaps it was the fact that he had an audience.

"Why do you keep checking your watch?"

Chris pulled his right hand over to their bound wrists and pulled up the sleeve of his jacket so that they both had a better view. What John couldn't see was the inscription on the back of the watch that warmed his skin.

*20 years ~ love Carol*

The letters were so faint that Chris had to hold the watch at a certain angle to see them when he dressed each morning. Somehow, she'd found the perfect watch for him to obsess and geek out about: a vintage mechanical Poljot with an alarm in perfect working order. Crafted in the former Soviet Union with eighteen jewels. The seller had even included pictures of the back removed so that Chris could see the inner gears.

"I know what makes you tick," she kidded when fastening it around his wrist after their modest dinner at home. "Now you can figure out how that fancy alarm works so that you can get up early and exercise."

Chris returned his right hand to his side, allowing the face to slide back underneath the sleeve. "The alarm is set for the same time she took her last breath. When it goes off, I jump." He swiveled his gaze to John, all ridiculous and bloody. "Whether you're with me or not."

John squirmed but made no effort to untie them. "Wh-what time would that be?"

"Let's leave that as a surprise, shall we?"

"That'll be murder, you know."

"Sue me."

Pink tainted John's cheeks again. "You're a very funny guy." His tone suggested the exact opposite.

Chris lost all humor. "Then untie me."

John raised his chin a tad. "No."

"So, it's your choice then."

But Chris already knew he wouldn't jump and pull John to his death. Worse yet, an injury that he'd be sued for. Probably would settle out of court if Chris agreed to counseling or whatever. Wouldn't Carol get a laugh out of this backwards situation? She always found the chink in his armor.

"You asked me before about a time I'd rather forget." The words tumbled from Chris's mouth unbidden. Spilling secrets. He blew a hard breath through his lips, making them sputter. A scent on the breeze caught his attention: ripe apples. Probably from the orchard on the way in. The fruit up high would be riper.

John jostled their bound hands as he adjusted his seat but remained silent.

"When Carol told me she was sick again, I couldn't…I didn't want to hear it. But she smiled and repeated herself. She always smiled."

From the corner of his vision, Chris saw John's own grin. It hurt.

"Of course, I didn't go to that appointment," Chris continued. "I had a sermon I was busy with and couldn't spare the time." He reached out and glanced at his watch again.

"The first time she was sick, I was there for every step of the way. The drives for chemotherapy. Learning how to run the laundry. Making sure she was propped up on the bed so that she could sleep for more than an hour at a time."

There was a certain laundry detergent Chris discovered she loved. And he learned why she tossed an old tennis ball in the dryer. Softer and fluffier blankets and towels. Especially her favorite red blanket, all velvety. She'd tuck it under her chin when she slept.

"People always say that their husband or wife never complained," Chris went on. "Carol did exactly one time. Her port became infected, and she asked for more pain medication. That was it. When she went into remission, the recurrence rate was so low, that we had a party to celebrate the new half of her life."

Red and white balloons. Just like her blood cells, she said. Chloe made a cake. A few families from the congregation came over to the backyard party.

"It was just a follow-up appointment."

Carol kissed him on the cheek. "I'm wearing my lucky jumper," she said, looking down at the pearl buttons on the navy V-neck.

"What is so lucky about it?" Chris held his finger to the place on the concordance he needed to keep reading.

"It's the jumper I was wearing when we went last year. When I got my remission notice."

"Oh…oh, yes."

She laughed, filling the corners and crannies of his study with happiness. "You didn't have a clue then either, love. I'll be home before supper."

The bridge moved ever so slightly. Chris scooted side to side to encourage blood flow to the parts of his legs that tingled. Shocking that John remained quiet the entire time.

"Breathe, focus," John mumbled before they made eye contact. "So you didn't go to that appointment, then?"

"No." Grief washed over him like a cold bucket of water dumped on top of his head. "I didn't. I didn't even look at my watch until I was hungry and checked the time. Then I panicked because she should've been home over an hour before. She answered her mobile right away. She was just round the corner, picking up some of my favorite bread.

"Maybe I should've guessed when she didn't talk through dinner, or that she cooked my favorite steak and garlic bread."

Suddenly, Chris's throat became dry. He tried to clear it and it only made him cough. The mint tin he always carried luckily was in his right pocket, so he flipped it open with his thumb. Shaking a single candy into his mouth, Chris waited until saliva flooded again before speaking. Why share this with John? It'd be better to move away from everything precious.

"Do you want a mint?" He held the tin close enough for John to choose one.

"Mmm," John said, using a sad excuse of a British accent. "Lovely."

Right. Topic change.

"So, why are you here?"

John's eyebrows furrowed as he contemplated. "I…" he started slowly. "I think I'm here because God sent me."

Chris smashed his eyes closed. John would never stop.

"Hey, I love the way the Lord works." John grinned when Chris looked back at him.

"No, I mean why are you here," Chris said, motioning to the area around them. "You know, in the U.K."

"Oh!" John chuckled, his head bobbing side to side. "I'm on a work assignment. The new construction on A12. I had today off. I like to photograph old bridges and buildings, and your country is chock full of them. It's just a hobby of mine."

The more he talked, the more animated his body and deathlike his grip on the beam. At least it wasn't about Jesus or Carol.

John nodded to the bridge below. "You know, this bridge is

famous. It's one of the last remaining wooden truss bridges in all of England. It was built by this eccentric old American guy."

Of course it was.

"He settled here in England and wanted to build a bridge. It's funny," John continued, smiling once more. "There's no meaning, there's no purpose, it doesn't do anything. It wasn't on a main road or even to his house. You guys call it folly."

There was an itch on Chris's back that he couldn't reach. He flexed his shoulders for some relief. "Pointless is what I call it."

John's lips tipped down and his shoulders raised. "I read about it and wanted to come see it in person. It's just my hobby. Dunno. Do you have a hobby?"

Nope. Not going down personal street again. "Shouldn't you really be out preaching the gospel rather than taking pictures of old bridges?"

That made John stop talking. For a moment. "Probably, yeah. Truth be told, I feel very close with God when I'm out with my camera taking pictures. It's nice."

"If God exists, why doesn't he send me a sign?"

John snorted a laugh. "I don't know. You're the one who used to be a pastor. You would know better than me. I couldn't even get my tract straight."

"Oh, come on, something." Against his better judgement, and for the sake of keeping John far from his personal life, Chris continued down that path. "Something like, some sort of sign that proves his existence—"

His rumbling train of thought was interrupted by a ringing mobile.

The mobile that vibrated against his left breast.

On the third ring, Chris finally worked it free of the pocket and slid it open to answer the unknown number.

"Hello?"

"Is this Christopher Arnold?" The woman's voice raised on the wrong syllable, ar-NOLD. In the background, it sounded like children ran circles around her chair.

"Yeah." But it was better than conversation with John. "Yeah, that's me."

"Good afternoon. Can you hear me okay?"

"Yep."

"Good. I am calling today to speak with you about an opportunity—"

"Hang on a second." Chris let his eyes fall shut. This was really happening now? "Can I—"

"… to build a more secure future—"

"Can I stop you there?"

"You never know what tomorrow will hold."

Chris gritted his teeth. "Are you trying to sell me something?"

"It's a low-cost opportunity—"

"No," he said through his teeth. "I said are you trying to sell me something?"

"Life insurance should be available to everyone at affordable rates," she prattled on.

"Right. Well, I don't need life insurance where I'm going."

"Are you headed on holiday to Florida? We're going to Disney World next year." A dog started yapping into the chaos.

"No," Chris snapped. "It's not Florida."

"Well, where are you off to?"

"It's none of your business."

"No need to be rude, sir. I don't have to give you a quote."

Chris's thermometer popped. "Listen, at the same time, can you take me off whatever list it is you've got me on, please?"

"I don't have the authority to do that, Mr. Arnold."

That was it!

"Well in that case, can I speak to the manager?"

"I have no way of transferring you directly to him. But I'd be happy to take your information and pass it along."

Daft girl. "No, I'd like to speak with the manager now."

Static then a garbled noise filled the earpiece. "Hello?" The children and dog disappeared. "Hello?" A faint rubbing noise. "Hello?"

"Drop dead," came the polite answer just before the click ending the call.

"I can't believe that," Chris said, tucking the mobile into the pocket again.

"What?" John leaned forward.

"She told me to drop dead."

John's robust laughter echoed all the way down the canyon, echoing back. "I can't believe she told you to drop dead!"

# CHAPTER 19

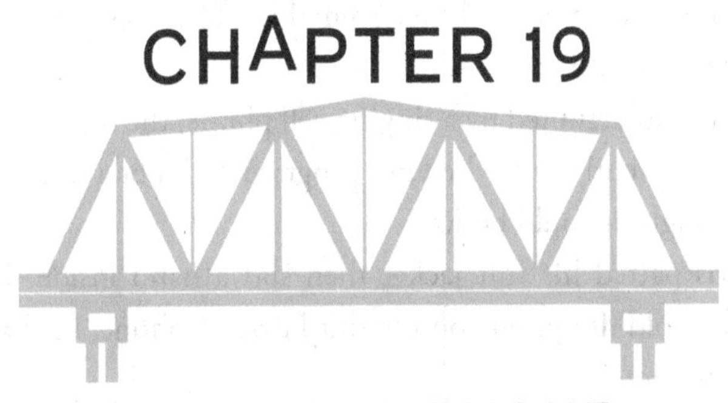

## DINOSAUR PHONE

*John*

"SHOULDN'T YOU REALLY BE OUT PREACHING THE GOSpel rather than taking pictures of old bridges?"

And just like that, John's forward motion to becoming Chris's friend ground to a halt. This man couldn't let anyone be kind to him.

"Probably, yeah." John's butt was nearly numb now, but the view was spectacular. The cloud-filtered light was perfect. And the shadows on the trees would've made for some great shots. "Truth be told, I feel very close with God when I'm out with my camera taking pictures. It's nice."

The smell of rain filled his one good nostril. Pity his camera was water-logged.

"If God exists," Chris said, reverting back to the nasal snobbish tone, "why doesn't he send me a sign?"

Like a Cracker Jack prize? A bubble of laughter slipped out. "I don't know. You're the one who used to be a pastor. You would know better than me. I couldn't even get my tract straight."

"Oh, come on, something. Something like, some sort of sign that proves his existence—"

He was interrupted by a ringing cell phone, the tone that most phones inherently ring when not programmed. For a split second, John thought it could be Joy.

Chris patted his suit jacket then slid a hand inside. He retrieved an old flip phone on the third ring. A phone. He had one the whole time!

"Hello?" Chris turned his head away from John, as if it would afford him two inches of privacy. "Yeah. Yeah, that's me."

John couldn't hear whoever it was on the other end, but when Chris became more agitated the further along the conversation progressed, John tightened every grip against the bridge that he could. Chris swung his free arm, and John squeaked.

"Breathe," he whispered, moving his body opposite of Chris's annoyed actions.

"Well in that case, can I speak to the manager?"

John dropped his head so that Chris couldn't see him laughing. What a typical thing for Chris to do.

"No, I'd like to speak with the manager now." His voice raised with every word. "Hello? Hello?" Chris held out the phone and then put it to his ear again. "Hello?"

The conversation must've ended because Chris placed the phone back into his jacket. His bushy eyebrows knitted together when he faced John. "I can't believe that."

"What?"

"She told me to drop dead."

No. Way!

Laughter burst out from deep inside John. All he could do was laugh and hold on tight so that they didn't, quite literally, drop to their deaths. "I can't believe she told you to drop dead!"

Oh, the irony of it all. Mister I-want-to-speak-to-your-manager planted on a bridge and wanting to jump. God's sense of humor for the win.

Once the giggles worked their way out of his system, John nodded to Chris's chest. "I didn't know you had a cell phone."

Chris didn't acknowledge him at first. "You mean a mobile." He pouted in silence for a few more moments. "Doesn't everyone have them?"

Duh. But John said, "Yeah."

Chris squinted. "Did you really think that because I'm suicidal I wouldn't have a phone?"

Well, that's a question John never pondered. "I don't know."

Chris offered the phone to John. "Here," he said, bouncing the phone between his long fingers, "use it to call your daughter."

Jenny.

Maybe, just maybe, John was wearing Chris down by reminding him that Chloe needed him. That's why he was suggesting Jenny.

John grabbed the phone but left it in Chris's grasp. She wouldn't answer because she was so upset. He'd missed her birthday again. Worst dad of the year. No, the decade.

"Go on," Chris said, letting go. "Call her."

"I'm not sure I'd know what to say."

Chris sighed, a faint smile touching his lips. He nodded to the phone. "I'm sure you'll think of something. Call her."

It'd be after one in the morning there. A phone call now would be as useful as an accordion player on a deer hunt. She'd be grumpy and tired, not interested in any excuses he offered.

"Come on now," Chris said, eyebrows wrinkling his forehead. "Give it a try."

He was right. She at least deserved an effort. With a flick of his wrist, the old flip phone's tiny pixelated screen lit up. One slight problem.

"I'll have to call Joy first." He felt his cheeks burn with embarrassment. "I don't know Jenny's number."

"It's fine."

"I'll pay you for the cost."

"No need."

John turned the phone over once before punching in Joy's number. "Where'd you get this thing? A museum?" Chris kept his ghost of a smile in place when John cradled the phone to his ear.

One ring.

Two rings.

Three rings.

She would never answer an unknown number.

The fourth ring hadn't finished before the line connected, first with a squelch, then Joy's worried voice.

"Hello?"

He'd never been so happy to hear her. John pressed closer to the phone, trying to erase the distance. "Hey Joy, it's John." His heart swelled with love for her. It wasn't perfect love, or even the good mushy stuff she watched on television. But he did love her.

"I almost didn't answer the phone because I didn't recognize the number. But then I remembered the overseas extension and thought…never mind. Why didn't you just use your phone?" Every word ran into one another on a long breath.

"Um, I don't have my phone anymore so I'm using a…" John glanced up to see Chris watching, face full of anticipation. "I'm using a friend's phone for now."

"What happened to your phone?"

It was blissful not to have to pick out her words between the statics and feedback from his damaged phone. And since Chris's phone was a relative to the dinosaurs, Joy couldn't see they were perched on a bridge.

High above his phone.

"Oh, it's a long story. I'll have to tell you about it when I get home."

"Are you okay? Is there any trouble?"

That would wait, too. She didn't need the play-by-play with Chris at his elbow. "No. Nothing's the matter. I just—"

"But you're not on your phone and I tried calling you."

"Just hear me out, Joy." John cleared a tickle in his throat. "I need you to forgive me for the way that I spoke to you earlier."

"Oh," she whispered into the phone. He knew, even across the globe, that tears crowded her eyes. He could hear it in the way she breathed.

"I've been so angry and bitter."

"It's okay."

They both knew it wasn't. The words she said held little value.

"I've been angry with God, too." There. It was out. His dirty little secret. It punched John in the chest and ached. "And I know that I need to forgive you, like really forgive you, instead of just saying it. It doesn't mean that it never happened or that we don't have to work hard to get past it, but I want to, Joy."

She sobbed into the mouthpiece. John wished for nothing more than to slide his arms around her shoulders and tuck her into his chest, right where she fit. The best he could do was allow a stray tear to fall unchecked.

"We can move on, honey," he murmured into the phone.

"We can," she cried, sniffing and then blowing her nose. She always kept a box of tissues near the bed.

John felt lighter than he had in months. The invisible weight of anger shucked for the time being. "I'm going to fight for you, Joy."

She burst into a new round of crying, a dainty little hiccupping noise that always made John soften.

"And something happened today that just...it made me realize that I love you."

A gasp sounded before silence. John nearly asked if she was still there, when Joy spoke again. "Do you really mean that, John?"

A knife sliced his soul into shreds. It'd been too long since he'd told her without being in the presence of Pastor Ryan or in front of someone or just in reply to her, at her insistence. His first and only love. His best friend.

"Yeah. I really do."

"And you'll fight for me? For us? Because I want that too."

"I just want everything to be better." Sure there'd be some duct tape on their past and some potholes in their future, but Lord willing, they'd be together for a long time.

"Good," she said, a nervous giggle. "I know Pastor Ryan told me to stop apologizing for it, but for the last time, before we move on, I'm so sorry, John. I had no right to hurt you that way."

John felt the familiar heckle start at the back of his throat before he squashed it. "I forgive you, Joy Lynn."

Joy laughed long and loud, something he hadn't heard in months. It rekindled a longing to get home. "You haven't called me that since our wedding day."

"You were a knockout that day."

He'd seen movies and been to other people's weddings. No one explained or could've even tried to describe how overjoyed he'd be when she was at the other end of the aisle. Joy left her hair down because she knew he liked it better that way. She looked straight out of a fairytale book, lace from head to toe and a train that seemed half a mile long.

John could hardly wait to kiss the bride that day. Or as soon as he got back.

"Stop. I'm an old lady now." Knowing Joy, she looked down as she spoke, dismissing her own beauty. The way the one side of her smile went higher right before she laughed. Her color-shifting hazel eyes that Jenny inherited. And he could go on and on about her body, but this call was by the minute.

"You're still a knockout," he assured her, a smile working its way up his lips.

"You…you mean that." Joy sounded astonished.

"I love you very much, honey." It was easier to say now that the feeling bled into his heart and pumped throughout his body. No more lies. No more pretending that it was all okay. God just gave him a second chance, and he wasn't going to miss it.

"I love you," Joy said.

"I really, really do, and—"

"I like hearing you say that."

They both laughed.

A twitching back muscle made John straighten. "I'm so glad."

"Me, too!"

"I'm really so glad."

"Me, too!"

They talked over the top of one another, repeating themselves until they dissolved into laughter again. Chris's loafer swung into view in the corner of John's vision. Right. Jenny's number.

"Let's put this all behind us, okay?"

"Okay."

"And we're gonna make it better, okay?"

"I wish you were home so that I could kiss your face off, mister."

John snorted and adjusted his grip on the bridge, wrist burning from the strap. "Okay. Hey, can you text me Jenny's number?"

"Don't you have it?"

"I mean text it to this phone."

"I'm such an airhead. Yeah, I'll do that right now so that I don't forget."

"All right. Thanks. I gotta get going now."

"John?"

"Yeah?"

"I love you."

And for the first time in nearly a year, he believed her.

"I love you, honey."

"Call me later."

"Okay. Bye."

"Bye!"

Usually, he couldn't wait to disconnect their calls. Now, he kept the phone against his ear a few seconds longer to try and hear anything else. Nothing but silence. But this silence was peaceful and pleasant. It held the promise of hope. John forgave her—really forgave her—and couldn't wait to get going on that pledge.

His wide grin stayed in place when he flipped the phone closed and rested it on his thigh, not ready to give up the conversation yet.

"How'd it go?" Chris sounded positively upbeat. He even looked cheerful and kinda smiled.

"Good." Fantastic. Stupendous. Amazing. "Real good." Like with a cherry on top.

Chris nodded toward the phone. "Well, that was the easy bit. Now you've got to call your daughter."

Although John knew that was next, Chris's words knocked the wind out of his proverbial sails. He'd rather call Joy back up and talk until she fell asleep on the phone, like they used to do when they were dating.

But that wouldn't change the fact that he had to mend things with Jenny. Who knew? The way this morning was turning out now, it might be easy peasy.

"Joy said she'd text me the number to your phone."

"All right then."

"You'll have to give me your account so that I can pay you back. I know how expensive overseas calls can be without a plan."

Boy, did he know! Three calls in two days made him see red when he got the bill after Jenny went with her senior class to Japan.

The dull gray phone started to ring and vibrate. It felt strange to be holding another man's phone, so John held it up for Chris to see the number on the tiny window. Chris waved it back without looking.

"Take it."

Chris snatched the phone. It rang again.

"Answer it."

Chris blew out a disgusted sigh and handed the phone back. "It's from the States."

In teeny digits, a number flashed on the screen.

John responded with a curt nod before flipping the phone open again and pressing the worn green button.

"Hey, Jenny."

# CHAPTER 20

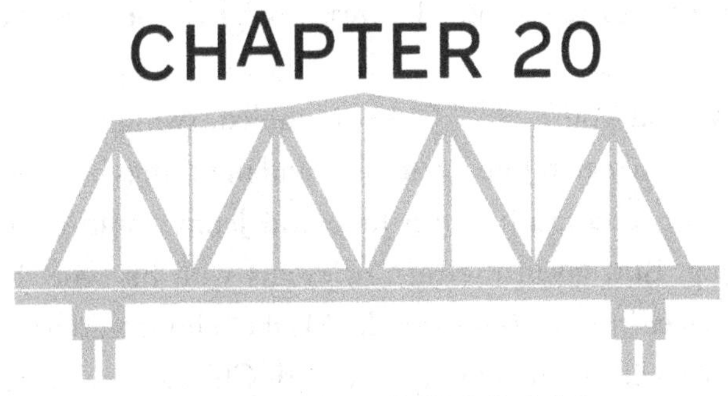

## REALLY, REALLY

*Chris*

THOUGH HE WAS TIED AT THE WRIST TO THE MAN, CHRIS did his best to allow John some privacy. Obviously, they'd been through the worst and John wanted to patch it up. He did a noble job of not blabbing about being on a bridge with a suicidal stranger. And there was something heartwarming, despite the lid Chris kept on it, about hearing John profess his love to her, after all they'd been through. It reminded him of how fiercely he'd loved Carol.

"I'm going to fight for you, Joy."

The level of conviction in John's voice even bolstered Chris. There was no doubt in his tone. Not even a hint of hesitation. He would have called it a jump-from-a-bridge level of conviction, if it were funny and they weren't in the spot high above a stream. It made Chris look down at his own wedding band.

Okay, it got a bit over the top and gushy when they exchanged "I love you" about ten times. Felt closer to a million. Then John progressed into repeating, “I’m really so glad,” between bouts of laughter.

“Say what you mean,” Chris mumbled, swinging his left leg out straight to catch John’s attention and put things back on track.

The conversation between John and Jenny could go all sorts of wrong. But, given the turn of events with his wife, it could equally steer into the positive side. Maybe John would have a better chance with Jenny than he had with Chloe. They never could see eye to eye, even before Carol passed. Once Chloe reached her teenage years, a strange phenomenon split the pair.

John prattled on more with Joy, but it all sounded encouraging. If Chris could help one more person before he left the planet, it’d be a job well done.

Almost.

Without reconnecting with Chloe, the job would never be complete.

Lost causes seemed to nip his ankles his entire life. Once, at boarding school, he found a bird with a puncture wound. Chris bound up the bird’s side and watered it one patient drop at a time for two days. On the third morning, it was stone cold against his side.

The first crush he nurtured with a gal who was in his basics class at the RAF academy ended with her laughter. At him. “Oh, I thought you were joking when you told me.”

Chris tried to resurrect hopeless marriages, strengthen grieving families. Sometimes it worked. Often, he’d see them again. Or they’d leave the church without so much as a goodbye or an explanation.

Made sense that Chloe would fall in line with those failures.

“I love you, honey,” John crooned into the phone like a man head over heels. Good for him. John flipped the phone closed and stared at it. Maybe he was trying to capture that feeling of triumph, of love winning over all.

It rubbed a bit of sunshine into Chris's soul. "How'd it go?" Though he got the gist from the play by play, it'd be nice to hear.

"Good." Chris clutched the phone in his left hand and the bridge with his right. "Real good."

Chris smiled and gave an encouraging nod to the phone. "Well, that was the easy bit. Now you've got to call your daughter."

John's beaming grin faltered to concern.

It'd be fine, Chris knew. If John could patch up his marriage after that, everything would work out swimmingly with Jenny.

Chloe knew how to push his buttons. And he hers. When she came back round to profess her faith in God, he didn't want to hear about her happiness. Quashed it like a bug with a cruel comeback and disdain.

John shook the mobile in his hand but didn't return it. "Joy said she'd text me the number to your phone."

"All right then."

"You'll have to give me your account so that I can pay you back. I know how expensive overseas calls can be without a plan."

It didn't matter. He'd prepaid the plan so that there were no loose ends for Chloe to deal with. Rent notice submitted and paid in full. The ironic life insurance policy Carol insisted he carry. He'd even paid the florist in advance to have fresh flowers delivered to Carol's grave on this date for several years. The headstone stood waiting for him now.

Chris was going to protest payment when the mobile began to ring. John automatically thrusted it toward Chris's face, who waved his free hand. He really didn't want to speak with Joy.

"Take it," John said.

Chris grabbed it.

The mobile rang again, but he really didn't care. Joy would endlessly question him. While Chris was genuinely happy for John, he was not prepared for explanations.

"Answer it." John never took his eyes from the old flip phone.

Chris glanced down at the small screen. An unfamiliar prefix. He thrust the mobile back to John. "It's from the States."

John looked torn between throwing the phone or throwing up just before he flipped the phone open and pressed the button to talk.

"Hey, Jenny." His enthusiasm waned and his smile ducked into a frown as he listened to his daughter.

"Yeah, I know, but it's very complicated, Jenny."

Ah. She came at him with guns blazing, as they said in America. Both barrels loaded. About her mom. If the girl only knew how much John loved her to guard that grenade.

"Jenny, you shouldn't be talking to me like that. I'm your father."

Saucy, that one. Like Chloe after secondary school. Her mouth embarrassed Carol on several occasions. "She'll come back around," Carol would say after Chloe stormed off.

John sighed into the phone before the telltale angry jaw muscle bounced. "Excuse me for earning a living so that you could have everything you need."

Right. Probably onto how he was never there. Been there, heard that one, too.

"Jenny, Jenny, now you listen to me," John said, squeezing his eyes closed. "Your mom tells me you were out at a club last night? What's up with that, Jenny? Since when do you go to a club?" Each word dripped venom and insinuation. John sat as judge and jury on this conversation. It would go poorly.

"Well, there's a lot wrong with it."

Chris tried to get John's attention, to steer him from the cliff he so blindly ran to, by waving his free hand.

John couldn't see with his eyes closed. "You weren't raised that way, Jenny. You're better than that."

An unintelligible squawk came through the earpiece. It wasn't a good sound.

"Yeah, and what do you do in a club?" John scoffed when she answered and continued on his tirade. "You were dancing, dancing today—what tomorrow?"

She must've really laid into him because John breathed a long exhale through his nose after a while. "No, Jenny I trust you. I really, really do."

To Chris, it sounded like John really, really didn't.

Whatever Jenny decided to pop off in the next moment lit John's fuse and his entire face flushed red.

"Jenny," he seethed through gritted teeth, "as long as you're living under my roof you're going to abide by—"

Enough. Chris couldn't watch John crash and burn when he'd flown so high with Joy.

"Give me the phone," he snapped, stretching to grab the mobile. His long arms gave him the advantage. "Give me the phone, give me the phone!" he whisper-shouted, still trying to reach the phone that John held just out of grasp.

John stilled and held up a finger. In warning?

"What?" Chris whispered.

"What?" John echoed just as softly.

"Be nice."

A simple concept. John knew it. He'd just repaired a misfit of a marriage. He'd even made Chris feel sorry for him. Almost like him. And if John couldn't be nice to his daughter and quit judging her, he'd lose her forever.

Don't lose anyone forever.

It made your heart shrivel up and harden beyond repair.

Chris relaxed his face muscles. "Just be nice," he whispered, pulling John's arm so the mobile came back to his ear. "Nice."

Jenny, on the other hand, could be heard giving her father a piece of her mind.

"Jenny," John spat, riled again, "the word of God says—"

Chris motioned like he'd slap John if another horrid word left his mouth. John caught on quick and paused.

"Happy birthday," Chris whispered.

"Happy birthday," John parroted.

Chris flashed a thumbs up. "Good!"

John's shoulders drooped.

"I'm sorry for shouting," Chris started and then waved until John looked up. "I'm sorry for shouting..."

"And I'm sorry for shouting at you. Not just now, but I mean like I feel like I've been shouting at you a lot lately."

A beat of silence. Birds bustled about, and Chris knew time was of the essence.

"I miss you," Chris whispered.

"I miss you." John allowed his eyes to slide closed again before speaking. "No, really I do. It's not nice to be away all of the time and I just...I really miss you and your mom."

"I love you." Chris overemphasized the way he mouthed the words.

"I love you. I mean, I know I haven't been really good at telling you that either. But it's true. I really, really love you, Jenny."

This time, it really, really rang true.

But there was still more to do, so Chris put his index finger up and spun it in a lazy circle with the next whispered suggestion. "Let's do something together."

John grinned a big John smile and nodded. "What do you say we do something together when I get back home? Maybe one of those father-daughter dates we used to have."

Little Chloe loved tea on the living room floor with her dolls. When Daddy came to tea, she'd run and change into a Sunday dress and smart shoes. Carol would try and help her bring the tray onto the rug.

"I got it," Chloe would chide, chubby hands wrapped around the edges of the silver tray. Inevitably, tea spilled and sopped up through the biscuits. He'd stopped attending their parties long ago. It wasn't like he meant to, but other things got in the way, and he forgot.

John continued nodding. "Yeah, yeah. That'd be great. Like a father-mother-daughter date thing."

He chuckled at something Jenny said. "It'd be great. And just..."

The pause and tone in his voice worried Chris. Intervention.

"Happy Birthday," Chris whispered.

"I love you and really, really happy birthday. Okay, bye."

For a grand moment, everything in the world was perfect. If Chris didn't think too hard about it, the loneliness didn't feel as deeply set into his bones. It didn't taint every thought or drudge Carol's memory into bitter disrepair.

Even the breeze wasn't so cold now that his suit had mostly dried. The air smelled like spring and the chittering birds reminded Chris of children on a playground.

"Thank you," John said, surrendering the mobile. If they weren't perched atop the bridge, Chris was quite sure there would've been a bro hug.

"Just trying to help." It felt strangely satisfying to know he'd helped John pave a path back to Jenny. Albeit a path of rocks and pebbles until the man learned to temper his judgment, but hope blossomed for the American family.

John wiggled his fingers on his free hand. "What are those cracker things you guys eat? They're, uh, what is it—java cookies?"

Now what was he babbling on about? "Dunno. Never heard of a coffee biscuit."

"You know, they're all spongy on the inside and they have chocolate on the outside." He described his thoughts with one hand. "There's a little bit of jam in the middle of them."

"Oh! You mean Jaffa cakes." Carol's favorite. Her recipe was the best in the entire U.K.

"Jaffa cakes! That's it. Crazy name." John looked over the creek. His left hand sank back onto its death grip. "Jenny will love Jaffa cakes. I'm gonna make sure that I get a couple of boxes and bring them home to her."

"And what about Joy?"

"Oh, Joy." John chuckled. "She's a lot tougher. I'm going to have to make a trip to High Street for Joy." His entire face beamed like he'd found the winning lottery ticket. That bro hug look on John's face returned until he nodded. "You know, Chris, I really have to thank you."

This was new. "What for?" Certainly not a ruined camera and being tethered to a suicidal man.

"You've opened my eyes to a whole lot of things." His eyebrows crashed down. "You know, you were right when you said I didn't really care about you. I mean, I do now, but it's like you're not this non-believer that I have to preach to. You're a really, really great guy."

Stuff and nonsense.

"You chaps like, really, *really* lay it on thick, don't you?" Give

John a year, two tops, and he'd forget most of this. He wouldn't even recall Carol's name.

John smiled, Chris's barb seemingly falling away. "You're like this really, *really* great guy that Jesus loves."

Both men looked away from one another. Chris knew Jesus loved him. The Bible told him so. It didn't mean that Chris loved Jesus.

"What was Carol like?"

John's soft tone startled Chris from his self-deprecation.

"She was beautiful, gentle, sincere." Everyone flocked to her wherever they went.

"She was passionate about her views." God permeated her speech and actions. She trusted that He would protect Chris and Chloe once she passed.

"She always had something to say." Which was handy since he did, too.

"She kept me in my place, that's for sure." Sometimes it was with a touch or glance from underneath her dark lashes that told him to check his motives.

"She was, well, she was extraordinary." Dark tendrils of loneliness wove their inky fingers around Chris in a familiar embrace.

"Sounds like a wonderful woman," John said, voice heavy with emotion that even touched Chris's tattered heart.

"She knew when she was dying that day." Chris swallowed past the lump in his throat. "I…I told her it was too soon, but she argued that it comes for everyone. I was upset that Chloe wasn't there with us, but Carol trusted that she'd come back."

A sob tried to work its way out, but Chris forced it back. "She knew I was angry with God. Especially a god that allows so much pain. And fear. She was so afraid, even though she had faith in her destination."

Chris had stroked Carol's hand, skin chilled despite the layers of blankets she burrowed beneath. "Sing to me," she murmured, eyes closing, blankets rising up and falling as she breathed slower and slower.

"Jesus loves me, this I know," she began.

"For the Bible tells me so," Chris continued.

"Yes, Jesus loves me," he sang to the stream and birds and John. "Yes, Jesus loves me. Yes, Jesus loves me. The Bible tells me so."

A tinny mechanical beeping blared from his right wrist.

"It's time."

# CHAPTER 21

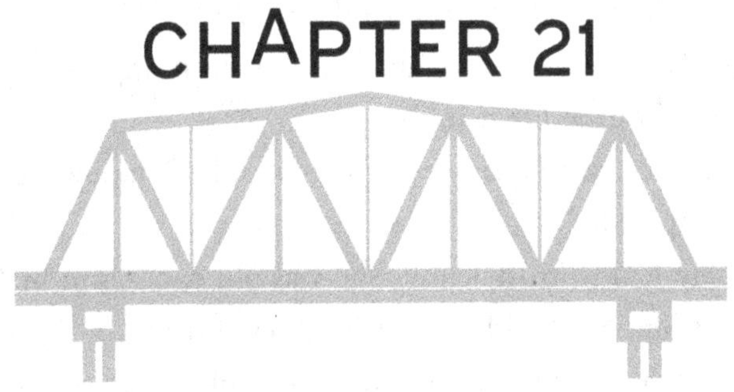

## JESUS LOVES ME

*John*

**"LET'S DO SOMETHING TOGETHER." JOHN TOSSED OUT** his line, hoping, praying for Jenny to just give him a chance to win back her trust.

"Okay." Jenny yawned and laughed into the receiver on the other side of the world. "Yeah, let's do something."

John hesitated with his suggestion. But go big or go home, right? "What do you say we do something together when I get back home? Maybe one of those father-daughter dates we used to have."

Jenny yawned again. "Mmm. What about having Mom come with us?" Another yawn.

"Yeah, yeah. That'd be great." They could sit in a diner booth together. Jenny across from him and Joy. He'd blow the straw wrapper at her face. "Like a father-mother-daughter date thing."

"Don't make us wear matching clothes or anything, Dad." Jenny mumbled something he couldn't understand. "Dinner sounds good."

He chuckled "It'll be great. And just…"

John imagined her at a club. Drunk men trying to touch her, or they might drug her drink!

Chris's face came into view from the side. "Happy Birthday," Chris whispered.

Yes. He had to trust Jenny. She was old enough to make her own decisions. Start with dinner. And reminders.

"I love you," John said, wishing he could make sure she was safe in her own bed. "And really, really happy birthday."

Her next yawn nearly sucked the words away. "Bye, Dad."

"Okay, bye."

If he wasn't straddling the top beam of a bridge, John would've hollered and jumped up and down like a popcorn kernel on a hot pan. Both of his girls wanted him. Praise Jesus!

And he wanted them, too.

In part, it was due to the man strapped to his right hand. John wouldn't have admitted his own fault or owned up to his hatred. He wouldn't have seen the despair in Chris's face that made him regret not reaching out to Joy and Jenny. Chris couldn't go back to Carol, but his devastation certainly prodded John to reconsider his anger.

Beside him, Chris stared off somewhere. His face was relaxed, and he looked content.

John held out the phone. "Thank you." Every fiber in his body radiated with gratitude for this man. Argumentative and stubborn, he'd led John to the path of redemption, even if he said that he didn't believe in God anymore. The irony.

"Just trying to help." Chris tucked the phone back into his jacket with a rare smile.

A thought blinked into John's mind. He needed to make sure to bring home gifts for the girls. Not the cheap touristy kind, either. Jenny liked all sorts of food. "What are those cracker things you guys eat? They're, uh, what is it—java cookies?"

"Dunno. Never heard of a coffee biscuit."

"You know, they're all spongy on the inside and they have chocolate on the outside." Orange marmalade was Jenny's favorite! She'd totally love them. "There's a little bit of jam in the middle of them."

Chris's entire face lit up with recognition. "Oh! You mean Jaffa cakes."

"Jaffa cakes! That's it. Crazy name." John looked down, and his stomach twisted. Grabbed the bridge with his left hand again, wishing he'd eaten for the umpteenth time. "Jenny will love Jaffa cakes. I'm gonna make sure that I get a couple of boxes and bring them home to her." Hopefully the customs guys wouldn't get grabby.

"And what about Joy?"

John chuckled. "Oh, Joy. She's a lot tougher." He quickly worked through his past presents and which ones fell flat: the vacuum and the blender were the worst. She liked unique jewelry or books. "I'm going to have to make a trip to High Street for Joy." He'd heard that was where the best shopping was in London. Until today, it hadn't even crossed his mind to shop there.

He needed to bring her back here, to England. Before the… before everything, they'd wanted to travel. Work always got in the way. John would go back and ask his boss for that vacation he usually cashed out. It'd take a while to organize, and Joy would have to get her passport. What could be more romantic than touring England together? Nestling into those stone cottage bed-and-breakfasts. Walking through tourist traps. Eating terrible food and drinking warm beer. Holding her hand everywhere they went.

"You know, Chris, I really have to thank you."

Chris looked gobsmacked, brows furrowing together. "What for?"

"You've opened my eyes to a whole lot of things." John wanted to present this the right way because he was still tied at the wrist to a man who wanted to jump. "You know, you were right when you said I didn't really care about you. I mean, I do now, but it's like you're not this non-believer that I have to preach to. You're a really, really great guy." John hadn't meant to bubble over with such praise, but it just ran away.

"You chaps like, really, *really* lay it on thick, don't you?" Chris shook his head, disdain tipping his lips downward.

"You're like this really, *really* great guy that Jesus loves."

Chris immediately stiffened and looked the other direction. Too much. Okay, John knew he could salvage this unconventional friendship. All he had to do was talk about the right subject.

And there was one thing Chris loved in the world more than himself.

"What was Carol like?"

Chris blew a long, slow breath out through his lips. "She was beautiful, gentle, sincere." A crooked smile budded. "She was passionate about her views." The corner of his mouth climbed as he sank into memories.

"She always had something to say." That was hilarious, considering the source. "She kept me in my place, that's for sure." It sure would've been fun to meet the tamer of this beast.

Another sigh sounded from Chris as his feet bounced. "She was, well, she was extraordinary." Love weighed Chris's voice. Pure, unadulterated love and devotion wrapped in profound sadness.

"Sounds like a wonderful woman," John said. His own heart mourned for her loss. For Chris's pain. The thought of losing

Joy—it was a dark chasm he never considered. Sure, he had contemplated leaving her and the whole mess behind. But now? Listening to Chris's heart break all over again?

"She knew when she was dying that day." Chris startled John. Chris's chin dropped to his black shirt. "I…I told her it was too soon, but she argued that it comes for everyone. I was upset that Chloe wasn't there with us, but Carol trusted that she'd come back."

John was devastated because of an affair, but Chris had lost *everything.*

A strangled sound came from Chris. "She knew I was angry with God. Especially a god that allows so much pain." His voice quivered. "And fear. She was so afraid, even though she had faith in her destination."

Chris stilled next to John, who dared to glance over and saw a single tear disappear into Chris's stubbled chin. His Adam's apple bobbled up and down.

"Yes, Jesus loves me," he crooned off-tune. "Yes, Jesus loves me. Yes, Jesus loves me. The Bible tells me so." He pushed out the last word with a sob.

Before John could say a word, he was interrupted by a watch alarm.

Chris's alarm.

"It's time," Chris said, face suddenly turning emotionless despite the tear stains.

No.

John's heart slammed into his chest wall. Chris couldn't kill or maim them both. He needed to hug Jenny and kiss Joy. Chris, well he needed to wake up and see his own daughter deserved to have him in her life.

"Look Chris, I…I don't have answers for all your pain and everything." Words sped out from somewhere deep inside of John. Jesus took the wheel because he had no idea what to say to keep Chris from pulling them both off the bridge. At this height, the consequences were dire.

John glanced down and back up to Chris, who now contemplated the creek. He still looked like a man who needed a friend. Someone to rant to and help him figure things out. John knew he could be that guy, if Chris would listen.

"I don't even have answers for my own life," John said. "But we've figured something out together today, haven't we?"

"God asks you to have blind faith in his word," Chris sneered, refusing to make eye contact.

"Yeah."

"Why?"

"I dunno," John said with a shrug. "I haven't studied about that. What did you learn about it?" Yes, get him talking.

"God demands obedience and patience for His will to be fulfilled. And the crazy part is that it may not even happen while we're alive. It's almost like trying to grasp the concept of eternity. You think you finally understand it and then another layer unfolds."

John nodded. "Eternity is crazy to think about."

"But faith is not. It's based on God's providence."

"Um. Big Christian word there."

Chris turned to glare at him. "Providence?"

John felt as ignorant as Chris's accented tone of voice implied. "Yes. Obviously not a city in Rhode Island."

The joke fell flat, and Chris sighed. "It means that God is directing, good or bad, everything in creation. He allows both to happen. We *mere* humans are subjected to his will. And told to have faith that it'll work out." He shoved an open palm into the air.

"I understand it now. Kinda," John said, nodding. "There's still parts I don't understand, but that's okay. Thank you."

"For what?"

"Explaining it in a way I can wrap my simple head around."

Chris's face scrunched together. "You're welcome, I guess."

"I'm okay with blind faith. There's something comforting in the thought that God knows it all and I don't. He's just asking me to trust that the outcome, good or bad, is what He wants."

Chris didn't react. Not a muscle, although his hair blew every which way in the breeze. It wasn't working. The alarm finally stopped, and Chris drew in a deep breath, fixing his gaze far below. John needed to reconnect.

Not Carol and the past. Not Chloe and the future. Change the approach.

"I mean, you don't believe in God." Chris glanced up there. Good. "Okay. I'm not going to argue with you. But I am going to tell you that I do believe in Him. Maybe I can't explain it right, maybe I don't understand it all. But I believe that He's good. And He's done amazing things in my life."

Better not to list them all at the moment, though John wanted to just to emphasize the point.

"Maybe I messed a lot of it up and everything," John continued when Chris remained mute and passive. But he was paying attention. "But…but He's just done amazing things, and Carol knew that."

If she were here, what would she do? John tried not to show his panic, even when Chris shifted his hand. Carol would remind him about God because she was extraordinary.

John cleared his throat. "Jesus loves me, this I know," he sang, trying to get Chris to join in by motioning with his hands.

Chris glared hard at John. "She didn't know what she was saying." Each word oozed with spite.

"She *did* know what she was saying!" How she loved this daft man was a mystery. "The Lord loved her, man."

"He took her away from me." Chris looked like he'd swallowed sour milk. If he didn't stop moving his free arm, they'd both end up in a world of trouble.

"So, tell me how does this make all that better?" John felt his mouth go slack. "What about Chloe? Think about Chloe." If he had both hands free, John might strangle the understanding into Chris.

"I grew up without a dad," John said. "He abandoned us. I *still* feel that today, Chris. And I'm not a young lady who lost her mother to cancer either."

John could reason away the torn and dirty clothes he'd grown up in. It didn't matter now how kids picked him last for gym class. He wasn't a child anymore, but the sting of his dad leaving felt like ripping off a new bandage every time. Even when he tracked and followed leads on the internet to see where he ended up, it didn't happy-clappy the feeling of being left behind. On purpose.

Chris pursed his lips, contemplation easing across his face. Thunder rumbled in the distance.

"You're right." He chuckled the type of understanding laugh after the punchline makes sense. "You're right. I should think about Chloe. And Carol." He nodded slowly. "Everything you said makes sense."

This had to be a joke. Like the time Joy conned him into believing that her writing group ran late and for him to join her for dinner at the pizza parlor. He showed up in ripped work jeans and a stained t-shirt for his own surprise birthday party.

Besides, Chris was the king of scorn. There's no way he'd change his mind after a small monologue rehashing the same reasons John had been making all morning.

But what if? What if Chris really did change his mind and wanted to consider Chloe's feelings? It was worth a shot. Jesus could change Saul to Paul. He could certainly change Chris's decision.

"Really?" John tried to mask the distrust in his voice and failed.

Chris nodded. "Really. Untie me." He yanked up on their wrists.

"You're not playing games with me here, are you?"

"No. I'm tired." Chris sounded exhausted. "I need to rest."

Maybe it was the way Chris's face seemed steeped in weariness or how his entire countenance fell from snobbish to broken, but John believed him.

John unwound the strap once before stopping. Chris still looked as sapped as before. John worked the camera strap from his wrist before releasing Chris.

"Thank you," Chris said, rubbing the pink mark. "I'm busting for a pee."

John burst into laughter, grateful not to plummet to his death after surviving numb butt muscles. His thighs would pay for it tomorrow, but praise Jesus, they just had to climb down now. "You're telling me, man. I'm ready to explode. Talk about the Lord doing miracles!"

# CHAPTER 22

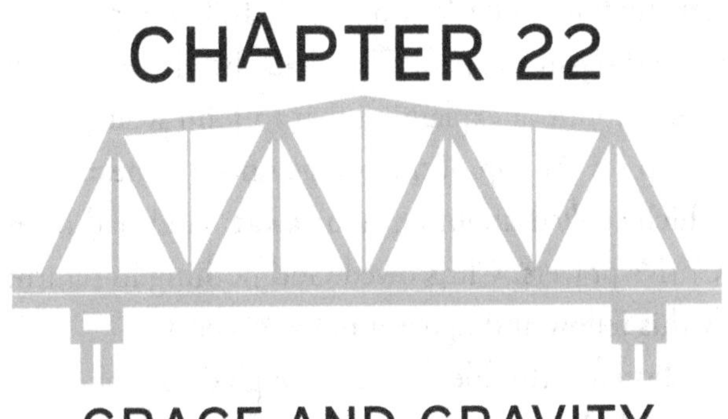

## GRACE AND GRAVITY

*Chris*

**"SO, TELL ME HOW DOES THIS MAKE ALL THAT BETTER?"** John snapped, words peckish and fast. "What about Chloe? Think about Chloe."

If only John understood that this *was* for Chloe, so that she didn't have to deal with a failure of a father the rest of her life. She wouldn't have to call and be sent to voicemail, her messages deleted without ever being heard. If she had a family one day, they wouldn't be tainted by his spiteful soul.

No, this wasn't the easy way. This was the only way for her to come out unscathed.

Every thought was about Chloe.

"I grew up without a dad. He abandoned us. I *still* feel that today, Chris. And I'm not a young lady who lost her mother to cancer, either."

John had no right to meddle in the emotional side of this. Being part of Chloe's life as a broken man was far different than

John inserting himself back into Jenny's, full of hope. No amount of hope could repair the pain Chris had already caused Chloe.

And no amount of explaining that to John would satisfy him. They'd be up on the top of the bridge until the next storm came along, which looked about an hour away. God hadn't answered any of Chris's prayers. Chris owed God nothing in return. Better to pacify this fellow and figure it out another day.

In the distance, thunder rolled through dark clouds.

"You're right," Chris said as convincingly as he could muster. He added on a believable chuckle. "You're right. I should think about Chloe. And Carol." Nodding unhurriedly, Chris carefully constructed his response. "Everything you said makes sense."

Like all of the times a husband would agree to something in counseling, the tone of his voice and wording precise. It was a thorough lie to agree to something one had no intention of doing. In this case, Chris just wanted to go home. John had his family back and obviously wouldn't leave until Chris climbed down. So, that's what he'd do.

"Really?" John's eyebrows shot up, eyes wide.

Chris nodded to sell it. "Really. Untie me."

"You're not playing games with me here, are you?"

"No. I'm tired. I need to rest." The extra details always helped blanket the lie to an untrained ear.

John grinned, all teeth showing. He looked so proud as he unwound the strap once before pausing. Chris gave a weary smile. John finished unbinding their wrists.

"Thank you. I'm busting for a pee." There was the truth of the matter. His bladder would force him down.

John tucked the black plastic strap back into his flannel pocket and laughed. "You're telling me, man. I'm ready to explode. Talk about the Lord doing miracles!"

Chris hesitated, then motioned down to the bridge deck. "Shall I go first?"

"Yeah, please."

"That way." Chris pointed to the inside of the framework.

"Yeah."

John stayed put until Chris swung his leg over the top post and eased himself down to the first diagonal beam. John mirrored Chris, keeping watch like a parent ready to catch a child if they fell. Chris had no intention of allowing that to happen. The reset button had been pressed on his plans, that's all. John couldn't follow him around for the rest of his life.

When Chris hopped down from the railing, pain zapped up both legs and his feet were on pins and needles. He hissed through his teeth and rubbed both palms on his thighs to get the blood circulation back into proper working order. The sooner that happened, the sooner he could convince John to leave.

What once was such a definite decision now swayed because of this intrusion. If Chris still believed in God, he would've chalked it up to providence. But he didn't. John happened to pick the same bridge at the same time.

John landed several meters away, and his body obviously felt as battered as Chris's. John clutched the railing for a few moments and then backed into the center of the bridge, eyes on Chris the entire time. He smiled, full of hope and happiness.

It was a stand-off. Two men on a bridge: one believed in God's grace and the other in gravity.

Chris wiped his hands against one another. "Um, well…thank you, I think." Not the sentiment intended, but useful nonetheless. He extended his hand. A proper shake and then John would leave, none the wiser that this plan would carry on without him.

John smiled and opened his arms. "Bro hug."

Bracing for impact, Chris widened his arms since the inevitable would happen. John wound his arms around Chris and squeezed. Chris awkwardly patted John's shoulders, hoping it would shorten the entire experience. It worked! John stepped back, grin still in place.

Chris offered a handshake, which John promptly accepted.

Time for this pity party to end. Chris pointed behind his shoulder, opposite of the way John had to go to retrieve his camera. "I'm going that way." The only thing in that direction was forest and fields and solitude. No one to talk about God or Chloe.

John's face washed in concern. "You okay?"

Chris shrugged. "Erm, yeah." He glanced around. It needed to be better, convincing. "Yeah, I'm fine. A bit tired, but I need some rest." So dumb, since he'd just said that before.

He took two steps backwards. John remained rooted to his spot in the middle of the bridge. "So, thank you."

"Okay." John opened his mouth like there were a thousand things to say, yet he offered up a smile instead.

Turning on his heels, Chris took a few tentative steps. Oddly, he almost wanted to stay and talk with John. He hadn't *really* talked with anyone in such a long time. But John came into his life at the most wrong place and most wrong time. It'd do no good to either of them. They would've been the Punch and Judy in the Christianity realm, always at odds. Exactly God's timing to bring along a friend when he'd depart the world.

"Um," John said behind him.

Chris stopped. They could talk on the phone once he left the country. That might help Chris's loneliness, just having someone to chat with. Chris turned around, heart and head in a wrestling match to the death. The sun broke through the clouds and warmed the side of his face.

"Is there an easier way to get down from here?" John jerked his thumb over one shoulder.

"Uh, yeah."

Figured. John wanted to move on with his life.

"Yeah, sorry," Chris said motioning his hand in a semi-circle. "There's a path past the brambles. It'll take you right to your camera." And out of Chris's miserable existence. His head smothered his heart into submission. Again.

John turned and cupped a hand over his eyes. "Okay," he said, turning to face Chris again. "I think I can see it down there."

"All right." Alone again. Overhead, the clouds darkened, of course. "Take care."

"Yeah, you too."

Chris stuffed his hands into his jacket pockets, turned, and took a step, listening for John to do the same. John lumbered away, trainers grinding into the gravel. Good for him. Get on with fixing things with Jenny. And his wife. Not everyone had those chances.

As Chris walked away, he liked to think that they'd make it, John's little family. That their father-daughter-mother date would involve pancakes or something of the sort. Joy needed to realize what a terrific man she'd married. Not many marriages made it past an affair. Maybe they'd sit together in church and John would remember seeing the man on the bridge and pray for him.

Chris stopped his advance toward the forest. He half-turned around, almost expecting to see John looking back at him like in a movie. John plodded on toward the pathway. And his new life.

Away from Chris.

Like a piece of rubbish.

It was silly to think that John would think much more of him.

If he walked carefully, Chris knew he could make it back to

the highest point without John even hearing him. An odd peace blanketed the feuding thoughts in his mind with each step. Chloe would be okay alone. He wasn't abandoning her. He was helping her move on. She'd have all the good memories of her mother.

Chris let the dark thoughts settle back into their familiar spots. They released the harsh reality of being alone. Failure as a father. A pastor who didn't believe in God. A man with no wife. Unattainable happiness. The further the dark judgments leached into the corners of his mind, the steadier Chris's steps.

It didn't matter. If he did this, actually followed through, everything would stop hurting. Forever. Because if you don't believe in God, then Hell didn't come into play. And Earth was certainly more painful than any everlasting punishment.

He stepped back to the place it'd all begun before the sun pushed into the gray sky. It'd take too long to climb again, and this would have to do. Aim for the hard earth. One last thing that he could do right.

Ducking under the handrail, Chris's shoes barely fit onto the ledge. He pushed his hands against the bridge supports and drew in an unsteady breath. If only Chloe would understand and forgive him.

He closed his eyes. It didn't stop the war in his mind, that small voice screaming for him to carry on. Even the bright spot in his thinking told him to keep calm in British fashion. Soldier on. Push past it all.

A breeze tickled his nose with ripe apples.

*So sorry, Chloe.*

*Apologies, Carol.* He tried to go on. He really did. It all seemed useless.

Strong arms wrapped around Chris's waist and held tight, pulling him backwards.

Chris latched onto the bridge and tried to propel himself forward.

"No," John groaned. "You can't."

A monumental tug, and Chris still couldn't break free.

"Oh, God, please help me." John's fingers slipped a little when he yanked.

Suddenly, the railing gave way and they both went backwards, Chris stumbling to the side and John landing square on his rear near the opposite rail. For half a moment, Chris hesitated when John looked to the side, terrified, head hanging above the stream.

But it was a blip. A moment he needed to seize. Now that the railing had given way, he had a clear shot at it. Chris strode back to the gap and braced himself, determined. Not even a begged plea from John could stop him.

Until his mobile rang in his pocket.

Chris froze. Gravel crunched behind him as John stood.

"It might be for me!"

John's desperation made Chris reach for the phone. He'd chuck it and then be done with it all. It rang a second and third time until Chris held up the screen. John now pushed his head next to Chris.

The mobile rang again, echoing. Chris stared at the screen. This day kept getting worse and worse.

John pressed into his back. "It's Chloe."

Chris made no effort to answer when it rang again. John carefully reached over Chris's shoulder and plucked it from his hand the next time it sounded.

"Hello, Chloe."

Nothing good would come of this. If he believed in a god, it would be the god of horrible timing.

"No, I'm a…a friend of your dad's." John grabbed a fistful of

Chris's jacket from behind. "I'm standing with him on a bridge, and he wants to jump. He's very serious." John's voice dropped a notch.

Chris closed his eyes.

When she barged into his flat one night, after following him home, he'd tried to dissuade her from being part of his life.

"I love you, Dad."

But she only thought she knew how to help him. "You don't understand."

Chloe sighed. Her keys clattered onto the kitchen table. "Well, help me and maybe we can get through this together."

"It's pointless."

When she apologized for missing Carol's funeral, the cobra inside struck out. "And you think that's gonna make everything all right?" he yelled, flinging a hand in her direction. "Saying sorry?"

Chloe flinched. "No, Dad. I don't expect anything." Her voice quivered.

Chris needed to hurt her to make her stay away. When she left that night, he was sure she got the point. Until the next day when she called. He sent it straight to voicemail. Then he ignored her texts and left them unread.

It took nineteen days for her to stop.

Nineteen days Chris waited for her to reach out. Nineteen days he snubbed her.

On the twentieth day, he checked the mobile to make sure it was in working order. Turned it off and on. Gave it a good shake. With a stiff upper lip, he powered it down for the night. The random texts afterwards were easier to ignore. If she cared more, it would've been every day for weeks. Or months.

She really didn't understand, even if she loved him in some

way. How could she really love him when all they did was shout at one another?

But she had tried for nineteen days. He didn't even give it a crack.

"Wait, what?" John asked, flabbergasted. "What do you mean 'again'?"

# CHAPTER 23

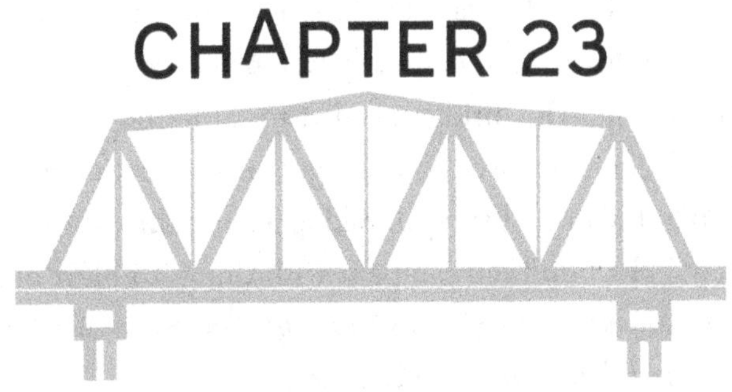

## TWO SECONDS

*John*

**IT ALL FELT FAKE AND REAL AT THE SAME TIME WHEN** Chris offered to shake John's hand. John squeezed and clapped his left hand to the back of Chris's, a handshake sandwich.

Chris used his free hand to point over the back of his shoulder, loosening his grip on John's hand. "I'm going that way."

John stretched and looked. Nothing but trees and, well, more trees. The map didn't show any other route to get here other than the one he'd used. Perhaps Chris meant to go that way to relieve himself.

The nagging feeling of something being off peaked when Chris flashed a particularly fake smile.

"You okay?" John asked, knowing full well he wasn't.

"Erm, yeah." Chris shrugged his shoulders, eyes bouncing from spot to spot. "Yeah, I'm fine. A bit tired, but I need some rest."

When Chris backed up a couple of steps, John stayed put. Being right in the middle of the bridge and far away from the edge was the best thing. He heard the lumber groan and splinter when they climbed down. God definitely watched over them while they were up on top. This bridge needed to either be torn down or blocked off. Someone was going to get hurt sooner or later.

"So, thank you," Chris said, raking a hand through his hair.

"Okay." His mind ran rampant with things to blurt out. *Jesus loves you. Why don't you give me your phone number? Want to catch some dinner? I'd sure love to meet Chloe.*

Instead, John smiled. Chris was safe, and the fine line to make sure he stayed that way necessitated silence.

John watched Chris turn and take a couple of steps. He glanced back toward the berry bushes. "Um."

Chris turned around, eyebrows hiked into his wrinkled forehead.

"Is there an easier way to get down from here?"

The wrinkles melted from Chris's face. "Uh, yeah." He scratched one temple. "There's a path past the brambles. It'll take you right to your camera."

The sun broke between the clouds. He shielded his eyes from the sunlight to try and see the path. Nope. Not a marker or anything. Just the overgrown murder thorn bushes.

"I think I can see it," he said, turning to face Chris again. It had to be there. This was the kinder answer.

"All right." Chris drew in a sharp breath and nodded once. "Take care."

"Yeah, you too."

It all seemed too fast, hurried. Chris needed Jesus.

Shoving his hands into his jacket pockets, Chris turned and walked away with wide strides. That meant it was time to go home for John.

Back to Jenny. To a daddy-daughter-mom date. They hadn't

taken the boat out in quite some time. It'd be fun to pack a lunch and go tootle around the lake. Maybe moor on the west side and take a hike up to the waterfalls.

He'd have to be careful not to lecture Jenny. John tossed up a prayer to God asking for the right way to approach her about the life choices she made. He was old and knew life wasn't kind with consequences. Sitting down with Joy and talking about Jenny would help.

Joy would be waiting for him at the airport this time. John hoped she'd be wearing red. She looked beautiful in red. Any color, but red made her cheeks look pink and set off her blue eyes. If she showed up in pajamas, he wouldn't care. As long as she made it there.

It was good to be happy again. John stopped and looked over his shoulder to make sure Chris had made it to the other side.

Head down and eyes on his feet, Chris marched back toward the center of the bridge.

John spun and sprinted. He needed to make it, to keep Chris from jumping because that was exactly what he was intending to do. But John was behind, because no matter how fast he ran, Chris had already made it to the chosen spot and ducked under the railing.

Chris braced his hands against the diagonal supports.

"Please, no," John whispered, skidding in the gravel and within reach.

John reached over the railing and wrapped Chris into a bear hug, latching his hands together against Chris's cold belt buckle. John threw his weight backwards.

Chris reacted opposite, thrusting himself toward oblivion.

"No," John cried out. "You can't!"

He had too much to lose. He had Chloe. He said he was wrong and he would think about Chloe and Carol.

But Chris struggled to break John's hold. When John's fingers lost their grip, he begged for help. "Oh, God, please help me." Because He was the only one who could stop Chris.

As if his prayer had been answered instantaneously, the wood railing cracked between the men. Both tumbled backwards. Chris remained on his feet, backpedaling. John fell onto his back and skidded across the gravel. He opened his arms to try and stop his body before it slid off of the other side. When he stopped, John twisted his head to the side, high above the creek.

He looked up at Chris, who advanced back to the open area. "Chris, please don't do this!"

By the time John scrambled to his feet, Chris's cell phone was ringing. It was the same tone as when Jenny called. And if Joy was trying to call him—

"It might be for me!"

John approached Chris from behind with careful steps while Chris fumbled in his jacket for the ringing cell phone. John angled his head over Chris's shoulder to see the tiny screen.

"It's Chloe," John said. Talk about providence.

Chris held as still as a statue, phone ringing away. John reached up and grabbed it before Chris decided to drop it into a watery grave.

John smashed the green button. "Hello, Chloe."

"Dad?"

"No. I'm a ..." Stranger? Random American? "A friend of your dad's." He reached up and grasped Chris's jacket for good measure. "I'm standing with him on a bridge, and he wants to jump." John dropped his voice to emphasize the matter. "He's very serious."

"Oh, not again," she gasped.

That wasn't the answer he expected.

"What do you mean 'again'?"

"Last time, I found out because the hospital called. He was found unconscious." Chloe took a shaky breath. "He cut his wrists. The neighbor called the police because they had no hot water and his shower had been running for hours."

"I—I had no idea."

Chris shoulders slumped, each hand resting on the diagonal supports.

"They called me because I was listed as his emergency contact after his first attempt." Chloe sniffed. "This is the third time now."

"I'm sorry," John offered, heart sinking. She sounded so sad, so lost, and he wanted to hug her and tell her that it'd be okay.

"He was mad at me last time, after I took him home when he was released. Even when I told him that I love him. He told me that I didn't understand." A sob bubbled through the receiver and John waited until she'd gathered herself. "I offered to help him, to get through this together."

"I'm trying to help him now," John said, releasing his grip on Chris's jacket. Let him hear the one side of the conversation. "Please don't cry, Chloe. Your dad loves you, too." John hoped those words punched Chris in the proverbial gut.

"I don't know," Chloe said, blowing her nose. "He told me that I didn't understand and that it was all pointless."

John angled himself so that his side of the conversation went right into Chris's left ear. "Well, I don't think it's pointless that you're trying to help him."

"I asked him if Mum's faith was pointless. He reminded me that she was dead. And I apologized for missing her funeral. It was so selfish of me."

"Chloe," John said, softening his tone. "We all make mistakes. I'm glad you apologized for missing that."

Chris dropped his chin to his chest.

"I only wanted to make my peace with him. I wanted to apologize and make it right since I'd become a Christian."

"Praise God!"

Chloe scoffed a proper British huff of air. "He told me I was better off without him then."

John held his breath. He didn't. He couldn't. It was cruel. Who would say that to their own child? John turned and covered his mouth, not sure how to comfort Chloe. Every part of his mind raced back to staring out the window, asking his mom when his dad would be home. The sinking pit of disappointment that rooted and turned to anger.

The same anger that transformed into rage and nearly destroyed his marriage.

John inhaled to offer his apology again and the phone was yanked out of his hand.

"Hey!"

Chris held up his index finger and glared.

"Hello, Chloe." Chris turned his back on John. "I know."

"I am." He was what? John hoped he was sorry for everything.

"I do." And taking it all back for hurting her.

"No." Promising not to leave her alone.

"I'm really sorry, Chloe," Chris said, tone monotonous and unemotional.

He really hadn't changed his mind! He had a daughter who loved him, and he didn't even care!

"Goodbye." Chris flipped the phone closed.

Faster than a striking rattlesnake, Chris spun around and

grabbed John by both of his jacket lapels. "You had *no* right," he seethed through his clamped teeth, lifting John's jacket up.

Of all of the things John wanted to spout off, the simplest truth popped out. "The Lord loves you, Chris."

"Don't you preach at me!"

"He wants you to live!" John felt his feet slipping on the gravel as Chris pushed him backwards across the bridge deck.

"But I want to die!" Chris shot back, tears forming in his eyes.

"Chloe needs you."

The simple statement stopped Chris. The hatred in his face softened. "Go home!" He shoved John, releasing his grip on the jacket.

John stumbled a step, glancing at his feet. If one rail broke, they all could snap with the right pressure. The sound of gravel made him look up.

Chris stepped toward the open railing again.

John swiped at the linen jacket, catching it in his left hand. Like a rope pull, he worked Chris backward a step, one hand over the other until Chris turned and swung his fist. John yanked his head back just in time, air whooshing past his ears.

Every time Chris pried a hand away, John clamped on with the other on the opposite side of Chris's body. The number of drunk employees John wrestled through the years came in handy as their feet slid in the gravel. Chris took ahold of John's jacket and shoved him toward the deck. Chunks of rock bit into John's palm, but he hung onto Chris's wrist.

"Let go!" Chris fumed, smacking and batting at John.

"You promised to think about Chloe!"

They grappled, both hanging onto the other's shoulders.

"Stay out of this!"

"I'm literally in the middle of it," John panted, trying to sweep his legs out. His lungs burned and arms felt like rubber, but he wouldn't stop until Chris was safe.

"Fine!" Chris ceased pulling and dropping his hands from John's shoulders.

John held fast. "You're lying again."

Chris reacted in high-speed, ducking, turning, and trying to break from John's grasp. John saw that Chris had nearly made it to the edge, so he practically laid backward from a standing position, all strength and power, desperate to stop Chris from jumping.

Somehow, the buttons on Chris's jacket withstood the pressure. But the man inside the suit raged. Chris twisted, kicking at John. He connected with John's knee, and John howled, forcing himself to hang onto Chris.

"Stop fighting," John yelled, weariness spreading.

"Let go then."

"If I let go, are you going to jump?"

"Yes."

John readjusted his grip, pushing through the pain. "Don't leave Chloe, man. Don't be that guy, Chris."

"Shut up."

They switched positions, legs propelling them in a circle, while Chris tried to force John to release him.

"She doesn't care that you're sad now. She loves you."

"I said shut up!"

Chris swung both arms between John's, raising his fists near John's face. They caught one another's stare for a fraction before Chris smashed both fists in opposite directions. The blows broke John's hold.

Chris advanced and latched onto John's lapels again, clearly having the advantage. "You…you…" His cheeks flushed red. And then he froze, furious face inches from John's. "Go back home and leave me alone," Chris growled. He let go and shoved John backwards with both open palms.

John staggered back a step and then two. Chris stepped in the opposite direction. John's off-balanced third step didn't land on the bridge. Or anything at all.

"Chris!" he yelled, flinging both arms to the side to catch the bridge uprights. Chris's eyes widened in horror.

John's two middle fingers touched the edge of a vertical brace. The corner of the wood dug into the crease just below his fingertips before they slipped. John flailed out with both arms, winding around and around and around like a broken windmill. He couldn't scream or inhale. He just felt the horrifying sensation of plummeting to the creek below.

He wouldn't get to kiss Joy. Or dip his finger in whipped cream when Jenny wasn't looking and smoosh it on the tip of her nose. She was the best kid, and he wanted to tell her.

It wasn't two seconds. It felt like an eternity and a blink at the same time, his vision filled with a gray cloudy sky framed by the trees.

Every nerve in his body exploded in agony.

Then it all went black.

# CHAPTER 24

## SUNSHINE AND A RAIN CLOUD

*Chris*

"YOU HAD *NO* RIGHT!"

Meddling American! Sticking his nose into other people's business. Chris grabbed the lapels of John's jacket, wanting to smack the ever-living grin off his stupid face.

"The Lord loves you, Chris."

Was he going back to that? Now? "Don't you preach at me!"

"He wants you to live!"

Chris propelled John backwards by the jacket, disgusted by the mantra. "But I want to die!"

He heard his cry echo: *die, die, die*. Tears crowded the corners of his eyes and desperation clawed his throat. To live and have hope or to put it all to rest.

John hunched over, straightening his jacket. He showed both hands in defeat. "Chloe needs you."

She didn't. Chris just needed to repeat that until his heart believed it. She'd be fine. Adjust her sails and carry on.

"Go home," he sighed, releasing John with a push. His head

pounded like a jackhammer, and the twinge at the base of his skull ached. Carol always knew how to rub those out.

"First, you need to stop allowing stress to play havoc in your life," she'd whisper, moistening the tips of her fingers with the peppermint lotion she loved. Then the magic fingers would rub and smooth away his pain while he groaned.

"You sound like a beluga," Carol laughed once.

"I believe it helps the healing."

"To make whale sounds?"

"Yes. If I let all of the noise out, my pain will go away."

Just like the fall from the bridge would make it all disappear. Chris took a step toward the broken rail. He jerked to the side when John pulled him from behind. He twisted and tried to hit John with a right hook. Swing and a miss.

The men grappled with one another. It reminded Chris of the video he saw of a hawk and snake, each trying to kill the other. Chris was able to use John's slouchy jacket to force him to the bridge deck, but John somehow ensnared Chris's wrist.

"Let go!"

"You promised to think about Chloe," John gasped.

They latched onto one another's shoulders and spun like a pair of fully-clothed Sumo wrestlers.

"Stay out of it," Chris spat.

"I'm literally in the middle of it." John kicked at Chris, who moved his longer legs out of reach.

They'd collapse soon if they kept at it. Chris needed the upper hand. John wanted to be in control, so let him think along those lines.

"Fine," Chris said, releasing John. He couldn't straighten because John held onto his shoulders.

"You're lying again."

It was the window Chris needed. He spun in the gravel and ducked under one of John's arms. He could stretch out his leg and reach the edge of the bridge. The rest was up to gravity.

Chris supposed he should be falling forward from the deck but found his entire body being dragged backwards by his jacket. He regained his footing, turned, and kicked John squarely in the knee, pain shooting through his toes.

John held on like a Velcro monkey. "Stop fighting!"

"Let go then."

"If I let go, are you going to jump?"

"Yes!"

Ugh. Blew it. He should've made promises. Talked pretty words.

John's fist shifted on Chris's jacket. "Don't leave Chloe, man. She loves you."

"Shut up!"

She didn't. She couldn't. Chris tried to move off again, and John spun them in a half circle.

"She doesn't care that you're sad now. She loves you."

"I said shut up!"

Chris brought his longer arms down and under John's. He swiftly raised both fists then thrust them in the opposite direction, crashing into John's biceps. Instantly, John's grip released and his arms fell.

With a short stride forward, Chris used John's imbalance to gain the upper hand. He grabbed onto John's jacket lapels again. Victorious rage swirled in Chris's belly. "You…you …" It cooled as quickly as it had sparked. "Go back home and leave me alone."

Chris jostled John backwards in a final act of domination. He turned, only to see the full rail in front of him. How had they turned around?

"Chris!" John's strangled cry flushed every part of Chris's body cold. By the time he turned his head, John's fingers slipped from the bridge supports and his trainer kicked gravel across the bridge.

Chris jerked his hand out toward John's flapping arms.

John disappeared under the bridge.

"John!"

Chris dashed the few meters, sliding on his knees. It hadn't even been a couple of seconds and John splashed into the water below.

"John!"

Panic throttled Chris into action. John couldn't die. All he'd done the entire day was try to save Chris. God couldn't… He wouldn't…

Chris raced across the bridge. The path seemed kilometers away and the stupid slip-ons weren't helping, sliding here and there.

"John! I'm coming!"

If John could hear him, if a friendly voice could keep him awake. "Please, God, please," he pleaded.

Chris nearly passed the muddy pathway, and he fell once he'd stepped foot on the slight slope. He cursed the whole world, dragging himself up.

"Sorry, God," he mumbled. "John!"

The turns and grade made him stumble more than once, but Chris kept running and yelling to John. At the edge of the field, where the grass morphed into river rock, he yelled once more and heard the most amazing sound in the entire universe.

John moaned, obviously in pain. "Chris," he said, then succumbed to another groan.

"I'm coming!" Chris watched where his feet landed. The last

thing he needed to do was dash his head against the rocks trying to save John.

"Chris," John called out again.

He floated in the stream, wedged between some rocks on the shore. Chris waded into the water and grabbed onto John's arm so he didn't go further downstream. "I've got you now." Chris pulled John onto the rocky shore while John hissed and moaned the entire time, clutching his sides.

John shivered hard when Chris propped him onto a fallen log. Water dripped from his quivering chin, but he offered a sloppy grin. "I can't believe that happened." A pain made him hold onto his right side.

Chris pulled John's legs from the water. Thank God. Thank God John made it.

A chuckle from John, and Chris finally made eye contact. "I—I told you the bridge wasn't high enough." A burst of laughter made John writhe in pain. But his smile remained, every muscle genuine.

Chris couldn't believe it. For once in his miserable existence, God had answered his prayers. And had he fallen, Chloe would've had to pick up the pieces again while he recovered. Chris landed on his rear end next to John, back against the log. "I thought you were dead," he said, voice low and embarrassed. "I almost killed you."

"Hey," John said, waiting until Chris looked over. "Whatever it takes."

Guilt plummeted Chris into despair. He stared at his hands—the hands that had pushed John. He almost killed John! John, who had a second chance at life. John, who sat on top of a bridge with a stranger because he knew it was what Jesus wanted. John, who reminded Chris every step of the way that Chloe needed him.

"I'm sorry," Chris mumbled. If he could grovel, approach on his belly, it'd be more appropriate.

"It's no problem."

Chris swiveled his gaze to John again. "No, really. I'm sorry." Pent up grief flooding his eyes with tears. "Please forgive me. I've really messed up this time."

A massive shudder worked through John's body, and his pain made him grunt. Of course, he was cold!

Chris shrugged off his jacket. "Here, put this over you." He squatted and adjusted it to cover John's shoulders.

"You, ah, gonna call an ambulance?"

"Oh, yeah, right. Of course." Chris gingerly retrieved the mobile from the inner jacket pocket. "Here it is."

"Oh," John said through blue lips, "it's so cold! Why is England always so cold?"

This man could turn anything positive. Even nearly dying. And Chris wanted more of it, to soak in the happy-clappy clichés of turning lemons into lemonade.

Chris flipped open the phone and paused. "Uh, when you're out of hospital, we could get together, you know. Have a cup of tea."

Every hope hung on the suggestion, and Chris prayed he didn't sound desperate. Because he was sure they'd disagree. They were vinegar and honey. Sunshine and a rain cloud. But maybe, they could help one another. John could honestly vent to him about the dark parts. And Chris could allow the positivity to warm his cold heart.

"Oh," John said, trying to adjust his body to get a better look at Chris. "A cup of tea sounds great." He smiled a big John smile, all teeth and optimism.

"Right." Chris's finger hovered over the phone keys. The words stuck in his throat because he'd never admitted it aloud before. Now, right then, he wanted nothing more than to show John that he was worth saving and that he'd keep his promise. "And maybe…you could help me talk to my daughter."

"Whatever you need," John said, eyebrows flicking up, "bro."

Chris chuckled, and John groaned. Chris dialed emergency services and described their location to the operator without success.

"Why don't you take my keys and go honk the horn?"

"I'm not going to leave you, John."

"It's not like I can get up and run anywhere."

Just like him to make jokes. Chris half ran, half walked back to John's car, nabbing the camera and bag on the way through the meadow. The fragrance of apples cheered him more than anything as he ducked under the low branches. He'd make this right. Carol would be proud of him. Today marked the first step on a new path.

It felt like an hour before the responders arrived and Chris had to lead them back through the overgrown orchard. Rain started to fall again. He called out once they'd reached the field. John yelled back, and Chris felt his heart relax a tick. But it wasn't until Chris slid down the bank and hobbled across the rocks that he breathed easier.

"Thank goodness it started raining," John panted through a brave smile.

"You're American?" asked the paramedic with the backpack.

"Born and raised."

"How'd you get to be here?"

"You mean at the bottom of a creek bed?" John laughed and hissed. "Oh, that hurts."

"I gather that you fell from the bridge."

Chris's entire mind plunged into regret.

"I did." John glanced at Chris. He grinned. "But I'm okay. I think."

The other medic positioned a wooden board beside John, laying out instructions on how they'd brace his neck and move him. Then they'd strap him on.

"Can my friend follow us to the hospital? He can drive my car." John lifted his chin in Chris's direction.

His friend? The same person who'd pushed him into falling twenty-two meters.

"Sure," the paramedic answered. "He won't be allowed in. Hospital rules."

"It's okay. He can wait for me. I'm sure it won't take too long." John winked at Chris. Winked! Like a practical joke.

The excruciating sounds John made as they moved him onto the backboard grinded into Chris's soul. He bit his lip as they fastened a white neck collar into place, then tethered John down.

"Is this yours?" The paramedic held out Chris's jacket in her blue-gloved hand.

"Uh, yeah." He grabbed it.

"Thanks for letting me use it, Chris." John waved his foot. "It actually kept me warm until the rain started."

That was the first lie Chris ever heard John utter.

John chattered like a jay between the painful moans on the entire hike back to the ambulance. He cracked jokes and made the medical personnel laugh. He even invoked a grin or two from Chris.

"Hey, you found my camera!" John side-eyed the bag on top of his car as they passed. "Thank you."

"Of course," Chris answered, humbled yet again by John's gracious nature.

Once John was moved onto a gurney, they waved Chris off.

"Just follow us to the hospital. I'll send someone out if I have to stay!" John yelled as they loaded the gurney into the ambulance.

"All right. Do you want me to call Joy?"

"No!" The rest of John's plea, if there were more, was swallowed as the doors banged shut.

Chris hustled to the car and tossed the camera and equipment into the passenger seat. Thank goodness it was automatic. His hands shook so violently, he'd have been there until next year if it had been a manual. As it were, Chris pulled out well after the ambulance left, but caught up with it down the road. The car smelled new, and worship music played from the radio, of course. John's petrol level showed him to be a man that liked to be prepared with the needle near full.

The car park at the hospital was full. Chris circled like a lazy crow on a breeze until a spot opened up. He backed into the space. As a stroke of luck—no, providence—he was just able to see the front doors.

The quiet was too noisy, so Chris turned the key until the radio turned on again. He recognized a few songs and hummed along, not ready to sing the words. But his heart rejoiced knowing that John was in good hands, that any moment, a nurse or orderly would inform him that John would stay overnight but would be released the next day.

Oh, but what if he wasn't all right? When the dark thoughts threatened to trample the hope of John's recovery, Chris twisted the radio dial to nearly full volume. The speakers rattled about Jesus' love. It chased the shadows away for the moment, but Chris knew that loud music would not remedy his problems. He needed help.

His phone rang from the passenger seat. Chris nabbed it and flipped open the screen. Chloe. He let it ring once more while he gathered some courage. He had a promise to keep.

"Hello, Chloe."

"Dad!" She sounded gobsmacked.

"Yes, hi." He lowered his forehead to the steering wheel and closed his eyes.

"Are you all right?"

"I'm okay. It's been…" He trailed off, not knowing how to describe his day. Tragic? Terrifying? Fulfilling? "It's been an interesting day."

"But you're okay?"

"I'm fine."

"Before, when I called," she said, hesitant, "another man answered your phone."

"Yeah, that's John."

"John, yeah. He said…well, he said you were on a bridge, Dad."

"I was."

"Oh." Chloe sounded ever so much like a frightened little girl again. She inhaled loud enough that he heard. "I'm glad you're okay."

"Me, too." For the first time in as long as he could remember, he meant it. Chris sat up straight again and leaned into the headrest. He opened his eyes to see John waving, walking toward the car.

"Look, Chloe, I really need to go." He opened the car door. This man was truly unbelievable!

"Dad!"

"I promise I'll call you," Chris said, smiling at John.

"Right." Chloe sighed into the mouthpiece.

It stopped Chris. "Chloe," he said, making sure John heard, "I promise I will call you back. But I have to go right now."

"Okay."

Chris slapped the phone closed and stepped forward. "Look at you!"

"Nothing's wrong. No broken bones, no nothing. Just bruises. They warmed me up with this cool blanket thingy that runs hot air all over. Then I was fine." John held out his jacket. "My clothes are still damp, though, and they told me to stay warm."

"Yeah, yeah, let's get you home!" Chris could drive him, make sure he had what he needed, and then call for a car.

John stuck out his hand. "I guess we saved each other today."

Chris looked at John's hand. He felt a grin slide across his lips. "Handshake? Nah. Bro hug."

"Gently!"

# CHAPTER 25

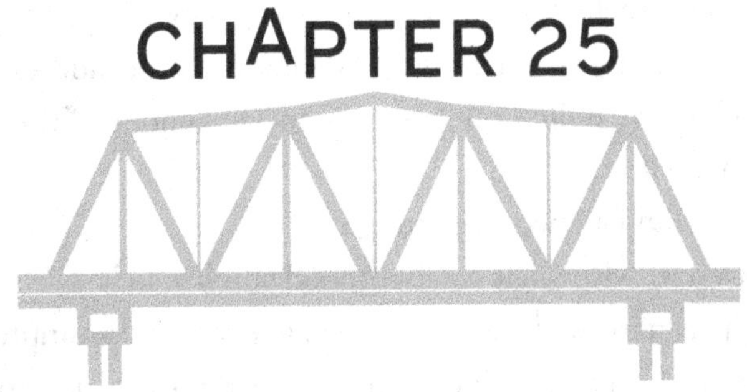

## IT'S A DATE

*John*

THE DROP INTO THE PASSENGER SEAT SENT SHARP pains wrapping around John's ribcage. He tried to grit his teeth, but a hiss of pain escaped.

"I'll never stop being sorry for that," Chris said, holding open the car door. His face crunched into concern, and he offered his hand to help.

"No," John said, shifting into the middle of the seat. Pain fanned across his abdomen. "I'm good." He waved Chris off, despite the agony. "Really."

Chris gingerly closed the door, leaning into it until the latch clicked. John pulled his seatbelt on while Chris jogged around the front of the car. Chris jammed the key into the ignition, and the small engine spun to life. "What's your address?"

"I can drive myself once we drop you off."

"Absolutely not. I'll call myself a car."

John knew from the set of Chris's jaw there was no argument.

"Okay." He reached into his damp jacket only to pat an empty pocket. "Well, this is interesting. My phone has my address."

"Oh." Chris pulled out his own ancient phone. "This won't help at all, will it?"

"No," John laughed, regretting it.

"Let's start with what neighborhood you live in."

The pair narrowed down the area after forty-five minutes and then stopped for a late lunch. Chris popped into a drug store for some aspirin.

"You didn't call Joy, did you?" John swallowed a pair of pills with some water.

"No. You told me not to."

"Did she call or text?"

"Nope."

"Good." John glanced over. Chris looked puzzled. "I don't mean good that she didn't call, but I don't want her to worry, especially since nothing is really wrong. She'd be upset that she's there and I'm here and want to fly over."

"I get that. I wanted to stay with Carol."

"That's different." John's body screamed for a warm shower and bed. "I'm just bruised."

"Right, but you should tell her. Especially since you're injured." Chris drove down the street toward John's rental. "You could leave out the part about me pushing you."

The laughter was worth the pain, so John held onto the bar above the window. Chris found a parking spot around the block and ambled next to John to Mrs. Pottifer's rented apartment. "Come on up," John said, twisting the keys in the lock. It smelled like she was boiling a pot of garlic as they pressed down the narrow hallway made even darker with brown peeling paint. Chris had to turn sideways to walk with the camera bag under his arm.

The three sets of stairs were annoying before. Now, they were downright laborious. "Just at the end here," John panted on the top step.

The streetlight across the road spilled a beam of light into the window and across the floor. John flicked on the light switch. "You can throw that there," John said, pointing at the bed while tossing his keys onto the bedside table.

"Let me at least get you some dinner," Chris said, shuffling into the only open space near the door.

"Are you offering to help me, Chris?" He chuckled and then moaned. "I'll pass. Lunch isn't settling great—probably from the medicine," John said, shucking his flannel to the floor. "At this point I just want a hot shower."

"Oh." Chris glanced at the bathroom. "I'll leave you to it, then."

"Wait! I don't even have your phone number."

"Do you have a paper and pen?"

John handed him both from the nightstand drawer. "I'm going to go get a cheap phone for the next couple of weeks that I'm here. That way I can call you." There was no way he'd let this guy go at it alone. "Besides, you said you wanted help talking with Chloe."

Chris's eyes jerked up. "I did," he said, hesitating to finish writing his number. "I did." More confident now, he finished by pecking the pen to the paper. "I made you a promise, and I intend to keep it."

"Good!"

"All right, then, I'll just go."

"Can I call you tomorrow?"

"Yes, of course."

"I'd like to take you up on the offer for tea, although I must admit that I prefer coffee."

"Figures," Chris deadpanned before a grin streaked across his face. "Then I'll talk to you tomorrow." He grabbed the door handle.

"Yup! Tomorrow." John pushed his weary body off of the bed. "Bro hug?"

Chris stepped forward and wrapped his arms around John. He smelled like a wet dog. And hugged like a longtime friend.

John relaxed once the hot steam rolled out of the open bathroom door. He shed his clothes to the floor and allowed the day to wash away. The camera. The fall. Joy and Jenny. He couldn't wait to go home.

Once he was out and into his pajamas, John crawled into bed. He checked the camera. It powered on! Through the small screen on the back, he scrolled past his pictures of the Tower and Westminster bridges. The particular shot of the Leadenhall Building on an upward diagonal that he was proud of. John turned off the camera and barely had the strength to move it to the floor.

He turned off the lamp next to his bed and scooted down, working his feet back and forth to warm the sheets.

"Well, God, you barely got me through this day," he whispered, balling the covers under his fist. Joy thought it was funny how he slept that way. "I don't know how I survived that fall other than you. I can't even..." His throat constricted, and tears flooded his eyes. "Please let me be a good friend to Chris. Don't let this be for nothing."

Exhaustion carried the rest of his prayers and thoughts away once his heavy eyelids closed. "And don't let Joy find out yet," he mumbled, slipping into oblivion.

It felt like John had barely fallen asleep when someone knocked on his door. He concentrated to make his eyes roll forward and open.

"Mr. Palmer?" Mrs. Pottifer's slippers shuffled on the wooden floor. "There's someone here to see you."

"Okay," he croaked. John moved his arm to throw back the covers, to shock himself awake with the chilly air, and was smacked with pain. He groaned and stilled.

"John?" Chris called from the other side of the door. "Are you all right?"

"All right is a relative term." John moaned again, pushing his aching body up to a sitting position. "Hang on a sec."

"No hurry. Your coffee is just getting cold, that's all."

John chuckled, sliding on his cheap slippers and hobbling toward the door. He needed aspirin or ibuprofen. Unlocking the door with his left hand, John pulled hard on the handle, as the door tended to stick, no matter the weather.

"Good morning," he said, eyeing the two paper cups Chris had stacked in one hand and the brown bag hanging from the other. "Let me get that." He grabbed the top cup and shut the door before immediately pulling it open again. "Just kidding! Come on in."

"I wasn't sure if you liked a bagel or donut, so I brought you one of each." Chris shoved the bag at John.

"Thank you." John set it on the bed and motioned to the chair in the corner where he read at night. "Have a seat."

Chris shed his jacket and hung it on the back of the chair. "I got your coffee black. Hope you don't mind." He slurped from his own cup.

"Not at all. Too many years on too many job sites to complain about coffee." It was brewed strong enough to curl the hair on a hog. "It's good."

"How are you feeling?"

"I think even my toenails are sore." Chris's crestfallen expression made John switch tactics. "I'll be fine. I'm just not as young as my brain thinks. My body doesn't have the bounce it used to."

Chris hummed into his plastic lid.

"Have you heard from Chloe?"

Chris slowly, methodically lowered his cup to rest on his knee. "Not since I picked you up at the hospital."

"At least you let her know that you're okay. That's important." Trust didn't happen overnight. Or over long conversations on a bridge. Brick by brick. Talk by talk.

"Oh," Chris rummaged around in the pocket of his blue jeans. "I got you something."

"You didn't have to get me anything."

Chris hiked his eyebrows and offered a cell phone.

"Hey! It's not from a museum!" John grabbed it and flicked his thumb across the screen.

"I had the salesman program Joy's number into it so she would stop calling me." Chris scoffed. "She's called about ten times already. I told her you were worn out from the hike yesterday and would be calling her."

John checked the time. "Eh, it's close to midnight. She's probably asleep."

"Probably not."

John found the contacts and the only two numbers listed were Joy's and Jenny's. "Thanks," he said, nodding to keep his tears in check. He must really be exhausted.

"No problem."

"I'll just be a minute." John grabbed a sweatshirt from the dresser drawer and headed outside. He dialed Joy, and she picked up on the first ring.

"John?" Her voice pitched high with panic.

"Hey honey. I'm sorry it took me so long to call you. Chris brought my new phone to me just a few minutes ago."

"I've been so worried about you! I thought you may have been hurt or something." If only she knew…

"Nah. That bridge was pretty far off the road, and I was on it for a few hours. Got to know Chris. He's a pretty great guy!"

"He sounded like a snob." Oh, that's right. He hung up on her and then tossed the phone into the creek.

"He's really not that bad. His wife passed away recently, and he was having a bad day."

"Oh," Joy said, voice lowering. "I'm sorry. I didn't know."

"Of course you didn't, honey." The smell of rain hung in the air, and the sidewalks were damp. "You're up pretty late."

Joy giggled. "I'm binge watching a documentary on Chernobyl. Didn't really help my nerves waiting for you to call." She yawned into the receiver. "Jenny came home for dinner tonight. She even folded the laundry before she disappeared into her room."

John took a deep breath to launch into a tirade about how Jenny needed to help around the house. He stopped. Well, God made him think about it and then he stopped. "I'm glad she's home tonight."

"Me too. I need to go to bed. I told Muriel that I'd come in early to church to help fold the bulletins."

"Aw, okay." John held the phone close to his ears, wishing to catch a whiff of the lotion she used every night before bedtime. "I love you."

"I love you, too. Glad you have a new phone."

"I'll call you before I go to bed."

"Okay. Love you."

"Love you, too."

John stared up at the sky, grateful to breathe the heavy air. Because it all could've gone a different way the day before.

He made his way back inside. Chris stood next to John's unmade bed holding his Bible. He held it up. "Looks pretty well-used."

"It is."

"I see you use different color highlighters."

"Yeah. I don't have a rhyme or reason. Just whatever is on hand."

Chris replaced the Bible. "Fancy some lunch? I'd be happy to have you over for a sandwich. You can run your laundry while you're there."

"Great!" John glanced at the heap of smelly clothes on the floor. "That sure beats wasting an afternoon in the laundromat."

Later, while John's clothes clattered in the dryer, and the two rested on their elbows across the kitchen table from one another, John finally worked up the courage to ask Chris a question.

"So," he took a sip from his water bottle, "when are you going to call Chloe again?"

Chris didn't react. Only his eyes moved, looking around the room behind John. "I hadn't thought about it."

"Hrm."

"I guess that's part of the problem. I need to think about her."

"That's a good start."

"It felt…good, yeah, good, to talk to her yesterday. She sounded so happy that I'd answered."

"The last time she talked to you, she told you that she loved you."

Chris crossed his arms. "I remember."

"I'm just reminding you," John said, placing both hands flat on the table. "She loved you then and she still does."

"I don't know why."

"Me neither, bro." John waited to catch Chris's stare before smiling. "What was it you told me with Jenny? Be nice?"

Chris glared, jaw muscles bouncing.

"Perhaps you can call Chloe today. Or tomorrow. Just tell her again that you're all right. You and I went home after the two of you talked, and you're trying to work through some things."

"That's putting it mildly."

"Yeah, well mildly is better than nothing at all."

Chris's lips tipped down and his forehead wrinkled as he nodded in agreement. "Baby steps."

"Amen, brother." The look of disdain on Chris's face made John reel it back a notch. "You could set your alarm for a specific time every day to call her. It doesn't have to be a long conversation. Ask her how her day went. Tell her that you need milk."

"I don't want to give her my grocery list."

"No, I mean just share with her." John walked two fingers across the table. "Baby steps."

Chris inhaled deeply. "I think Carol would like the idea of me using the alarm for that."

John nodded. An idea dashed into his mind. "My assignment ends in sixteen days. I was wondering, would you like to have dinner a couple of times before I go?

"Sounds splendid. And I promise there will be no bridges involved."

John's leg bounced all the way from Washington D.C. until his plane touched down on the tarmac at the airport about twenty minutes from his house. Although he wanted nothing more than to rush from the airplane and run to the baggage claim area, his aisle partner had other ideas. John could do nothing other than sit patiently until someone from farther back on the plane stopped to let them into the exit path. John slung his backpack straps onto both shoulders. He wanted both arms free: one for each of his girls.

Of course, there was construction in the concourse. The extra detour added a couple of minutes that felt like hours. Finally, John saw the triple sets of escalators leading down to baggage claim. He stretched onto his tiptoes, trying to see over the other people. Where were they?

A burst of red moved from his side view. Joy waved with one hand, the other clutching her purse. Just Joy.

And that was fine because as soon as John reached her, he held her face with both hands. Their eyes flicked back and forth before he kissed her. Joy's arms wrapped around his middle. He broke their kiss and lowered his forehead into the crook of her neck.

"Oh," she said into his ear, "I'm so glad you made it home in one piece."

"Me too, honey. Me, too."

# CHAPTER 26

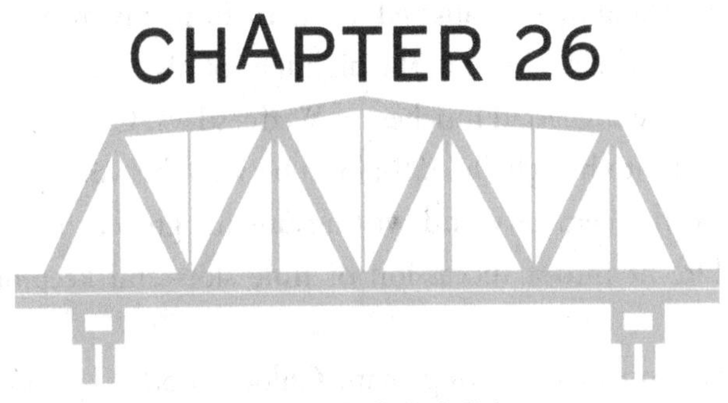

## PSALM 121

*Chris*

"DAD! I'M HERE!"

Chris pulled the loop of his shoelace taut as the front door slammed closed. He was as nervous as the first time he went to church with Carol.

"You here, Dad?" Chloe called from the kitchen. Her footsteps slapped against the linoleum.

"Just tying my shoes," Chris called, sucking in a breath to steady himself. She needed to know what he'd been through, what he'd decided to do about it all. And like her mother, Chloe was sure to have an opinion about everything.

"Hello," she said, popping her dark curls through the doorway. "Come on. We'll be late for lunch."

"Do you have a hot date or something afterwards that I don't know about?" Chris stood and shrugged on the coat from the peg next to the door.

"Maybe I have," she said, laughing.

He missed hearing that. Now, when they would talk on the

phone each night, she laughed a lot. In turn, his own laughter came easier. Their calls were the highlight of his day.

When she suggested lunches on Wednesdays, Chris made sure to fit them into his schedule. Right in between his volunteer work at the nearby cemetery and writing out his grocery list for the week. Life fit into a succession of time slots and keeping to a schedule.

"Have you met a young man, Chloe? Should I employ my network of spies to gather intelligence on him?" Both of Chris's elbows touched either side of the narrow hall when he zipped up his coat and wound his scarf around his throat.

Chloe chucked a look over her shoulder. "As if you have an army."

"Oh, ho!" He took a long stride around her to reach the front door first. "So there is someone."

Pink crept into both of her cheeks. "Let's go."

Chris smiled and pulled the door open. A blast of winter wind chilled his nose. Chloe linked her hand through the crook of his elbow when they both reached the sidewalk. Chris tucked her hand close for the short walk.

"How'd your meeting with your boss go this morning?" He knew she would never be forced to give up this secret man's name. It had to be her idea. His little darling meeting someone who made her blush was something to wait for.

"Good. She agreed to present my idea to the board for consideration."

"Excellent! I knew you could do it."

"Thanks for helping me get the details worked out."

"Just trying to help."

Chris walked steadily, but his mind tripped back to the last time he'd said that phrase. John had him trapped by the wrist on top of the bridge. They'd just patched up John's relationship with Jenny with Chris's suggestions. Ironic that his own daughter now clung to his arm. John would love to see that.

"Can I ask you something, Chlo?"

"Not if it's about a guy."

"No, no. Something far less dramatic and rather pathetic." The lights of their favorite diner were in sight now. "When we are seated, would you take a picture with your mobile and send it to me? My old one doesn't work so well, but I'd still like to see it and maybe share it with a friend, if you don't mind. If that's okay with—"

"Dad," Chloe interrupted, halting on the sidewalk. She grinned when he looked down. "I'd love to take a selfie with you."

"Good," he mumbled, pulling her back into pace to get out of the frigid winds. "Good."

When the door to the diner opened, Chris inhaled the comforting foods he loved: bangers and mash, meat pies, leek soup. It reminded him of Carol's cooking, and that was a good thing. Memories of Carol brought Chloe to mind and reminded him to choose life.

It wasn't easy. After his evening call to Chloe, the flat was quiet and still, save the cars driving by and the next-door neighbor's telly. Books helped, especially fiction. But even they didn't stave off the loneliness at times.

Those were the moments he'd fire off a random text message to John, with turtle-like speed, having to press each key to find the correct letter. One of these days, he needed Chloe to get him into the twenty-first century with a new mobile.

The waitress recognized the pair and seated them at a table in the middle of the floor. Old Chris would've stamped his feet at the audacity and said he'd wait for a booth. New Chris thanked their server, pulled the seat out for Chloe, and hung his jacket from the back of the chair.

After putting in their order, Chloe got up and crouched beside Chris. "Okay, you've got to look at this small circle. Right here." She pointed to an impossibly tiny dot.

"That's a camera?"

"Yup. Now I'll turn the camera round to this one for a selfie. There is a camera on the back, too."

"What? Two cameras?"

"You sound like an old man. Okay, look at the camera now."

Chris couldn't help but look to the screen first. Chloe had Carol's nose and smile, soft and genuine. Carol would be so proud of her. He looked at the tiny dot.

"All done," she said, returning to her seat. Her finger flung across the screen. "I got a couple of good ones!"

"A couple? I didn't even hear you take one."

Chloe swung the mobile around for Chris to see. She was lovely. He looked ancient. But...happy.

The time to tell her had arrived.

"Chloe." Chris waited for her to look up from her mobile. She was smiling at the screen.

"Dad."

"I need to talk with you about something."

Her smile melted and eyes widened. She took a quick breath and placed her phone face down on the table.

Inside the diner, Chris only heard his own breathing: inhale, exhale. Inhale, exhale. The chattering people and clinking dishes fade away. This was much harder than it ought to be. But he didn't want to hurt her ever again.

"I know I don't say it often, because I'm still learning even as an old man, but I love you."

Panic streaked across her face, nostrils flaring and color rushing from her cheeks.

Chris reached out and clasped her hand. "Chloe, I'm okay. You know that I wasn't for a very long time. Even when you tried to reach me, I pushed you away. Especially after your mother died."

Two tears pushed up and over her lids, racing down opposite cheeks. Chris reached into his shirt pocket for a handkerchief and passed it to her.

"I'm glad you stuck around for me far longer than I did for you," he whispered, emotions gathering in his throat and making it hard to speak. "I don't deserve such a fine daughter."

"Dad," she uttered.

"Right," Chris sniffed. "I've made the decision to check myself into treatment. It'll be inpatient, for six weeks." Chloe's lips parted, but she stayed quiet. "It's out in the countryside. You'll… you'll be happy to know that it's a Christian facility."

Her tears started again. She dabbed them with his handkerchief and nodded for him to continue.

"I didn't mean to upset you, but I wanted you to know ahead of the meal so that you can ask me any questions. Any at all."

Chloe nodded. Their food was delivered. He must've been stalling for some time, then. Beside his fish and chips, he noticed the mushy peas he'd forgotten to have removed.

Across the table, Chloe had a few bites before she launched into the Spanish Inquisition.

How did he hear about the facility?

Did he have references?

Why one in the countryside?

Could there be visitors?

Chris hesitated before answering that one in particular. "Yes, and no." He chewed through a bite before continuing. "I need to get better, Chloe. Not just for you, but for me. I can't go on living like this because I don't want to live when I'm like this."

"I thought it was better now."

"Oh, it is much better with you." His brave smile was mostly for her watery eyes. "I know that God brought me through this for a reason. *That* I am willing to admit. Beyond that, I'm not sure how to function. Everything I invested in your mother, I buried when she died." It felt like demons latched onto his heart and tore it open again with their talons and teeth.

"I miss your mum. But I also miss being your dad. And that's why I have to go."

Chloe gave a heroic nod. "What about visitors?"

Oh, she was good.

"For the first three weeks, none."

"None?"

"Not a one." He held up a hand before she tore into a rant. "I knew this before I applied. I'm an obstinate man. You, of all people, know that best. I need a program that can mold me into someone better."

Her sad smile encouraged him.

"I'm doing this for me, Chloe, not for you. You'd hate to bring your young man round to meet your depressed and suicidal dad."

"Dad!" She leaned forward. "That's not even funny." A giggle broke through her tears.

"And if you bless me with grandchildren, who'd want to play with a grumpy miserable grandpa?"

"You'll still be grumpy."

"Jesus can change many things, but I'm afraid you're right about that one."

The pair finished off their meal and Chris paid, as usual. Chloe glanced at her phone, and Chris knew their lunch date had come to an end. She'd already ordered a taxi, and it waited at the curb when they exited.

Chris hugged his girl. Every centimeter he could squeeze, he held tight to soften the last blow. "Give your old dad a kiss, now, Chloe girl."

She obeyed and pecked him once on the cheek before wiping off her lipstick with her thumb. The winds tossed her loose hair wildly about. The car beeped its horn.

"I will see you in a few weeks then," he said, bracing his hands around her elbows.

"You're leaving now?" she screeched, and the tears crowded the corners of both eyes.

"No. I've got to go pack. They'll send a man around to collect me at quarter past three."

"Dad." She sounded like a little girl all over again, and it nearly broke his resolve.

"Chloe Marie Arnold. You'll be all right. I'll write you letters or notes and keep them until I can give them to you myself."

"I love you, Dad."

Chris couldn't answer. He wrapped her back into an embrace. He'd have to store up this feeling to last for a long while.

Chloe turned around to wave when her car pulled away from the curb. Father and daughter stared at one another through glass and distance, one hand raised, until the car turned the corner down the block. Chris allowed himself to sob on the walk back to the flat. He resorted to using his scarf to blow his nose since his last handkerchief was with Chloe.

All of the details were in place, exactly as he'd done before the day he met John. Technically, John was to blame for this treatment center. Sure, the idea of going to treatment was his own, but John insisted on a Christian facility.

"Wouldn't Carol get a kick out of that?" he laughed.

She would, actually.

The packing list was short and fit neatly into his old plaid suitcase. With only two pairs of shoes allowed, neither with strings, Chris had purchased some cheap trainers instead of hauling the slip-ons along. Not exactly practical for the physical exercise portion of the program.

Unlike before, the card he wrote out for Chloe poured out his hopes and dreams for new memories together. He propped it against the toaster and checked his watch.

It was almost time.

The drive was much longer than he'd anticipated. Anthony, the driver, asked several questions, which Chris answered politely before staring out of the window. Green, green, and more green flew past the glass until the car slowed and made its way up a narrow driveway. Gravel crunched under the wheels. The brakes squeaked when they rolled to a stop in front of the two-story manor, straight out of a BBC special. Anthony hopped right out and fetched Chris's suitcase from the boot. Chris, on the other hand, wrung his hands until they felt warm before exiting the car.

The orderly who met him at the doorway wore a cheerful yellow jumper with a black name badge.

"Hello, Mr. Arnold." She held a clipboard in one hand and extended the other for a handshake. "I can call you Chris if you'd prefer. I'm Julianne."

He inclined his head toward her. "I can see that. It doesn't matter what you call me." This was a terrible mistake. He strangled the handle of his suitcase with his left hand while stretching out his right to greet Julianne.

"You don't have to decide right now. Just follow me, and we

can get you started." Her brown flats clicked against the gray slate tiles across the lobby. It smelled like fresh cinnamon sticky buns.

It took a little more than an hour to process his forms, go through his clothing to make sure he'd brought in no weapons or medications, lock his watch and wedding band into the safe, and be shown to his new room for the next month and a half. A plain green bedspread over the single bed next to an ornately carved table. Across the room, a door to the bath. A tall wardrobe nearly filled one wall in the bedroom. The window faced south. A dark gray storm rolled across the horizon.

On the bedside table, a small brown Bible. His name was etched in gold letters on the bottom righthand corner. Chris picked it up. Tested the feel of the weight in his hand. He opened the pages to the ribbon marker and read it to his empty bedroom.

"My help comes from the Lord, the Maker of heaven and earth. He will not let your foot slip, He who watches over you will not slumber."

Chris slapped the Bible closed. His chest felt tight and heavy. A quick rub of his knuckles against his chest bone didn't help. "Okay, just breathe," he mumbled to himself, before standing. "Breathe."

A flash memory of John standing on the bridge teased a grin.

"Breathe," he repeated aloud. "Visualize success, bro."

# CHAPTER 27

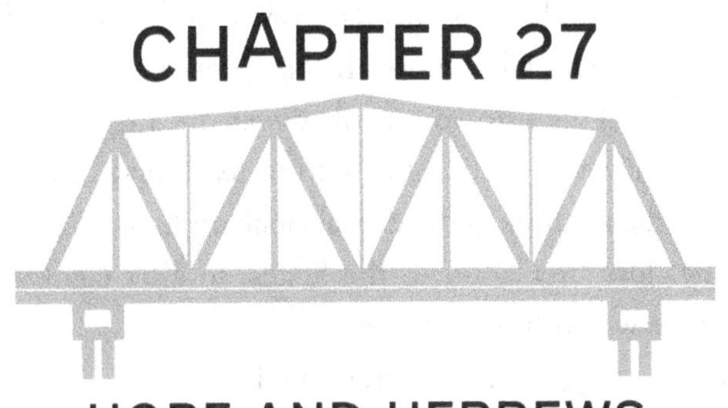

## HOPE AND HEBREWS

*John*

SUNDAY AFTER CHURCH, JOHN HUNKERED DOWN IN HIS squeaky office chair to make his weekly phone call to Chris. The sermon topic had been about hope. It reminded John of the bridge and his camera at the repair shop. The water damage wasn't significant, but the shutter speed had never been the same. Chris weighed on his mind during the entire service. Joy had even had to press her hand to still his bouncing knee.

True, they still didn't talk about sermons or dissect passages by the Apostles, but Chris and John hashed out a strange friendship of over-Americanized words and British snobbery. They talked about the weather and their jobs and their girls. Every once in a while, God would bounce into their conversations, but never with depth.

Today, that would change. God brought hope back into their lives, and the sermon was John's green light. Chris had so much to teach him.

John propped his feet up on the desk and dialed Chris's number. According to the wall calendar, it was only a couple of weeks until Joy's birthday. Chloe's was the day after, they'd discovered.

It rang until the auto-voicemail answered. Chris never learned to program it, even after Chloe tried to teach him several times. John smiled and checked the digital clock on his desk set to London time. Just after noon in the States, so after eight at night there. Chris would still be awake.

Maybe he was, you know, indisposed.

John switched to a text message. There was a funny joke he saw on the bulletin.

**How does Moses make his coffee?**

Two days later, John tried with a friendly "Hello!" text. Nothing crazy. It seemed strange Chris hadn't sent anything back.

John sent a text and called every day. For two weeks. He left messages and prayed for Chris after nightmares woke him in the middle of the night.

When Chris's number displayed on John's phone screen, he bolted from the middle of a meeting for a new multi-million-dollar contract.

"Hello?" he yelled into the phone, crashing into the hallway wall. "Chris, hello?"

"He brews it."

www.ingramcontent.com/pod-product-compliance
Lightning Source LLC
Chambersburg PA
CBHW010819250626
47156CB00011B/3122

* 9 7 8 1 9 4 1 7 2 0 5 8 5 *